Now You See Them

The Brighton Mysteries

Elly Griffiths

ISIS

LARGE
PRINT

First published in Great Britain 2019
by
Quercus

First Isis Edition
published 2020
by arrangement with
Quercus
An Hachette UK company

A catalogue record for this book is available from the British Library.

ISBN 978–1–78541–902–7

Published by
Ulverscroft Limited
Anstey, Leicestershire

Set by Words & Graphics Ltd.
Anstey, Leicestershire
Printed and bound in Great Britain by
T. J. International Ltd., Padstow, Cornwall

This book is printed on acid-free paper

For Lesley Thomson

CHAPTER
ONE

May 1964

At first Edgar thought that he wasn't coming. They were all there in church: Edgar and Emma, Bob and Betty, Queenie in the front pew sobbing into a lace-edged handkerchief. Even Mrs M was there, her hair white now but striking as always in a black cape with a fur collar. Ruby had caused a stir when she entered the church, followed, as ever, by Joe. There were even a few photographers waiting outside, just for the chance to snap the star of *Ruby Magic*, the nation's favourite TV show. Ruby swept up to the front to sit with Queenie, who welcomed her with a hug. "Isn't she lovely?" said someone. Edgar looked at Emma but her face was expressionless.

And then, as the wheezy music started up, a door banged at the back of the church and Edgar knew. The photographers must have known too because there was a shout outside, something like, "That's him." Edgar couldn't resist looking round and there he was, in the blackest suit with the thinnest tie, taking off his hat, unchanged by the last eleven years. Max.

1

The music stopped and started again. The undertakers began their slow journey to the front of the church. On top of Diablo's coffin was a wreath of red roses and his disreputable old panama hat. The sight of it brought unexpected tears to Edgar's eyes. He remembered his first sight of the old magician — he'd seemed ancient even then — on Inverness station, wearing the hat and drinking from a hip flask. Max had been with him, wearing last night's dinner jacket, and absent-mindedly shuffling a deck of cards.

"Captain Stephens? We've been sent to meet you. I'm Max Mephisto. This is Stan Parks, otherwise known as The Great Diablo."

"Dearly beloved." The vicar was as creaky as the church organ. "We are here to mourn our friend and brother Stanley."

Diablo was never Stanley, thought Edgar. He had clung to his stage name long after retirement, much as he'd stuck to the vocabulary; everyone was "darling" or "dear boy", non-showbiz types were "civilians". But Diablo himself had fought in the First World War and sometimes surprised you by coming out with that vernacular too, referring to "gaffs" or "gaspers" or "copping a Blighty". He'd never married, although there had been girls aplenty, and had no children. "Not that I know of, dear boy." Edgar could see the familiar leer now. Diablo had spent the last fourteen years of his life with Queenie and she had nursed him devotedly towards the end. The other mourners were mostly old pros in moth-eaten coats and gallant hats. Edgar and Max had served with Diablo in the Second World War

2

when they had been part of a shadowy group called the Magic Men. Their job had been to use the techniques of stage magic — camouflage, sleight-of-hand, misdirection — to aid the war effort. They had created dummy tanks and dummy soldiers. They had built a fake battleship out of an old cruiser and some barrels. And now, Edgar realised suddenly, they were the last members of the gang left alive. Bob had only known Diablo through Edgar but his wife Betty was an ex-chorus girl who understood the show-business world with its ever-shifting cast of characters but curiously enduring loyalties. Ruby, Max's daughter, had known Diablo well. She'd called him Uncle Stan — which, in Edgar's mind, justified her front-row seat. Did she know that her father was in the church? She gave no sign, if so. She had her arm round Queenie and they were crying together. Joe Passolini, in a sharp single-breasted suit, looked appropriately sombre but, as the vicar extolled "Stanley's" virtues, he turned round and winked at Edgar. As far as Edgar could tell, Joe took nothing entirely seriously. Except money, that is.

The vicar had embarked on a long story about "treading the boards". He could have done with some of Diablo's material. What was the one about the six-foot Lascar from Madagascar? In the days when pros used to buy jokes from each other and lease them for the season, Diablo had once confided that this particular gag had cost him three and sixpence. "You were robbed," said Max. "Not at all," Diablo had retorted. "It raised quite a titter at the Alexandra in Scarborough."

But now the Alexandra and the Royal and the Palace· Theatres would know Diablo no more. The organist launched into "Abide with Me" and the pros sang along lustily. Emma sang too, in her clear soprano. On Edgar's other side, Bob muttered the words in a kind of embarrassed drone.

"Swift to its close ebbs out life's little day."

"Goodbye, Diablo," whispered Edgar as the coffin went past him. He felt that they should be applauding, surely that was the sound that Diablo would want to accompany his last appearance? Queenie and Ruby followed, as befitted the chief mourners. Ruby was wearing a black dress with a short white jacket. She'd cut her hair and it swung about her ears. Joe was carrying her handbag.

"In life, in death, O Lord, abide with me."

Edgar and Emma filed out with the rest of the congregation. Max was standing by the door.

"His final curtain call," he said. "Not a bad crowd either." This was so much what Edgar was thinking that he almost laughed.

"Hallo, Max. When did you arrive?"

"Flew in from Los Angeles last night," said Max. He kissed Emma on both cheeks. "Mrs Stephens. You get more beautiful every time I see you."

"Maybe it's just as well that you don't see me very often," said Emma.

"Ruby telephoned and told me that Diablo had died," said Max. "I couldn't miss the old boy's final performance."

Max had been in America for eleven years, during which time he'd become a film star and married a leading Hollywood actress. Edgar had seen Max once in all that time, when he'd visited England five years ago on the death of his father. Max was now Lord Massingham although Edgar was pretty sure that he'd never use the title.

"Joyce!" Max turned away to greet Joyce Markham, a theatrical landlady otherwise known as Mrs M, who had once been his lover.

"Hallo, Max," she said. "Long time, no see."

Edgar remembered how the landlady had the ability to make the most harmless cliché sound like a double entendre.

"You're looking as lovely as ever, Joyce," said Max. But, in the daylight, Edgar thought that Mrs M looked her age, whatever that was. She had a certain dignity though as she kissed Max on the cheek. "Congratulations on your marriage," she said. "I'm a diehard Lydia Lamont fan. I never miss one of her films."

Max had starred with Lydia in his first Hollywood film, *The Conjuror*. They had married shortly afterwards and now had two children. Edgar had only ever seen Lydia Lamont in film magazines, but she was clearly the possessor of what the caption writers called "a luminous beauty". She was also at least twenty years younger than Max.

"Well, if it's not my favourite policeman." Mrs M greeted Edgar affectionately. "And your lovely wife. I miss those happy days in Brighton."

The happy days had included several nasty murders but Mrs M seemed determined to remember them fondly. She told Edgar that she'd sold the boarding house in Brighton and had moved to Hastings.

"It's where we all end up," she said dolefully, as they joined the slow procession behind Diablo's coffin. Hastings had certainly been the end of the line for the old magician but he'd had over a decade of happy years before he'd been called to the Great Box Office in the Sky. Edgar asked if Mrs M still took in theatrical lodgers.

"Just one or two in pantomime season," she said. "I can't imagine a Christmas without a Buttons or a Dame in the house. But variety's dead. There are no weekly shows any more."

Variety was dead and so was Diablo. Edgar had a sudden squeamish shrinking from the thought of seeing Diablo's coffin being lowered into the ground. It was ridiculous. He was a policeman, he'd seen enough death over the years. He'd lost his brother in the war and Jonathan had only been nineteen, not Diablo's three score years and about thirty. But he followed Mrs M's black feathered hat under the lychgate to the graveside. Emma took his hand as if she understood. Max had turned aside to light a cigarette.

"I am the resurrection and the life, saith the Lord."

This was the moment for the reveal, for the magician to stand up in the box and wave to the stalls and the Royal Circle. But, instead, Queenie and Ruby scattered earth on the coffin lid and the gravediggers picked up their shovels. A seagull flew overhead calling loudly and

Edgar had a moment's fantasy that Diablo's soul had been reborn in this appropriately nomadic and disorderly bird.

"Edgar!" Queenie gave him a fierce hug. "Thank you for coming. Diablo was so fond of you. I hope you'll come back to the house for some tea."

"That's very kind," said Edgar. He didn't want to go back to the boarding house on the seafront but he did want the chance to talk to Max. He introduced Emma who said all the right things. She'd been fond of Diablo too, even though he had tried to give their daughter Marianne a bottle of whisky for her seventh birthday.

Emma had never visited Queenie's boarding house but she'd seen plenty of others like it. It was a tall, Regency house overlooking the sea. She knew that inside it would have elegant lines, elaborate cornices and probably a sweeping staircase. It would also have serviceable carpets, wipe-clean walls and a long table for those endless late breakfasts. The rooms upstairs would be divided, each making two or three smaller rooms, the ceilings too high for their width.

Queenie had laid on a magnificent spread, though, and the theatricals got stuck in with relish. Emma saw one moustachioed lounge lizard in a white suit taking two plates of sandwiches into a secluded corner.

"Can I get you anything?" asked Edgar.

"Maybe just a cup of tea." She looked at her watch. One o'clock. This was lunch rather than tea; no wonder people were so hungry. Perhaps she should eat something. She had to get back at three to collect the girls from school. Most of the other children walked home alone but Emma thought that Sophie, at six, was still too young. Mavis was looking after the baby but she always made it clear that the ten-minute walk to the school was too much for her varicose veins.

Looking round the room she saw Ruby sitting on the window seat, lighting a cigarette. Joe was hovering with a cup and an ashtray. There was the usual buzz of "That's her", "That's Ruby Magic", but Ruby seemed unconcerned. Perhaps she was used to it by now. There had been photographers waiting outside the house too, avid to catch Max or Ruby, both of whom had ignored them. Ruby looked pensive, thought Emma. Maybe she was sad about Diablo or maybe the visit to Hastings had stirred up bad memories. Emma rather despised herself for being more interested in where Ruby got her dress and jacket from. The dress was the fashionable shorter length and it made Emma feel dowdy and middle-aged in her full skirt. Emma and Ruby were almost the same age but Ruby had never been married and had no children. That was the difference.

"Tea?" It was Max, not Edgar, proffering a cup and saucer.

"Thank you."

They sat on a small ottoman, rather closer together than was comfortable.

"So, Mrs Stephens," said Max, "how's married life?"

"We've been married for ten years now," said Emma, rather tartly. She wasn't sure that she liked Max's new habit of calling her Mrs Stephens. As a child she'd hated her maiden name, Holmes (the source of much teasing when she entered the police force), but now she rather missed it.

"I should ask you how you're enjoying being a husband," she said. "But it's not something men get asked, is it?" Max had been married for almost ten years too, soon after meeting Lydia Lamont on the set of *The Conjuror*. But Emma had only seen him once, briefly, in all that time. Tea in a London hotel, five years ago, made uncomfortable by the squirming presence of Sophie, then just over a year old.

"I'm enjoying it very much," said Max. And considering that he was married to one of the most beautiful women in the world, maybe this wasn't surprising. He grinned at Emma, teeth very white in his sun-tanned face. Max was fifty-four, Emma knew, but he seemed, if anything, younger than when he left England. Then she realised that Max was showing her a photograph.

"Rocco, aged six," he said. "Elena, four."

The colour picture showed two beautiful dark-haired children standing on either side of a large dog. In the background a vast white house, vaguely Spanish in style, glimmered against a blue sky.

"They're gorgeous," said Emma.

"How old are yours now?"

"Marianne is eight, Sophie is six and Jonathan's just ten months."

"Great names."

"So are yours."

"Elena's after my mother. Lydia says that Rocco's a more suitable name for an Alsatian."

This was interesting. It was the first personal thing that Emma had ever heard about Lydia Lamont. She noted that, whatever Lydia's objections, Max had got his way about the name.

"What's the Alsatian called?"

"Bob."

Emma laughed and, hearing his name, Bob walked over, carrying a plate piled high with sandwiches.

"Hallo, Bob," said Max. "Still fighting crime?"

"Someone has to," said Bob. Emma hadn't seen Bob for a few months but he was always the same, still boyish despite increased girth and slightly receding hair. Betty, who was talking to Ruby, looked the epitome of respectability in a black-and-white check suit. It was hard to believe that she had once posed on stage as the Lady of Shalott, naked apart from a few well-placed flowers.

"Oh, you've got tea." Edgar emerged with two cups. He was always the last person to get served in a bar or café. Emma used to find it lovable but now she found herself contrasting Edgar unfavourably with Max, and even Joe, both of whom had fought their way to the tea urn.

"I'll drink both," said Emma, smiling at her husband. "We ought to go in about half an hour."

"So soon?" said Max, getting out his cigarette case and lighting up. Emma could just read the inscription on the silver: "For MM with love, LL".

"I have to collect the girls from school."

"Don't you have a nanny?"

"We have a woman who helps but she refuses to walk anywhere," said Edgar.

"Well let's meet up for dinner in Brighton," said Max. "I'm staying at the Grand."

Of course he was.

"We'd love that," said Emma. She drained her second cup of tea and was aware of a maid hovering at the edge of the group. She didn't think anyone had maids any more. This poor woman even wore a uniform.

"Please, m'm. I've got a telephone message for the detective inspector."

"Yes?" she heard Bob say. "I'm Detective Inspector Willis."

Emma still couldn't get used to the fact that Bob was the DI now.

CHAPTER
TWO

After Bob had taken the message, he and Edgar conferred in low voices for a while. To avoid looking as if she was listening, Emma wandered over to Ruby, who was still sitting on the window seat.

"I keep thinking how much Uncle Stan would have loved this," said Ruby. "He adored reunions. Telling all those Magic Men stories."

"About the time they were adrift at sea for days and days," said Emma. "And Diablo kept them alive by singing 'Burlington Bertie'."

"Those were the days," said Ruby. She stubbed her cigarette out in her saucer.

Emma was trying to think of a neutral topic of conversation when Ruby said, "Was Max showing you pictures of his adorable children?" There was definitely an edge to this and "adorable" was said with what was clearly meant to be an American accent.

"He did show me a photograph," said Emma carefully.

"Very much the proud father," said Ruby, getting another cigarette out of her case. She seemed a bit lost without Joe to light it for her.

"He's proud of you too," said Emma.

"You wouldn't know it," said Ruby. "I've barely seen him since he went to America. He's only here today because of Uncle Stan. Oh, and because of the film."

"He said that you telephoned him to tell him about Diablo," said Emma. "I think he's here for you too."

They both looked over at Max who was talking to two women who were obviously once chorus girls. All three of them were laughing and Max did not look like a man with fatherhood on his mind.

"I went to visit them in Hollywood," said Ruby. "They've got this massive house with a swimming pool. Lydia spends all day drifting about in a negligee getting photographed by gossip magazines. The children are quite sweet though. Although they've got American accents."

"Well, they are American, I suppose."

"I suppose," said Ruby. "I just never thought that Max would have American children." She had succeeded in lighting her cigarette and inhaled deeply. Ruby might be a glamorous TV star who called her father by his first name, thought Emma, but she still sometimes sounded like a disgruntled child.

"How's Edgar?" said Ruby. "I hear he's a superintendent now."

"Yes, he is," said Emma. "He's fine, although it's a lot of work." The previous superintendent, Frank Hodges, had spent most of his time on the golf course but Edgar was made of sterner stuff.

"Do you miss it?" said Ruby. "Being a policewoman?"

Emma was surprised. In all the years since she had married Edgar and left the force ("married women can't be police officers," Hodges had decreed) no one had ever asked her this. Most people seemed to think that she must be delighted with her life: handsome husband, three healthy children, charming town house in Brighton. And, by and large, she was.

"Yes," she said. "I do miss it. I was good at it."

"You were," said Ruby. "I remember." Were they both thinking about the days when Emma was a detective sergeant — one of the first women to have this title — and Ruby was engaged to Edgar?

"You've been so successful though," said Emma. "Are you happy?" It was rather a personal question but she really wanted to know.

"Oh I'm deliriously happy." Ruby flashed her famous TV smile. "The show is more popular than ever and I'm seeing a rather delicious new man."

Emma glanced over at Joe who was now deep in conversation with Max, who had once been one of his clients.

"Oh, not Joe," said Ruby. "We're just friends, whatever the papers say. And he's my agent, of course. No, this is someone *entirely* different." Her voice lowered and she leaned forward.

"Emma. There you are. I think we should be going now. It's nearly two."

Ruby laughed. "Still the same old Edgar."

Emma didn't like her tone.

"What was the message for Bob?" asked Emma as they drove back along the coast road, the bland white hotels on one side, the sea on the other. It was a beautiful

14

spring afternoon, blue and gold, seagulls riding in on the waves.

Emma was sure that the message was confidential but Edgar usually shared work details with her. He said it was because he valued her advice but Emma noticed that he didn't always take it.

"A girl has gone missing," said Edgar after a pause. "She left a note saying that she was going to London but her parents are worried. She's only sixteen and still at school. Roedean," he added, with a sideways glance at Emma.

"Goodness." Emma had been a Roedean girl herself. She liked to say that the school, an imposing building on the cliff edge outside Brighton, had been like a prison and that her only happy years were when the pupils were evacuated to the Lake District in the war. But, as she grew older, she found herself feeling almost nostalgic for the place. It didn't mean that she was going to send her daughters there though, whatever her parents said.

"How long has she been missing?" she asked.

"Only a day," said Edgar. "The school informed the parents this morning. The girl, Rhonda, was last seen in her bedroom last night. The father's an MP, quite important, and he's kicking up all kinds of fuss."

Emma could imagine her own father doing the same, though he wasn't an important MP, just a businessman with enough money to send his daughter to a posh private school. "What does Bob think?" she asked.

"He thinks — and I quote — that she's gone to see 'the bright lights of London'."

Emma laughed. "Has Bob ever been to London, do you think?"

"He went once," said Edgar, "but he didn't like it." He was laughing too.

"What about the note?" said Emma. "Was it in Rhonda's handwriting?"

"You're still a detective at heart, Sergeant Holmes."

"I was the best sergeant you ever had," said Emma. "Make sure you have a look at the note."

Edgar dropped Emma at the school gate. The girls were at Bristol Road Primary, a council school whose intake made Emma's parents shudder every time they encountered them at end-of-term plays or the disorganised free-for-all that counted as Sports Day. But Emma and Edgar had met the headmaster on a previous case and liked him. If Marianne and Sophie passed the Eleven Plus then they would go to the grammar school in Hove, which was unrelentingly middle-class. "Why put them through that, darling," said Emma's mother, "when Roedean is so close?" There were many answers to that but Emma was saving her ammunition for nearer the time. At the moment the girls loved their school, playing hopscotch in the concrete playground or running madly around Queen's Park with their friends. And at least they had local friends, which is more than Emma ever had.

"Mummy!" Sophie came hurtling out first. "I drew you a picture."

"It's lovely." Emma took the sheet of paper, still wet with poster paint. "What is it?"

"How can you say it's lovely when you don't know what it is?" Marianne had appeared. A tall girl with Emma's blonde hair, she could occasionally look alarmingly grown-up.

"It's a lady shark," said Sophie. "We learnt about fish today."

"How can you tell it's a lady?" asked Marianne, as they began the walk up the hill towards home.

"They've got bigger teeth," said Sophie. "Did you buy me a present from Hastings, Mummy?"

CHAPTER
THREE

Edgar found Bob in his office facing a large man with a red face and an intimidating moustache, the sort RAF officers had sported during the war. But he was to learn that Sir Crispian Miles had avoided military service due to bad circulation and excellent connections.

"At last!" Sir Crispian managed to give the impression that he had been waiting for Edgar for hours, possibly years. Edgar recognised him as the type who always starts a meeting with a sense of grievance and, having been introduced to an official, immediately demands to see their superior. Bob's ears were pink and he said, "I'm dealing with your complaint, sir."

"My complaint!" Sir Crispian appeared to be swelling in his chair. "My daughter goes missing and you call it a complaint. It's a crime. And when I got here, I was told that the detective inspector and the superintendent were at a funeral. It's a disgrace. Why do I pay my taxes?"

Edgar was willing to bet that Crispian paid as little tax as his accountant was able to contrive.

"DI Willis and I are on leave today," he said. "We were attending the funeral of a close friend but we came in as soon as we were notified."

"I made them telephone," said Sir Crispian. "I wasn't about to be fobbed off with some constable."

Edgar took the seat next to Sir Crispian, wanting to emphasise that Bob was still in charge.

"Sir Crispian's daughter Rhonda has gone missing from school," said Bob, in the wooden voice he adopted for relaying evidence. "She was last seen at approximately nine last night."

"Twelve hours," barked Sir Crispian. "Twelve hours before I was informed of this. I'm going to sue."

"I'm sure you've already been through this with DI Willis," said Edgar, "but could you tell me what happened from the time that Roedean first reported Rhonda missing?"

He thought that Sir Crispian was going to explode again but, after a couple of deep breaths, he said, in an almost reasonable voice, "The housemistress rang me. Bloody impertinent woman. She said that Rhonda had left a note saying that she was going to London."

"Have you seen the note?" asked Edgar.

"Of course I've seen the note," said Sir Crispian. "I motored straight down from Surrey."

"And was the note in Rhonda's handwriting? Did it sound like her?"

"What d'you mean, did it sound like her?"

"Did it sound like her letters home to you, for example?"

"I never read them. M'wife reads bits out to me sometimes. But it looked like Rhonda's handwriting, all right. The teacher thought so too."

19

Where was Lady Miles? wondered Edgar. Surely she would want to accompany her husband on his visit to the school. But, then again, he couldn't remember the last time he'd visited his daughters' school. Emma took them there in the morning and collected them in the afternoon. She went to all the plays and sports days too, often accompanied by her parents. Edgar could rarely get time off work. But if something like this happened, he told himself rather defensively, he would be there like a shot. The thought made him feel superstitiously anxious and less willing to judge the Miles family.

"What else did Rhonda's teacher say?" he asked.

"She said that Rhonda had last been seen when a teacher called in on her at lights out. Rho shares a bedroom with another girl but she was in sickbay. The teacher said good-night to Rhonda, said she seemed her normal self but, when Rhonda didn't turn up for breakfast, the housemistress sent a junior to call for her. The girl found Rhonda missing and the note on her desk."

"Did anyone see her leave?"

"Apparently not. What a shower."

Edgar thought about Roedean school, which was visible from Emma's parents' house. In fact, it was visible for miles around, a Gothic-looking mansion high on the clifftop. The coast road was in front, the South Downs behind. There were a few houses nearby, grand 1920s villas like the one owned by his parents-in-law, but these were hidden behind gardens and gates. Further back was the golf course and the beginnings of the council estate, the grey houses making their way up towards the Race Hill. If Rhonda escaped in the night, she would have had to walk along the unlit coast road or hike over the fields. That is, unless someone was waiting for her with a car.

"What did the note say, exactly?"

"I've got it here." Sir Crispian opened an official-looking briefcase and pulled out a piece of notepaper in a rather lurid pink.

The letter was brief.

I'm going to London for a bit. Don't worry about me.
See you later, alligator
Rhonda.

"See you later, alligator," said Sir Crispian. "What does it *mean*?"

"It's a line from a fifties pop song," said Bob. "Bill Haley and his Comets."

"A pop song!" Sir Crispian started to swell again.

Edgar cut in. "Did the school, the housemistress, think that this was in character for Rhonda? This note, for instance?"

"She didn't seem that surprised," said Sir Crispian. "Everyone at the school seemed to think that Rhonda was obsessed with some film star. Bobby something. They thought she might have gone to see him. But Rhonda's not like that. She's a good girl. A hard worker. She won a chess competition recently. It was in the paper. She's not the sort to moon over some long-haired idiot from Hollywood."

"What do you think has happened to Rhonda?" asked Edgar.

"It's obvious," said Sir Crispian. "She's been abducted. I'm a rich man. Someone wants a ransom."

"Have you had a ransom demand?"

"No." Sir Crispian sounded almost disappointed.

"And why did the school think Rhonda might have gone to see this film star?"

"Apparently he's here, in London, making some god-awful film. It's with that magician, Max Mephisto. I used to like him before he went all American."

Max hadn't mentioned any film to Edgar. Was that the real reason why he was in England? Edgar felt a stab of hurt on Diablo's behalf. He exchanged a look with Bob.

"We should follow this up," he said. "Find out where this film star is staying. I suppose you can't remember his full name, Sir Crispian?"

"I certainly can't." He sounded affronted at the very thought.

"Don't worry. I know someone who will know."

"Bobby Hambro," said Emma. "He was a child star. He's only about eighteen now but he's a fully fledged matinee idol. His last two films were 'box office smashes'." Edgar could hear her putting quotation marks around the words. "*Puppy Love* was the first, *Only You* was the second."

Reading *Film Frolics* was one of Emma's weaknesses; her photographic memory was one of her strengths.

22

"Have you heard anything about a third film?" asked Edgar. "Possibly filming in London now?"

"I heard that he was in England looking at locations for a new film. I don't think they've started filming yet. Apparently it's an adaptation of Little *Lord Fauntleroy*."

"I thought he was a child?"

"He's a teenager in this version. A golden-haired, lovable teenager. In fact I think it's called something like *Golden*. Ruby mentioned something about a film this afternoon. Maybe Max is going to be in it too."

"That's what I'd heard."

Edgar thought of Sir Crispian saying that Rhonda was "not the sort to moon over some long-haired idiot from Hollywood". He sympathised. He dreaded the day when Marianne and Sophie became interested in boys. But, all the same, he thought it was possible that Rhonda could have fallen under the influence of the golden-haired Bobby Hambro. He wondered what part Max could possibly be playing in an adaptation of *Little Lord Fauntleroy*.

"Do you know anything else about Bobby?" he said. "Where he's staying in London, for example."

"What do you think I am?" said Emma. "Directory Enquiries?" But she didn't really sound annoyed. He could hear the wireless playing and the girls arguing in the background. It made him want to be at home. By the time he got back from work, there was usually barely time to eat supper before the girls were preparing for bed. It sometimes felt as if he was missing out on the best part of the day. When he'd said this once to Emma she had replied, tartly, that she'd be willing to swap.

"Film stars usually stay at the Ritz," Emma was saying. "I'll see if there's anything in the magazine . . . Here it is . . . Oh!"

"What is it?" said Edgar. It reminded him of the times when Emma was his sergeant and would sometimes go off following a hunch without telling him what it was.

"It doesn't say where Bobby is staying but it does say who his London agent is."

"Who is it?" said Edgar but he thought he had guessed.

"Joe Passolini."

Joe, a Londoner of Italian heritage with a sharp line in suits and trilbies, was Ruby's agent and had once been Max's. Edgar had never really spoken to Joe but he had a nasty feeling that the agent — who was certainly Ruby's confidant, if not her lover — knew everything there was to know about him.

"Joe will be back in London by now," he said.

"I don't think so," said Emma. "I think Ruby went back alone. I bet Joe will be having a drink with Max at the Grand, trying to get him back on the books."

As usual, Emma was probably right.

CHAPTER
FOUR

"Here's your poison." Joe Passolini put the glass on the table in front of Max, who eyed it with disfavour.

"Didn't they have any ice?"

"Apparently not."

"This is the Grand. Of course they'll have ice." Max heard himself sounding like his father and stopped, though it was an effort. "Sorry. It's living in America. They put ice in everything."

Joe took an appreciative sip of his whisky. "Ah, the Big Apple." To Max's knowledge, Joe had never visited America but he had based his whole persona on a New York gumshoe, down to the trench coat and the fedora. He peppered his London vernacular with American-isms and had a distressing tendency to call women "honey".

"I'm based in LA," said Max. "That's not the Big Apple. It's more like a giant wasp."

"A *vespa*," said Joe who liked to use Italian words with Max, as if to emphasise their shared heritage. Max's mother had been an Italian opera singer. "You know that's what they call those little motorbikes," he added. "The ones the mods ride."

Mods, young men in sharp suits who lounged about in coffee bars, listened to R&B music and occasionally roused themselves to have fights with rockers, had yet to surface in LA but Max had seen plenty of them in Brighton. He thought that Joe's single-breasted suit and thin tie owed something to the movement.

"Are you a mod now, Joe?"

"Nah." A switch back to cockney as Joe lit a cigarette. "I just like the schmutter." A quick detour into stage Yiddish.

Max took out his cigarette box, having declined one of Joe's.

"Pity Ruby couldn't have joined us," he said.

"She's got a hot date back in London," said Joe. "Took the car back." He blew out smoke in what Max saw as a slightly aggressive fashion. He wanted to know who Ruby was seeing in London but knew that he didn't have the right to ask. While he was in England, he'd try to catch up with Ruby's mother, an ex-snake-charmer called Emerald. Now rigidly respectable, Emerald wasn't his biggest fan but she might be able to reassure him that Ruby was happy.

"So, Maxie," said Joe, who, despite numerous requests and occasional threats, could not seem to break himself of this nickname, "what do you think about this here film?"

"I don't know," said Max. "I can't quite see myself as the Earl of Dorincourt. Wasn't he about ninety in the book?"

"Forget the book," said Joe, who had almost certainly never read the Frances Hodgson Burnett classic. "In this version the earl is a handsome, dissolute aristocrat. That's why you'd be perfect."

"Because I'm dissolute?"

"Because you're a bona fide aristocrat. Lord Massingham and all that. The producers are in a tizzy about it."

"I haven't said yes yet."

"Just come to London and meet Bobby," said Joe. "He's a sweet kid."

"I know the type. Hollywood's full of child stars. Horrible grinning moppets."

"Bobby's just a farm boy from Ohio at heart," said Joe. "And he really wants to do this film with you."

"I can't afford the time," said Max.

"Are you signed up for something else?" asked Joe.

"No," said Max. The truth was that he didn't have another film on the horizon. Every script he was sent seemed to require him to be a moustache-twirling British villain, or in love with a woman a third of his age. He didn't want to admit this to Joe though. "And I don't want to be away from my family," he said.

"Bring them," said Joe expansively.

"Lydia's too busy," said Max. Though Lydia had, in fact, just finished a film and he knew that she'd relish the chance to visit England, especially if it included a visit to Max's ancestral home. She had sulked for hours when Max announced that he wouldn't be using his title. She said Lady Lydia Lamont had a ring to it, although Max could have told her that she would actually be called Lady Massingham.

"Ruby would like to see a bit more of you," said Joe, looking at Max through cigarette smoke. "She was really cut up about her uncle Stan."

"She was fond of Diablo," said Max.

"She needs her dad."

"Don't push it, Joe."

"And you'd like to spend some time in dear old Blighty, wouldn't you? See your friend Edgar again."

"I can see him now," said Max, because Edgar had just walked into the bar.

"I thought I'd find you here," said Edgar.

"I'm nothing if not predictable," said Max. "Do you want a drink?"

"Actually," said Edgar. "I wanted to talk to Joe. I guessed that you'd be here." He didn't say that the intuition had actually been Emma's. Edgar thought that Max looked rather irritated at this interruption.

"Would you like me to go?" said Max now, still with that slight edge.

"No," said Edgar, "of course not." In the past he had involved Max in his cases, needing his insight into the theatrical world and, even more, his support and friendship. Somehow they had slipped back into the old days of the Magic Men, where Max was the ideas man and Edgar, supposedly, the one who kept them within the bounds of reality and the law. But they hadn't worked on a case for eleven years. Max was a Hollywood star now; he probably had no interest in the work of a small-town policeman.

Despite Edgar's protests, Max bought him a drink and they moved to a quiet table in the glassed-in area over-looking the sea. The sun was setting behind the West Pier, turning the sea red and gold.

"A girl has gone missing," Edgar told Joe. "She's a big fan of Bobby Hambro and we've reason to believe that she's gone to London to look for him."

"All the girls love Bobby," said Joe. "You should see the crowds outside his hotel every evening. All young girls, screaming his name. 'Bobby! Bobby!' It's like Frank Sinatra all over again. We've even had girls fainting."

"Where's he staying?" asked Edgar.

"The Ritz."

Emma was right again.

Edgar got a black-and-white photograph out of his pocket. It had been given to him by Sir Crispian Miles and showed a round-faced girl with a fringe and chin-length hair. She was grinning, showing teeth that seemed rather too big for her face. Looking at Rhonda Miles, Edgar had some sympathy with her father's view that she was not the sort of girl to lose her head over an American film star.

"Her name's Rhonda Miles and she's got bright-red hair, apparently," he said. "You haven't seen a girl like this hanging round the Ritz, Joe?"

Joe was looking at the photograph with an expert eye, as if Rhonda were auditioning for a role as a showgirl. "Can't say I have," he said. "But they all look the same to me. That's how I know I'm getting old."

Edgar was pleased to see that Max didn't return Joe's rather lascivious smile.

"How long has Rhonda been missing?" he asked. Edgar felt grateful to him for using her name.

"Since last night or early this morning. We can't be sure. She left a note saying that she was going to London."

"Then Joe can't have seen her. He's been in Hastings all day."

"I just wondered if she'd managed to get to London another time," said Edgar, feeling slightly wrong-footed. "Her family don't live that far away and it was half-term recently."

"It's possible," said Joe. "Bobby's been in London for a few weeks and there've been girls outside every night."

"Can you keep your eye out for a redhead?" said Edgar. "I've alerted the London police and they'll be checking up on Bobby's fans. I think they'll want to talk to him too."

Joe looked faintly alarmed now. "Look, Bobby's just a simple country boy. He won't want to be mixed up with the police."

"He won't be mixed up," said Edgar. "He'll simply be helping them to find a missing girl. I'm sure he'd want to help, especially since Rhonda's a fan of his."

"Oh yes," said Joe. "Bobby's got a heart of gold." But Edgar thought that he still looked rather concerned.

"Do you think something's happened to this girl?" asked Max, holding the picture up to the light. "How old is she?"

30

"Sixteen. This picture's a few years old. I've asked her father for a more recent one."

"Sixteen-year-olds can usually look out for themselves. I ran away from school three times. I left at sixteen. Went straight onto the boards doing card tricks. My father disowned me. The first of many times."

But Max had been reconciled to his father by the end. At least he had been back in Lord Massingham's will and had inherited the title he now refused to use. But Edgar knew that Max's childhood hadn't been easy. He'd lost his mother when he was six and had hated his boarding school. But Roedean seemed a much gentler place and, as Max said, sixteen-year-olds were usually fairly hardy.

"We don't have reason to believe that Rhonda is in danger," he said. "But the family are concerned. Bob Willis is going to the school tomorrow."

"Are you letting Bob loose in a girls' school?" said Max. "He'll be terrified."

"It's been ten years since you've seen Bob," said Edgar. "He's the DI now, married with two children. He's grown up a lot."

"Really?" said Max. "I had a long talk with him this afternoon. He seemed exactly the same to me."

Edgar couldn't help smiling at this. "I've got a new WPC," he said. "She can chaperone him."

"A new woman police officer," said Max. "Is she as good as Emma?"

"No one's ever been as good as Emma," said Edgar.

★ ★ ★

After Edgar and Joe had gone, Max stayed in the bar, nursing his lukewarm whisky and thinking about Brighton. He hadn't been back since he left Mrs M's boarding house eleven years ago, motivated only by a desire to get as far away as possible from the town where a woman he loved had been murdered. Florence. He thought of her now, watching as the lights on the West Pier were extinguished one by one. She had been part of a tableaux show where nearly naked women recreated scenes from art or history. The nudity was permitted only if the women didn't move. There was a horrible salaciousness about the act, leering punters leaning forward in the hope of a drape slipping or a woman coughing, but Florence as Cleopatra had managed to rise above all that. She was so simply, perfectly, beautiful that she did, in fact, look like a work of art or a Shakespearean scene come to life. Florence had been clever too — she had shown Max radio sketches that she had written and they were really good, funny and original without being at all mawkish. Florence and Max had become lovers, although Max had been living with Mrs M at the time. They were in love, he told himself now, almost defiantly. It had been the real thing. Max had wanted to live with Florence, to see that perfect face every day. He had wanted them to have adventures together, to travel the world. It excused everything, that kind of love. But Florence had been killed, her body posed in a grotesque re-enactment of the Cleopatra scene. And Max had never been the same again.

Was that true, he thought now, or was he dramatising things, like any aging pro in the bar late at night? Had the death of Florence really been the defining moment of his life? The day that she died, he had gone on stage as usual and had got through his act. Though it had been a near thing, saved only by Ruby's brilliance and quick thinking. The next night a Hollywood agent had come to the theatre and offered him a part in a film. Max had left with barely a backward glance. He hadn't thought about Mrs M, who had been deeply in love with him. He hadn't even thought about Ruby, his daughter, who had just been through a painful break-up with Edgar. He had simply thought about escaping. He had gone to America and, on the set of *The Conjuror*, had met Lydia Lamont, an actress then just ascending into stardom. Had he been in love with Lydia? It was more, he thought, that she had been in love with him. Or rather she had fallen for the character he played in the film, a Svengali-type villain who could only be redeemed by the love of a good woman. Lydia threw herself into that role with gusto.

Max remembered the moment when an on-screen kiss became something more serious. He had looked into Lydia's big blue eyes and had seen the promise of escape, a different life, a different identity. When he was in Cairo during the war Max had seen a man performing the Indian Rope Trick, the rope ascending upwards, seemingly without human interference. Lydia had been his rope; he had grasped onto her and she had taken him towards the light. And, for the most part, it had been a happy marriage, an outstandingly successful

33

one by Hollywood standards. Lydia was beautiful, of course, as Florence had been, though angelically blonde where Florence had been dramatically dark. But you can grow used to beauty. Max found that he no longer really noticed his wife's looks except in the rare moments when she herself seemed unconscious of her appearance, first thing in the morning, for instance, or when playing with the children. Lydia could be wonderful company, full of fun and an almost relentless gaiety. She had a temper too but that didn't bother Max; it was part of her charm. A deprived childhood had given Lydia an energy and ambition that sometimes made Max feel quite exhausted. But he thought that Lydia had been good for him, she had woken him up and revitalised him, stopped him from sinking into cynical middle age. And Lydia had given him Rocco and Elena. She could murder him tomorrow and he'd still be grateful to her for that. Jesus, why had that thought occurred to him? It was being back in Brighton. The place was making him morbid.

Max finished his whisky. He'd meet Bobby Hambro and discuss the film. If it sounded promising, he could bring Lydia and the children over for the summer. It would be good for them to get to know England. If the Vietnam war went on for much longer, they'd have to leave America anyway. Max wasn't going to let his son die fighting a ridiculous war for a foreign power. Thinking of Rocco and Elena, Max felt himself relax. He took out the photograph he had showed Emma earlier and looked at it. This feeling was, at least, simple and uncomplicated. He loved his children, he would die for them. And that included Ruby. If he stayed in England, he would make an effort with his elder daughter, try to make up for the missing years.

The pier was in darkness now. Max made his way out of the bar. Tomorrow he would go to London to meet this former child star. But he would walk around Brighton too. He would confront Florence's ghost. Maybe he would find that it no longer had any power over him.

CHAPTER
FIVE

If there was one thing WPC Meg Connolly hated it was being compared to DS Emma Holmes, now Mrs Edgar Stephens. The way people talked about Emma, it was as if she was this combination of Marilyn Monroe and her name-sake Sherlock. There was an old sergeant called Hobbs, he kept going on about how DS Holmes had solved the Lansdowne Road murders single-handedly. Except she had nearly got killed for her pains but Superintendent Stephens (then just a DI) had come to her rescue, giving her mouth-to-mouth and carrying her naked body (that bit was never explained) through the snow. The love story added to Emma's mystique at the station. Even DI Willis went pink around the ears when he mentioned her. Maybe he was in love with her as well although he'd apparently met his wife through the Lansdowne Road case too. Just Meg's luck that there were no juicy murder investigations these days.

The only time Meg had ever met Emma was at the Christmas party, a really grisly affair where you were meant to invite your "other half", which, in practice, meant wives only. Emma had been there with her two little girls, both very sweet, saying "thank you" with little bobbed curtsies when Father Christmas — Doug from the post room in a badly fitting wig — gave them their presents. Meg couldn't see what there was to write home about really. Emma was what her mother would call "nice-looking", she had shoulder-length blonde hair, good skin and no discernible make-up. Her fur coat had looked expensive but underneath she wore a black dress that had definitely seen better days. Afterwards Meg had worked out that Emma had been pregnant with her third child that Christmas. It hadn't showed but maybe that explained the baggy dress and the lack of lipstick. Either way, she wasn't exactly Mata Hari.

They drove to Roedean in DI Willis's car. It was normally the junior officer who drove but WPCs weren't allowed to take the wheel. Another thing to grumble about, though really, if you added them all up, you'd have no time for anything else.

The DI didn't speak until they got past Black Rock, when he said, "Emma went to Roedean, you know."

Dear God, not bloody Emma Holmes again. Meg pretended not to understand. "Emma who?"

"DS Holmes. Mrs Stephens as she is now."

"She's a Roedean girl? Aren't we all?"

DI Willis turned to look at her. "Did you go to Roedean then?"

Meg laughed. "No. I went to Fitzherbert in Woodingdean. My parents wanted me to go to Blessed Sacrament but I failed the Eleven Plus."

"Blessed Sacrament? Are you a Catholic then?"

"Yes," said Meg. "Good Catholic girl. Can't you tell?"

The DI's ears went pink again and he didn't answer. He'd sounded quite disapproving though. There was still a lot of anti-Catholic prejudice around, according to her mum, an expert on intolerance. Or maybe she'd been too jokey. She often got the tone wrong when talking to superiors. Maybe he just thought it was odd to call herself a girl. She was only nineteen but she knew that, at nearly six foot, she wasn't what most people thought of as girlish.

After a few more minutes, the DI asked, "Are you from Woodingdean?"

"No," said Meg. "Whitehawk." She was aware that this was probably the wrong answer. If Roedean was the smartest address in Brighton, next-door Whitehawk was definitely the least salubrious. Meg and Emma Holmes might have lived a few miles apart but socially there was a vast gulf between them. The DI digested this new information in silence.

The Roedean gates opened straight onto the coast road. The DI indicated and turned in but clearly someone was needed to push open the gates and clearly that someone was Meg. Nevertheless she managed to stay in her seat until the DI was forced to say, "WPC Connolly, would you . . .?" Once inside, the grey building loomed above them. Close up it looked more like a monstrous seaside villa than a castle, four storeys high with sloping gables and pebbledash walls. The main entrance had a sort of tower though, with a clock in the middle and chunky pillars, like chess pieces, below. The view was incredible, an uninterrupted sweep across the playing fields out to the sea. It was also, on this cold spring day, a rather bleak one. The sea was slate grey, capped with white, and, on the pitch in front of them, a group of girls struggled to control a lacrosse ball. Seagulls skirled overhead and, far below, you could hear the waves breaking against the cliffs.

In the entrance hall, in front of a magnificent double staircase, they were met by a tall woman in an academic gown. "I'm Miss Browning, the Number Four housemistress."

The DI obviously didn't know whether to shake hands or not. "I'm DI Willis and this is WPC Connolly."

Miss Browning did not say that she was pleased to meet them. Instead she gave them both a steady stare from under heavy brows. She was almost Meg's height and rather taller than the DI. "Come this way," she said. "I'll show you Rhonda's bedroom."

They set off down one of the longest corridors Meg had ever seen. They had occasional glimpses of girls in navy pinafore dresses, scurrying across courtyards or disappearing behind one of the many doors. It was a pity that they couldn't talk to Rhonda's fellow pupils, thought Meg. She was sure that they would know what had happened to her. She was equally sure that the DI would never ask to interview them.

"So you're the Number Four housemistress," she said, catching up with Miss Browning as they passed through another set of doors. "Where are numbers one, two and three?"

"I'm in charge of House Number Four," said Miss Browning. Meg could feel the DI's eyes burning into her back.

The end of the corridor was blocked by a tarpaulin and they could hear sounds of hammering and occasionally, and rather shockingly, a male voice. "We're having a new dining hall built," said Miss Browning. "Princess Margaret has agreed to open it."

"How lovely," said Meg. "I love the princess, don't you? She's so pretty."

Miss Browning did not answer this. Instead she opened a door and led them up a stone staircase. "This is Rhonda's room. She shares it with Stephanie but unfortunately she's in the san. with mumps."

The room was small and seemed full of furniture: two beds with mats beside them, two bedside tables and a large wardrobe. There was a sash window overlooking the sea and a silver-painted radiator. What struck Meg most, though, were the dozen or so images of a blond-haired man that looked down from every wall.

"Blimey," she said, without thinking. "Is that him? Bobby Whatsit?"

"I apologise for WPC Connolly's language," said the DI.

"I've heard worse from the girls, believe me," said Miss Browning with a trace of a smile.

The DI seemed to remember that he was investigating a case. He took out a notebook and asked, "When was Rhonda last seen?"

"A teacher went to check on her at lights out on Sunday," said Miss Browning. She was staring at a poster showing the blond man mounted on a black-and-white horse. "She said that Rhonda seemed her usual self. That was at nine-thirty. Fifth formers are allowed to stay up until ten on the weekends. When Rhonda didn't appear at breakfast on Monday, I sent a junior to fetch her. When the girl told me that the room was empty, I went to check myself. That's when I found the note."

"Where was it?" asked Meg.

"On Rhonda's pillow." The beds were both neatly made and covered with grey blankets. Meg wondered about the absent Stephanie. Had she minded the room becoming a shrine to an American film star?

"What did you do then?" asked the DI.

"I instigated a search for Rhonda. Then, when she wasn't to be found, I telephoned to Sir Crispian. He . . . well, you've met him. I'm sure you can imagine how he responded."

"Were you worried?" asked the DI. "What did you think had happened to Rhonda?"

"I assumed that she'd gone to London," said the house-mistress. She gestured at the walls. "Everyone knew that Rhonda had a crush on Bobby Hambro. I imagine she's gone to see if she can catch a glimpse of him. He's in England at the moment, I believe."

"Was that in character for Rhonda?" asked Meg. "To run away on the off-chance of meeting a film star?"

DI Willis was glaring at her again but Miss Browning seemed to take the question seriously.

"A few years ago, I would have said no," she said. "She was quite a serious girl when she came to us. Rather bright, good at mathematics, a prefect and keen chess player. But this last year she became . . . I can only say *obsessed* with this actor. She talked about him all the time, even tried to change her name to Bobby. Some of her friends called her Mrs Hambro. I think that, once she knew he was in London, she just had to try to see him. It was almost a sickness, in my view."

"She hasn't been seen in over twenty-four hours," said the DI. "Do you have any idea where Rhonda could be?"

"No," said Miss Browning, with another of her straight looks. "But, in my experience, sixteen-year-old girls are quite resourceful. I'm sure she'll turn up in a few days with an autograph book full of signatures."

But Meg, looking at the narrow bed, which had been angled so that, when Rhonda woke up, the first thing she saw was Bobby's bright-blue eyes, was not so sure.

But she had misjudged the DI. Before they left, he asked if they could speak to some of Rhonda's friends, to see if they could "cast any light on her disappearance". Miss Browning looked as if she wanted to refuse but instead she told them to wait in the visitors' room while she "rounded some girls up".

"It sounds as if she's going to lasso them," said Meg. She thought of Bobby Hambro in cowboy pose, coil of rope in hand.

"I wouldn't put it past her," said the DI. He was looking out of the window which, again, faced the sea. The room had comfortable sofas, a stone fireplace and several cabinets full of trophies. This was presumably where parents waited when they visited Roedean to see if it was a suitable place for their pampered darlings. It was certainly more luxurious than the dormitory block. Meg tried to remember if her parents had ever visited her school. Probably not. She was the fourth member of her family to go to Fitzherbert and any interest her parents may have had in their children's education had long since evaporated. Only her clever younger sister had made the journey to the hallowed halls of the Blessed Sacrament.

She got up to examine the trophies. Most of them seemed to be for lacrosse but, at the back of the cupboard, she spotted a small silver cup. "Presented to Emma Holmes for Public Speaking 1944".

"Look, sir."

The DI seemed tickled pink. "Look at that," he kept saying, rubbing his hands together. "Can you believe that?"

All too easily, thought Meg. She wondered what it would have been like for DI Willis to have worked with Emma; so clever, so perfect, so *posh*. Some of the other PCs liked to say that the DI wasn't the brightest, but Meg thought that he was sharp enough. The super wouldn't have promoted him otherwise. But he clearly couldn't hold a candle to the sainted Emma. Yet he also seemed proud of her, staring at that stupid cup with an almost doting smile on his face.

"What was Emma, Mrs Stephens, like to work with?" she asked. The DI looked at her as if this was an impertinent question (which perhaps it was) but he also seemed prepared to answer it. Unfortunately, at that moment Miss Browning came back into the room followed by three girls, one of whom was in a dressing gown and slippers.

"This is Moira, Joan and Stephanie," she said. "I thought you'd want to talk to Stephanie as she is Rhonda's roommate. She shouldn't be contagious any more."

Meg saw the DI back away slightly. Mumps was meant to make men infertile. The DI and his wife had two boys, maybe he wanted to try for a girl.

"I won't stay in the room," said Miss Browning, which Meg thought was rather decent of her. "But I'll be just outside." She addressed the girls who were sitting in a row on one of the sofas. "Answer the officers' questions truthfully now."

"Yes, madam," chorused the girls although Meg thought they looked worried all the same. And *madam*. Had they wandered into the previous century by mistake? Still, maybe it was how they talked in places like this.

When the door had shut behind Miss Browning, the three pupils looked at the DI with something very like terror. He turned to Meg and she took the hint. "OK, girls," she said, trying for the matey approach. She sat down too so they wouldn't be intimidated by her height. "You know that Rhonda Miles has gone missing. Her parents are worried about her and so are we. If any of you know anything about where she might be, please tell us. You won't get into trouble, I promise."

The three girls stared at her solemnly.

"Did any of you know that Rhonda was planning to run away? It's OK. I won't tell Miss Browning."

"I knew she wanted to see Bobby," said Stephanie. "He's in London, you know, scouting locations for a new film."

Something told Meg that Stephanie was also a film fan.

"Did she tell you what she planned to do when she got to London?"

"No." Stephanie had a round face, probably made rather rounder by the mumps. She looked as though she was usually cheerful and smiley but now she glanced nervously at her two friends, frowning slightly. "I never thought she'd actually go. I mean, she talked about it a lot. She talked about Bobby all the time. At night we used to make up stories about what we'd do if we actually met him."

"Are you a Bobby Hambro fan too?" asked Meg. That accounted for the preponderance of posters in the room.

"We all are," said Moira, a dark girl wearing badges proclaiming that she was both a prefect and a library monitor. "We're Bobby Soxers."

And all three girls made heart shapes with their fingers. "Bobby for ever," they intoned.

CHAPTER
SIX

Max stood looking up at Mrs M's boarding house. Eleven years ago the tall, stuccoed building had looked rather tired — the ground-floor rooms had been comfortable enough but things had become colder and more utilitarian the higher you went. Max still remembered the arctic chill of his attic bedroom before he had abandoned it to share Joyce's boudoir two floors below. But now the house gleamed with care and attention, freshly painted with wooden shutters at the windows. It was a family house. You didn't need to be a detective to work that out. There were bicycles chained to the railings and a rocking horse could be glimpsed in an upstairs room. Good luck to them. Edgar and Emma lived only a few streets away. Perhaps the children could play together. The front door was new too, gleaming black paint, the steps newly paved. Max remembered ascending those steps after the first performance of *Aladdin*. Mrs M meeting him in the hall wearing a midnight-blue dress and an inviting expression.

"You were the best Abanazar I've ever seen."

"Have you seen many?"

"To tell you the truth, darling, you were the first."

Not long afterwards they had ascended to the bedroom. Was it the one over the lintel, now with blue-patterned curtains? He stepped backwards, trying to look, and a passing errand boy looked at him suspiciously. Time to move on. It would be embarrassing for Edgar if he was arrested for loitering with intent.

Max continued up the hill towards the station. He'd forgotten how mountainous Brighton was. Or maybe his years in LA had left him unable to walk. He was certainly out of breath by the time he reached the road that ran from Roedean to the Pavilion. The hospital was on his right and, looking up at its solid Victorian columns, Max remembered the time that he'd taken Emma there after she'd been attacked. Edgar, though frantic with worry, had had to leave her to pursue the culprit. Max, still in a daze after Florence's death, had accompanied Emma in the ambulance. He still remembered that journey, the blue light illuminating the snowy streets, the whispered medical conversations around him. He'd prayed for Emma to survive, saying Hail Marys under his breath although his Catholic faith had died alongside his mother when he was six.

Well, his prayers had been answered. Emma had survived and had married Edgar. They had three children and Edgar was now the police superintendent. Were they happy? For years Emma and Edgar had been Max's idea of a perfect couple but, seeing them together at Diablo's funeral, he thought he sensed a slight fraying round the edges. Emma seemed dissatisfied, her intelligence turned to sharpness, and

Edgar was, as usual, harassed and over-worked. Well, nothing ever stayed the same. Behind the hospital, hideous new apartment blocks were rising into the air. Soon the Brighton skyline would look like a cut-price New York. Max turned his steps towards the station, hoping that he might see a taxi on the way.

London was changing too. The streets were full of cars and the girls wore skirts so short that Max found himself trying not to stare at them. He walked through Green Park wondering about this new breed of young people who seemed to possess everything and yet be so angry. Teenagers, they were called in America. Well, American teens had something concrete to worry about: the on-going war in Vietnam. What was the problem with British youngsters? Why did they hang round in coffee bars looking like they were waiting for the end of the world? There was a group of young girls outside the Ritz, some in school uniform and some in vestigial minis. They were standing in twos and threes and seemed somehow expectant. As he passed, one of them said, "That's Max Mephisto", but in an uninterested tone, as if they were pointing out an ancient monument.

Max made his way to the bar and ordered a Scotch. It was early to be on the hard stuff but he felt that he needed something to warm him up. His lightweight American suit had been the wrong choice for the cool spring day.

Joe, when he appeared, was wearing one of his mod suits, skinny and single-breasted. The man with him, whom Max took to be Bobby Hambro, was casually dressed in jeans and a polo-necked jumper. So casually that the maître d' stopped them on the way in. Jacket and tie was the correct garb for the Ritz. Whatever Joe said must have soothed the man's disapproval because Joe and Bobby were waved through to the bar.

"Maxie! Good to see you. This is Bobby Hambro."

Max's first impression was that Bobby, who had a surprisingly strong handshake, was certainly not a grinning moppet. The second was that if Bobby was eighteen he, Max, was the Queen of the May. Twenty-five at least was his guess.

"Lord Massingham." Bobby had a deep mid-West drawl. "I'm honoured."

"I don't use the title," said Max.

"I'm getting into character for Cedric," said Bobby, taking the seat next to Max.

"For Little Lord Fauntleroy?" said Max.

"He's not so little in this version," said Joe and it was true that Bobby, though not particularly tall, was extremely muscular. He seemed to find it hard to fit his tightly bejeaned thighs onto the bar stool.

"Drink, Bobby?" asked Joe.

"Just orange juice, please," said Bobby. Max scanned him quickly for crucifixes or other religious regalia. If Bobby tried to convert him he certainly wasn't going to do the film.

Bobby turned a blue-eyed stare in Max's direction. "How can I persuade you to do *Golden Heart*, Lord — Max?"

"By changing the name, for one thing," said Max.

"It's a quote," said Joe. "Something about golden hearts being worth more than coronets."

"That's kind hearts," said Max. "'Kind hearts are more than coronets, and simple faith than Norman blood.'"

"Amen to that," said Bobby, draining his juice. Uh-oh, thought Max. "The point is," the American continued, "golden is kind of like my thing. Because of the hair." He pointed to his head which was, indeed, covered with curls of burnished gold, the kind usually seen on Hollywood starlets.

"I've got points in this one," said Bobby, sounding more businesslike and less spiritual by the minute. "We stand to make a hell of a lot of money, Max."

"Keep talking," said Max.

The switchboard at the Ritz informed Edgar that Mr Hambro was not available. No, he couldn't leave a message. Edgar put the phone down feeling frustrated. The London police hadn't come up with any sightings of Rhonda, even though they had questioned Bobby's fans outside the Ritz and visited obscure cousins in Streatham and Thornton Heath. The DI and WPC Connolly hadn't gathered much from the Roedean trip apart from confirmation that Rhonda was obsessed with Hambro. "Almost a sickness," Bob reported the housemistress as saying. And apparently this sickness was shared by half the school. "It was down-right creepy," Bob had said. "They all made this weird shape with their fingers and said, 'Bobby for ever.' It was like some sort of cult."

50

Edgar took a turn around his office. It was a fairly spacious room but always dark because it was in the basement. Brighton police station, a collection of dank underground rooms in Bartholomew Square, had actually been condemned in the 1930s and the council was always talking about relocating them but Edgar doubted that this would happen while he was superintendent. He'd got used to the mice in the walls and the smell of damp. He'd even got used to the resident ghost. A previous chief superintendent had been murdered in this very room, injudiciously turning his back on a suspect armed with a poker. Henry Solomon was meant to haunt the building, joining the monks who had once lived in St Bartholomew's Priory and the nun who was said to be bricked up in one of the walls. Edgar had never seen Henry Solomon, although he did occasionally talk to him. "Where is she?" he asked now. "Where is Rhonda?" But the man in the oil painting above the fireplace remained irritatingly silent.

Edgar was steeling himself to ring Sir Crispian and update him when a scared-looking secretary appeared to tell him that the politician was in reception.

"Show him in," said Edgar wearily.

Sir Crispian didn't bother with any pleasantries. He sat down opposite Edgar and said, "Why haven't you found her?"

"I've got police from three forces searching," said Edgar. "I've just had an update from the Met."

"And?"

"They've spoken to the girls outside the Ritz. Apparently there's a group of hardcore Bobby Hambro fans who go there every day. None of them recognised the photograph of Rhonda."

"Of course not," said Sir Crispian. "She won't be hanging around outside a hotel. Someone has taken her."

"My officers went to the school today," said Edgar. "Her housemistress said that Rhonda packed a suitcase and was wearing her hat, cloak and outdoor shoes. That doesn't sound as if she was abducted."

Sir Crispian rolled his eyes. "Call yourself a policeman? She was lured away, of course."

"Why do you say that?" asked Edgar. It occurred to him that there might be something behind the abduction theory besides an unwillingness to accept that Rhonda had left of her own accord.

"Because it's happened before," said Sir Crispian.

CHAPTER
SEVEN

Emma was dispiritedly making a shepherd's pie. She used to rather enjoy cooking, in fact she'd even taken a cordon bleu course when she was deciding what to do after leaving school. But Madame Duvalier was mostly concerned with cooking things in cream and garlic or arranging tiny, shiny choux pastries on a lace doily. She didn't have to serve a meal for four people, one of whom was always late and two of whom invariably pronounced it disgusting. The lamb mince looked fatty and unappealing. Could she get away with adding a shaving of nutmeg? Probably not, after what happened when Sophie found raisins in her moussaka. Emma thought of meals at her parents house. For most of her childhood they'd had a housekeeper and a cook whose speciality was 'good plain meals': roast beef and Yorkshire pudding, apple pie and custard. Now Cook and Ada were both dead and her mother managed with a girl who came in twice a week to do what she called "the rough". But Emma's parents seemed to exist on poached eggs and rice pudding, especially after her father's last heart attack. Marianne said that rice pudding tasted "like feet".

At least Johnny was asleep and the girls were quietly watching the television in the playroom upstairs. Edgar hadn't wanted to get a set but he wasn't the one stuck at home with three children wanting his attention *all* the time. Look at my picture. Listen to my song. Read me a story. How do aeroplanes stay in the air? Why is the sky blue? I hate her. I hate you. I love you. It was all so wearing, even the love part, and then you add a baby who literally wants to be part of your body, feeding off you, clinging to you with those tiny limpet hands. Emma had never told anyone how she had felt when she realised that she was pregnant again. She had just regained her figure and her energy after Marianne and Sophie. She was beginning to wonder if maybe, perhaps, in a few years' time, she might be able to get a part-time job. And then that familiar queasiness in the mornings, the visit to the doctor for the ominous-sounding "frog test", the announcement to Edgar who was, predictably, delighted. Well, Edgar had always wanted a son, an heir that he could name after his dead brother, but Emma had been quite content with her girls. Oh, she loved Jonathan, who wouldn't love him with his little round face and merry eyes? It was just that, sometimes, she felt that Jonathan was slowing her down, the way children sometimes cling onto a parent's leg to stop them moving away.

The kitchen was a semi-basement so all she could see was feet going past: brogues, boots, the occasional clattering pair of high heels. She liked to imagine where they were all going. Some of them were probably going home to cook shepherd's pie but some might be off on

54

adventures, meeting a lover, solving a crime. Or committing one. As she watched, stirring the meat with one hand, a pair of gym shoes stopped at her top step. She watched the feet and their owner descend the area steps: capri pants, a fisherman's sweater, short brown hair, jaunty beret. Sam Collins.

"Sam!" Emma opened the door.

"Hi, Em. Something smells good. What are you making?"

"Shepherd's pie. You're welcome to stay and have some. It probably won't taste as good as it smells."

"You make it sounds so appetising. How can I resist?"

Sam Collins, a reporter on the local paper, the *Evening Argus*, had become a close friend in recent years. Emma still kept in touch with some girls from school but they were scattered around the country now, all with children and husbands with Hon. before their names. Vera lived nearby in Rottingdean but she only really cared about her horses. Sometimes it surprised Emma to think that now her only real friends were Sam and a mystic called Madame Astarte. They were also the only people who talked to her as if she was still Emma Holmes and not Mrs Stephens, the superintendent's wife.

They chatted while Emma finished assembling the shepherd's pie and put it in the oven. Then she made them both a cup of tea. They sat at the round kitchen table and, suddenly, the grey evening and the feet walking past seemed cosy rather than oppressive.

"How's work?" Emma asked Sam.

"Awful," said Sam. "They've brought in a new chief reporter. A man, of course. That job should have been mine."

Sam claimed that, when she'd been hired by post, the editor had thought that she was a man. When he found out the awful truth, he had tried to condemn her to a lifetime of making tea and tidying up the news room.

"At least you've still got a job," said Emma.

"Yes. But I haven't got a husband. My mother's becoming more desperate by the minute. I visited Lewes Prison the other day and she asked if any of the inmates were good-looking."

Emma laughed. "My mother was the same. I got married at twenty-five but she acted like it was my last chance. I'm never going to pressure my girls to get married. I want them to have a career first."

"Why first? Why not after they're married too?"

"It's hard," said Emma. She could hear the girls moving about upstairs. She prayed that they weren't going to come down. "It's hard to have a job and a marriage. Especially if you have children."

"I hear Max Mephisto is back in England," said Sam.

Emma thought that it was rather interesting that Sam mentioned Max straight after the conversation about marriage and good-looking men. "Yes. I saw him yesterday. He came over for Diablo's funeral. You know, his army friend. The magician. The Great Diablo."

"I saw him in panto once. Is Max still married to Lydia Lamont?"

"He seemed very married. Showed me pictures of their children."

"Pity. Anyway, that's not why I wanted to talk to you."

"This isn't just a social visit then?"

"No," said Sam. "This is work." She was carrying a bag like a postman's sack and, from it, she produced a sheaf of papers. "Is Edgar investigating the Rhonda Miles case?"

"How do you know about that?"

"I have my contacts. Bob Willis was at Roedean this morning, apparently accompanied by an enormously tall female police constable."

"That must be Meg Connolly," said Emma. "I met her at the Christmas party the year before last."

"Well, apparently Rhonda has disappeared and the theory is that she's gone to London to see Bobby Hambro. She's a Bobby Soxer."

"A what?"

"A diehard Hambro fan. There are lots of them about. Screaming teenage girls with raging hormones. The thing is, though, I think this is part of something bigger."

Emma's heart, which had soared when Sam mentioned the word "work", now began to beat faster.

Sam put three newspaper cuttings on the table. One showed a girl grinning by a chessboard, the second a group of nurses outside the Royal Sussex Hospital and the third a young girl wearing what Emma had recently learnt were "mod clothes": short black-and-white dress and knee-length boots. She had backcombed peroxide hair and was glaring defiantly into the camera.

"That's Rhonda Miles." Sam pointed to the chess player.

"And the others?"

"Louise Dawkins, student nurse. She went missing last month. The modette is Sara Henratty. She disappeared two weeks ago. They both left notes."

"And you think they're linked to Rhonda's disappearance?"

"There are similarities. Louise's note said that she was going back to her family in the Caribbean. As far as I know, no one bothered to check but her friends at the nurses' hostel said that Louise didn't have any close family. Sara was in and out of foster care. I don't think anyone cared enough to make a fuss about her."

"Were the stories in the papers?"

"No. I found out about Louise from one of my friends, a houseman at the hospital. Sara was living in a children's home in Moulsecoomb. I went there because we'd had a report that conditions were bad. One of the cleaners told me about Sara. This picture was in her room. You know how photographers are always taking snaps of the mods and rockers on the seafront."

The photograph was entitled "Mod Style" and showed Sara leaning against a Vespa adorned with multiple wing mirrors. Two boys in parkas lounged in the background.

"Sara's note said that she'd run away with a boy known as Peanuts. I tracked him down and he lives with his parents in Southwick. He'd gone out with Sara a few times but clearly had no idea where she was now. I've got the note here."

She held out a piece of pink notepaper. The writing was round and childish.

To whom it may concern. I've gone off with Peanuts. Don't try to find me. See you in the next life. Sara.

There was a heart next to her name. Emma felt her throat contract. *To whom it may concern* (i.e. no one).

"Was this her handwriting?"

"Apparently so. As I say, no one at the home seemed that worried. They were quite happy to let me have the note. Hadn't even reported it to the police."

"What about Louise's disappearance? Was that reported?"

"No. The matron at the hospital accepted the Caribbean explanation. She said that she always thought Louise would 'go back home' as she put it. This was her home! She was born in Hackney. Her friends thought it was odd though. That's why Pete, my doctor friend, contacted me."

"And you think something suspicious is going on?"

"Well, don't you? Three girls disappearing in six weeks. The difference is that, unlike Louise and Sara, Rhonda has parents who will make a fuss."

"You have to tell Edgar," said Emma.

"I'll leave that to you," said Sam. But at that moment Marianne and Sophie came flying into the room in the middle of an argument about ballet shoes. They stopped when they saw Sam but, as she was an old friend, soon started up again. And, from upstairs, came the angry sound of the baby crying.

Edgar greeted Sam warmly but Emma knew that he was constrained by her presence. They didn't talk about the case but, helped by a bottle of red wine that Sam produced from her postman's sack, discussed the new tower block at Black Rock, the chances of a fight between mods and rockers at the forthcoming bank holiday weekend and the odds of Brighton and Hove Albion making it to the first division. The shepherd's pie was actually quite good and the girls cleared the dishes without complaining too much. When Emma got up to put Jonathan to bed, Sam said that she'd better be off. "The news never sleeps."

"Nor does Jonathan," said Emma.

But Johnny went down quite quickly that evening. Emma oversaw the girls having their baths and getting into bed and went back downstairs. Edgar had done the washing up and was sitting at the table reading the *Evening Argus*. There was a picture of Ruby on the front page, emerging from the church after Diablo's funeral: white jacket, black dress, white skin, black hair. She looked lovely even in monochrome.

"Sam says not to believe everything you read in there," said Emma, putting the kettle on for tea.

"I won't," said Edgar.

"How's the Rhonda Miles case going?"

"It's not going anywhere," said Edgar, putting the paper down. "There's no sign of the girl and no real

60

leads either. Her father is demanding my head on a plate."

"Sir Crispian Miles?"

"Yes. How did you know his name?"

"I looked him up in *Who's Who*. Apparently he made his money out of a chain of butchers' shops before the war. Then he sold them to one of the new supermarkets, made a ton of money and became a Conservative MP. He got his knighthood two years ago."

"You know everything, Em."

"I'm just good at research," said Emma. "Sam's got a theory about the Rhonda Miles case."

Edgar looked slightly wary at the mention of Sam. "Tell me," he said.

He didn't immediately spring into action, as Emma had hoped, but he did take it seriously and looked at the newspaper cuttings before writing Louise and Sara's names in his notebook.

"What if someone has abducted them?" said Emma. "What if there's this madman out there and no one's looking for him?"

"Rhonda's father said that she was abducted when she was ten," said Edgar. "Someone snatched her on her way home from ballet class. The man's in prison now. The whole thing gave Rhonda's mother a nervous breakdown."

"But if he's in prison he can't have had anything to do with this disappearance."

"It doesn't seem like it but what are the chances of being abducted twice? I don't like it. I've asked Bob to follow it up."

"What did Bob think of Roedean?" asked Emma.

"I think he found it terrifying," said Edgar, "but he seemed to do a thorough job. Actually, I think he left a lot of it to WPC Connolly. She's a bright girl."

Emma thought of Roedean: of the chapel with the naval flags hanging from the rafters, of playing hide-and-seek in the rough ground they called Spiders, of the "bunny runs" between the houses. For the second time that evening she felt near to tears. It didn't help to hear Meg Connolly described as bright either.

"Did they look in the tunnel?" she asked.

Edgar looked up. "What tunnel?"

"There's a secret tunnel inside the school leading down to the beach."

"A secret tunnel?"

"Well, not exactly secret but it's only opened once or twice a year. We used to be made to scrub the steps as a punishment."

"That sounds positively Dickensian."

Emma waved this away, annoyed at the teasing note in Edgar's voice. "Maybe Rhonda got away that way. She could have gone through the tunnel and into Brighton on the undercliff walk. Ed!" Emma grasped his arm, all tears forgotten. "Let's go there now! You could get the keys from the caretaker. I know the way. We could be there in ten minutes."

Edgar smiled. "How could we leave the children? I'll tell Bob to send a couple of PCs in the morning."

Upstairs, Jonathan started to cry again.

CHAPTER
EIGHT

—

Meg was surprised, and rather pleased, to be asked to lead the second expedition to Roedean.

"You seemed to get on well with Miss Browning," said the DI.

"Did I?" Meg had thought that the housemistress had disapproved of her. She was too big and too common, with her Whitehawk vowels and her chat about princesses. But, then again, there were a couple of moments when Miss Browning looked like betraying the fact that there was a sense of humour hidden under the twinset and academic gown. Meg doubted whether she would be laughing today though.

A young PC called Danny Black drove them to Roedean in one of the new two-tone Morris Minors. People turned to stare as they drove through Kemp Town and Meg had to resist the temptation to turn and wave like the Queen.

"I feel ridiculous," said PC Black, grinding the gears.

"Let me drive then. My dad's got a Morris Minor."

"You're not allowed," said Danny.

Meg sighed. It was going to be a long morning.

★ ★ ★

Miss Browning was not delighted to see them.

"The tunnel? Why would you want to see the tunnel? It's only opened once or twice a year on special occasions. And on Roedean Day, of course."

"Who has the key?"

"Richards the caretaker."

"Is it possible that Rhonda could have got hold of a key and escaped that way?" asked Meg.

"Escaped? This isn't a prison."

"Could have fooled me," muttered Danny to Meg. Miss Browning eventually consented to get the key from Richards and they walked in single file back down to the main entrance gates. Even Miss Browning's back looked outraged.

The entrance to the tunnel was a wooden door next to the gates. Even from a distance they could see that it was padlocked but, as they got closer, they saw something else. The padlock was open and the door wedged ajar by a large pebble.

"Someone's been here recently," said Meg. Stating the obvious, of course, but isn't that what the police are meant to do?

"That's impossible," said Miss Browning.

In answer, Meg pushed open the wooden door. They were immediately met by the harsh, briny smell of the sea. They could hear it too, the hiss of the waves over the shingle beach. In front of them was a steep flight of concrete stairs. Danny turned on his torch.

A rope handrail was attached to the wall and Meg held on tight as they made their way downwards. She felt both excited and slightly scared. What would they find when they reached the bottom? Apart from her late grandfather, she had never seen a dead body. She didn't want to start with a sixteen-year-old girl. She could hear Miss Browning's sensible brogues behind her. What would the housemistress say if Rhonda's lifeless corpse awaited them? Would she weep? Shout? Rend her garments? Blame the police for incompetence?

The door at the foot of the stairs was also propped open by a stone. Through the gap, Meg could see the sea, grey and inhospitable. Slowly and carefully, Danny shone his torch up and around, showing the tunnel's low ceiling and the pebble-strewn floor.

"This stuff must have blown in from the sea," he said, kicking aside a piece of seaweed.

"There's nothing here," said Miss Browning, her voice echoing against the concrete walls. Meg thought that she sounded very relieved.

"Hang on," said Meg. "What's this?"

In the corner by the door she had spotted something blue. She picked it up. It was a broad-brimmed school hat. She hardly needed to read the nametape.

Rhonda Miles.

"The tunnel couldn't have been open," said the caretaker. "It's impossible."

"Well, clearly not, Richards," said Miss Browning. She was rattled, Meg could see. The discovery of the hat had cast a different light on Rhonda's disappearance. There was no more talk of a schoolgirl prank. Wherever Rhonda had gone, whether to London in search of Bobby Hambro or for a more sinister rendezvous, it was clear that her escape had been deliberate. Miss Browning hadn't even objected when Meg asked to speak to Richards, the caretaker. They were in his house now, a neat bungalow in the school grounds. Richards, a grey-haired man with watery blue eyes, seemed very put out by their presence. Mind you, it could just be because Meg and Miss Browning towered over him. The front room seemed uncomfortably crowded.

Richards said that he'd last checked the tunnel entrance a few weeks ago. "But it's always kept locked," he said.

"It wasn't locked today," said Miss Browning. "The door was propped open by a stone."

"Where do you keep the keys?" asked Meg.

"In the key safe."

"Can I look at it?"

The metal safe was next to the front door.

"Is it always kept locked?" asked Meg.

"Yes," said Richards. As he spoke, the safe door swung forwards. "Well, not always," he conceded.

"And your front door?"

"This isn't a police state, you know. Folk don't need to keep their doors locked."

It would have been fairly easy to get a key then, thought Meg. Someone would only have to open the unlocked door and reach round for the safe.

"Richards," said Miss Browning, warningly.

"Do the girls ever come here?" asked Meg, trying to keep any note of accusation out of her voice.

66

"It's out of bounds," said Richards, "but they come with messages sometimes."

"Did Rhonda Miles ever come here?"

"She might have done. Yes, she came once because her bicycle had a puncture."

"Richards does all the repair work," said Miss Browning, "and he helps prepare the girls for their cycling proficiency badge."

So it obviously wasn't unknown for pupils to visit the caretaker's cottage, thought Meg.

"Are the girls allowed to cycle?" she asked.

"In the school grounds," said Miss Browning. "And Miss Jones, the games mistress, takes them out on rides sometimes. They go up to Devil's Dyke. Very good exercise."

"Did Rhonda know where the keys were kept?" asked Meg.

"I couldn't say." Miss Browning was regaining some of her composure — and her authority.

But Richards said, "She did know because she saw me get the keys to the bike shed. She made a joke about me being the Keeper of the Keys, like in the Charlie Chan book."

So Rhonda read detective stories, thought Meg. And, by the sound of it, so did Richards.

"We need to take the hat back to the police station," she said.

"Could she have left it there on purpose?" asked Superintendent Stephens. "It seems so obvious."

Meg felt rather annoyed. The hat was her clue, the first real clue they had, and now the super was sneering at it. Of course, DI Willis hastened to agree with his boss.

"That's what I thought. Almost as if was left there for us to find."

The hat was sitting in the middle of the incident table. Meg had been careful to handle it with her gloves on. The super had an obsession about not touching evidence. He liked to dust everything for fingerprints and for other, less obvious, evidence. So far Rhonda's hat had yielded a collection of red hairs which were also on the table in a see-through bag. "One day," the super said, "we'll be able to identify people from a single hair." This was why some people called him eccentric.

"Why would someone leave the hat for us to find?" said Meg, aware that she was sounding truculent.

"Maybe it was Rhonda herself," said the super, "trying to put us off the scent. She placed the hat there so that we'd think she'd left via the tunnel."

"Why though?" said Meg. "I mean, Rhonda must have planned her escape. She stole the keys from the caretaker. That wouldn't have been so difficult though. The safe was by his front door and he admitted that it wasn't always kept locked. But, having gone to all that trouble, why leave a clue?"

The DI made a noise indicating that she should be quiet and stop answering her superiors back but the super just said, mildly, "That's a point. But it's hard to see how the hat came off by accident. It's quite large and there's a neck strap to secure it."

"You never do up the neck strap," Meg informed him, although Fitzherbert hadn't run to school hats, or indeed a uniform of any kind. "And she could have been carrying it, not wearing it."

"Or she could have been in a struggle," said Danny Black, perhaps emboldened by Meg's example to speak up. Usually PCs weren't invited to the incident meetings but, as they had found the evidence, an exception had been made. To Meg's annoyance, everyone took Danny's suggestion more seriously than they had taken her objections.

"That's certainly possible," said the super, looking concerned. "There have been no recorded sightings of Rhonda although we're keeping a close watch on the Bobby Hambro fans outside his hotel. I spoke to Mr Hambro today and he couldn't recall ever having seen a girl of Rhonda's description."

Meg would have loved to have listened in to the conversation between Superintendent Stephens and Bobby Hambro, Hollywood idol. She wasn't a Hambro fan herself. She was a Beatles girl.

"There's another line I'd like us to explore," the super was saying. He took two newspaper cuttings from his briefcase and pinned them on the board. Meg craned her neck to see. She was at the back of the room but luckily she could see over the men's heads. One showed a group of nurses, the other a mod girl standing by a Vespa.

"Louise Dawkins," said Superintendent Stephens, pointing to one of the nurses, "and Sara Henratty. Both went missing over the last few weeks. Both left notes."

"We think there might be a connection," said DI Willis. He'd clearly been briefed beforehand but he still sounded rather dubious. To be fair, though, he sounded dubious about most things. "All three girls are young. Louise is nineteen, Sara and Rhonda sixteen. They all disappeared, leaving notes saying not to follow them. Louise and Sara haven't been seen since."

"There aren't many similarities," said DS Brendan O'Neill, a large man famous in the station for his way with a billiard cue and with suspects. Rumour had it that he succeeded with the latter mainly by beating confessions out of them. He had always been friendly to Meg, probably because they were both Irish, but she was still slightly scared of him. "I mean," O'Neill went on, "that girl's coloured and the other one's a mod. Rhonda was a nice girl, she came from a good family."

"All three have names," said the super, "and all three are probably nice girls. Louise was a trainee nurse. She said in her note that she was going back to her family in the West Indies but, according to her friends, she didn't have any close relations left there. Sara was in foster care. She said she was going off with a boyfriend and no one bothered to check. It's true that Rhonda came from a different background. She was a pupil at an exclusive boarding school. Her disappearance was never going to go unnoticed. But three young women vanishing in Brighton over about six weeks. I think we should entertain the hypothesis that there's a link."

Entertain the hypothesis. Would the super never learn? O'Neill looked baffled and rather angry. Danny turned to Meg and made a face, eyes crossed hideously.

"Let's get going," said DI Willis. "DS O'Neill and DS Barker." Charlie "Chubby" Barker, O'Neill's long-time partner, a lugubrious man who, despite his nickname, was extremely thin. "You follow up on Louise and Sara. See if there's anything suspicious in their disappearances. Also check the undercliff walk. See if there were any sightings of a red-haired girl on Monday night or early on Tuesday morning. WPC Connolly." Meg jumped. She hadn't expected to be given a role. She'd thought that she would be back to traffic duty and finding lost dogs. She sat up straighter. "Yes, sir?"

"I want you to go up to London and talk to the Bobby Hambro fans."

"Talk to them?"

"Yes." The DI's ears were going red again. "I want you to mingle with them. Undercover. In plain clothes."

"You'll have to wear a miniskirt, Meg," said Danny.

Meg didn't mind. She even didn't mind all the sniggering in the room at the thought of her legs being exposed. She was going undercover. Like a real detective.

CHAPTER
NINE

Max was feeling uncomfortable. It wasn't just that he was having a rare evening alone with his adult daughter, or that she was cooking him something that smelt as if it was already burnt, it was also that he was sitting on what was closer to a medieval instrument of torture than an armchair. He'd chosen the chair, an egg-shaped thing with an orange corduroy cushion in the middle, because the only other alternatives appeared to be beanbags or a sofa that was already occupied by a Siamese cat. Ruby was obviously proud of her flat, which was in a 1930s mansion block, just off Kensington Church Street. She had shown him round proudly: white walls, op-art pictures, a bed covered in zebra stripes, a bathroom with pink furnishings, an open-plan kitchen/diner with bar stools and an American-style fridge.

"It's been in *Vogue*," she told him, leafing through the magazines on the glass coffee table until she found one that opened easily at a spread entitled "Ruby Magic at Home", showing Ruby curled up in the egg chair, and holding a frying pan in the kitchen whilst wearing a miniskirt and white knee-length boots.

"It's great," said Max. "Very modern."

"I suppose you're used to your mansion in Beverly Hills," said Ruby, her voice hardening.

"Of course not," said Max. But, in truth, he was, rather. He was used to space and light and seeing blue sky out of the window, rather than the flats opposite. He was used to swimming forty lengths before breakfast and having a Spanish chef who made him pancakes with blueberries and fresh cream. Ruby's flat was described in *Vogue* as "a with-it retreat for our favourite It Girl" but it seemed cramped and uncomfortable to Max. Or maybe that was just because his back seemed to have gone into spasm.

Ruby was in the kitchen now, clattering pans and occasionally uttering small exclamations of surprise and dismay. Max had offered to take her to a restaurant, to the Hungaria or the Ritz, but she had insisted on cooking for him at her flat. Now, he wondered why. Despite the photograph in *Vogue*, he got the impression that Ruby didn't venture into the kitchen very often.

"Ready!" she called. The cat, who was called Cleopatra, stretched and looked at Max out of insolent blue eyes. Max liked cats but this one seemed a particularly aloof specimen who had responded to Max's initial overtures of friendship with a sharp, almost certainly admonitory, meow. Max and Cleopatra proceeded into the kitchen where Ruby had laid the round table with a red table-cloth and a candle in a Chianti bottle. She placed a plate in front of Max. It contained a pork chop with a pineapple ring on it surrounded by an unknown gloopy substance.

"Ratatouille," she said. "It comes out of a tin but it's apparently just as good as the real thing."

Cleopatra was meowing impatiently and Ruby opened a different tin for her. Max found himself looking at its contents almost with envy. He'd brought a bottle of Barolo and opened it now, pouring them both generous glasses. He had a feeling that he would need it if he was going to be able to eat anything.

The chop and the pineapple were both slightly burnt but the pineapple had a cloying sweetness that contrasted oddly with the acidity of the ratatouille. Max took a swig of wine.

"This is delicious," he said. "Thank you."

"It tastes a bit strange," said Ruby dispassionately. "Everything I cook ends up tasting strange."

"Do you cook often?"

"No." She smiled at him, her old grin, a mixture of bonhomie and challenge. "Usually men take me out to dinner."

"I can imagine."

Max knew about Ruby's boyfriends. They even sometimes appeared in the American gossip magazines that were Lydia's main source of reading material: pop stars, racing drivers, the occasional minor royal and, of course, the ever-present Joe Passolini. But Max had no idea why Ruby was thirty-four (how *could* he have a daughter in her thirties?) and still unmarried. She was rich and successful and as beautiful as ever. Possibly more beautiful now than she had been at twenty, thinner and more stylish, her glossy black hair just reaching her chin, her brown eyes enhanced with mascara and dark eyeliner.

"It's good to see you," he said, manfully continuing to eat his chop. Ruby had pushed her plate away, almost untouched.

"It's been a long time," said Ruby. "Do you mind if I smoke?"

"No," said Max. He was surprised how many people in England still smoked. Lydia thought that tobacco was poison and made him take his cigars out into the garden.

He'd seen Ruby at his father's funeral. She'd been fond of the old monster and seemed genuinely sad at his death. Then she'd visited them in LA with mixed success. Ruby had got on well with the children but he could see that Lydia was not overjoyed by the appearance of a stepdaughter who was almost her own age and was, what's more, a successful performer in her own right. He'd made a fuss of Ruby and had shown her the sights of Hollywood but she'd seemed determined to be unimpressed. "It reminds me of the Blackpool illuminations," she'd said, when he'd taken her to see the famous sign in the hills.

"Is there a man at the moment?" he asked, as she blew out smoke. He fully expected Ruby to tell him to mind his own business but she just gave him the smile again and said, "Yes, there is, as a matter of fact, but I'm keeping him secret for the moment."

"How's the show going?" he said. "Joe said that ratings were higher than ever."

"Yes," she said. "People still seem to love *Ruby Magic*." The show, a comedy drama about a magician who used her powers to extricate her from the complications of her personal life, had been on the BBC for six years now. Ruby was wonderful in it, funny and clever and sometimes unexpectedly moving, but, even so, Max wondered whether it was reaching the end of its natural life. There were only so many romantic mishaps a girl magician could have.

"It was good to see Edgar and Emma again at Uncle Stan's funeral," Ruby said now. "I'd forgotten that I actually liked her."

Ruby had once been engaged to Edgar and, whilst Max had never thought that they were well-suited, he sometimes wondered whether Ruby had been more upset at their break-up than she admitted. He thought that she had been hurt at the speed with which Edgar had married Emma afterwards. He had certainly never heard her speak warmly about Emma before.

"She's an interesting woman," he said, rather cautiously. "I wonder if she finds life as a wife and mother completely fulfilling."

"I would say she was bored to tears," said Ruby.

"I'm having dinner with them tomorrow," said Max. "I'll ask her."

"I bet you don't," said Ruby. "Oh, stop pretending to eat that, Max. It's absolutely disgusting. I've got some cheese and biscuits somewhere."

After that, the evening was cosier. They took the cheese and biscuits, and the rest of the wine, into the sitting room and Ruby made Cleopatra move so that they could have the sofa. They talked about acting and magic and the Beatles' recent trip to America.

"I met them once," said Ruby. "They were nice. Quite shy actually."

"They're clever songwriters," said Max. "But all this hysteria about pop stars now makes me rather nervous. Strange things happen when people become hysterical. I remember that in the war."

"It's like stage magic," said Ruby. "People will see what they want to see."

Max had already decided not to go back to Brighton that night. He'd go to the Strand Palace where they always kept a room for him. It was nearly midnight but he didn't want to break up the evening. But then the telephone rang and Ruby disappeared for a long time. When she came back, she seemed rather keen for him to leave, mentioning last trains and the difficulties of finding taxis on Kensington High Street. Max took the hint. He wondered if the mysterious man was coming round. The thought made him rather uneasy.

CHAPTER
TEN

Meg emerged from Green Park tube station feeling unpleasantly conscious of the fact that the people behind her could see up her skirt. She'd had to borrow it from her younger sister Aisling and, whilst all the Connollys were tall, Aisling was at least three inches shorter than Meg. The pleated skirt that came just above Aisling's knees was mid-thigh on Meg and the waistband was uncomfortably tight. She'd teamed it with a chunky jumper, knee-length boots and a crocheted hat that she'd made herself. The outfit had looked passable in her mirror that morning but as soon as she reached London, she saw that it was all wrong. Girls wore shift dresses with little white collars, pale tights and buckled shoes. Boots were white, not brown with rubber soles. No one wore a jumper, unless it was a little twinset. The hat was OK but she was conscious that her hair, cut short so that it wouldn't have to be tied back at work, wasn't the shiny waterfall that cascaded down the backs of the beauties sauntering along Piccadilly. And — dear God! — why were all the women so small and thin? What had they done with everyone over five ten? Locked them up in the Tower?

At least she looked awkward so she'd probably fit in with the Bobby Soxers. They were gathered outside the hotel, about fifteen of them, teenagers by the look of them. Why weren't they in school? It was eleven o'clock on a Thursday morning. Shouldn't they be doing double French, or something equally tedious? She approached two girls who were reading a magazine, shiny heads close together, mousy and blonde.

"Hi!" she said. "Has he come out yet?"

The girls looked at her. They weren't hostile exactly but they were wary, suspecting an outsider in their midst.

"He's not due out until midday," said the blonde girl. "He's going into the country to look at locations for *Golden Heart*."

"How do you know?"

"The doorman told us," said Mousy Hair. "It's Pat today. He's nice. Not like Alan."

"No, Alan's horrible," said the other girl. "He called us silly little girls the other day."

"What a cheek," said Meg. "Well, he can't call me little." She thought she'd better get the height thing out of the way early on. She was bending her knees slightly but she still towered over the other girls.

"No," said Blondie. "How old are you anyway?"

"Eighteen," said Meg promptly. "Same as Bobby."

"I read somewhere that he's twenty-five," said Mouse.

"That's a bloody lie," said Blondie. She looked rather defiantly at Meg, perhaps expecting her to be shocked at such language.

Two other girls came over; they looked older and more confident, wearing leather jackets and capri pants.

"Who's she?" said one of them, who had short dark hair and panda eyes.

"I'm Meg. What's your name?"

Panda looked shocked at such affrontery but eventually said, "I'm Jean. Why are you here?"

"I'm a Bobby Soxer."

"Oh yeah? When's his birthday?"

"Second of April. He's an Aries."

"What's his favourite colour?"

"Blue."

"What are his sisters' names?"

"Erin and Kelly-Ann." Meg blessed the hour she had spent with Aisling's copy of *Film Frolics* which had included a Q and A with Bobby Hambro.

Jean looked at her appraisingly. Mousy seemed to think that she had passed the test though because she vouchsafed that she was Veronica and her friend was Isabel.

"Why haven't we seen you here before?" said Jean.

"I work in an office," said Meg. "I haven't had any time off. I've come all the way from Brighton."

This seemed to gain her some Brownie points. Veronica told her that she and Isabel were skiving off school. Jean said that she'd left school and that office work was for dummies.

"Have you ever met my friend from Brighton?" asked Meg. "She's called Rhonda. Got red hair in a bob."

"What's your game?" said Jean. "We had a policeman asking about Rhonda the other day."

Damn. She hadn't expected this to come up so quickly.

"Her dad's really square and overprotective," she said. "He doesn't like her coming here. He set the police on her."

"Rhonda was here a few weeks ago," said Veronica, "but we haven't seen her since."

"And we wouldn't tell the pigs if we had," said Jean. "We hate the police."

"Too right," said Meg.

In his underground office Edgar was reading about the first abduction of Rhonda Miles. It had happened six years ago, when Rhonda was ten. She was walking home alone from her ballet lesson when a car stopped and apparently offered her a lift. Ignoring all her parents' warnings about such an eventuality, Rhonda had got into the car whereupon the driver, Ernest Coggins, had driven her five miles to his caravan near Esher Common. He had locked Rhonda in the van and telephoned her parents demanding the almost pathetically small sum of a thousand pounds. Crispian Miles (this was before his elevation to the peerage) had asked his location and promptly driven there accompanied by three burly policemen. Coggins had been arrested and subsequently found guilty of abduction and extortion. He was sentenced to ten years which he was currently serving, Edgar was interested to see, at Ford Open Prison in West Sussex. The papers at the time were full of Crispian's coolness under pressure and Rhonda's recklessness at getting into the car. She was not even meant to be walking home alone but had quarrelled with her friend and taken a different, less salubrious, route.

It was a sad little story, thought Edgar, but interesting nonetheless. It showed that, even at ten, Rhonda was capable of deceiving her parents and gullible enough to believe a stranger offering her a lift. Would she be fooled again, especially considering this childhood trauma? Ernest Coggins was described in court as a fantasist who believed himself to be a master criminal. There was some suggestion that he had also had some political animus against Crispian Miles and that "communist literature" had been found in his caravan. One paper reported that Rhonda had cried on being discovered because she didn't want to be parted from Coggins' terrier, Lenin. This too was interesting.

All things considered, Edgar was not surprised, at two o'clock, to be told that Sir Crispian Miles was in reception and demanding to see him.

"What are you doing about my daughter?" were the politician's first words. "It's been four days now and, as far as I can see, you and your men have done precisely nothing to find her."

"I know this is very hard for you and Lady Miles," said Edgar, "but I promise you that we are doing all we can to find Rhonda. There's been a small development, in fact. Rhonda's school hat was found in a tunnel leading from Roedean to the undercliff walk."

"Tunnel?" Sir Crispian's eyes started to bulge alarmingly. "What tunnel?"

82

"There's a tunnel from the school to the sea," said Edgar. "It's usually kept locked but my men . . . my officers . . . investigated and found that it was open. Rhonda's hat was found by the door."

"What are you waiting for, then?" said Sir Crispian. "That must have been the way he took her, the abductor."

"We've been making enquiries along the length of the undercliff walk," said Edgar, "but no one recalls seeing a girl of Rhonda's description. We're also continuing to watch the Ritz in London. I've got an undercover officer, a WPC, there now."

"I don't know why you keep harping on about this Bobby Hambro business," said Sir Crispian. "Rhonda isn't the kind of girl to hang around outside hotels waiting to see some tinpot film star."

"We spoke to her friends at Roedean," said Edgar, "and they all agreed that Rhonda is a big fan of Mr Hambro. As indeed they all are."

"Don't know what the world's coming to," said Sir Crispian. "Teenagers. We didn't have teenagers when I was growing up. You were a child and then you were an adult. That was it."

Edgar didn't say that, at sixteen, Rhonda would be considered by many to be an adult.

"I've been reading about the Ernest Coggins case," he said. "That must have been very traumatic for your family."

"Yes," said Sir Crispian, his voice lowering in volume for the first time. "Edith, m'wife, she was never really the same again. Rhonda's our only child, you see."

He got out a large handkerchief and blew his nose loudly. For the first time he didn't seem like a bullying politician. Edgar felt his heart twist in sympathy.

"Was Rhonda affected by the kidnapping?" he said. "It must have been an awful experience for her."

"Rhonda just kept going on about Coggins' stupid dog. The one with a commie name. She kept on at me to get her a dog. That's why we sent her to Roedean. We thought it would stop all that nonsense."

Getting a dog wasn't exactly nonsense, thought Edgar. His daughters were also carrying on a campaign for a dog. Unlike Sir Crispian, Edgar thought that he'd probably capitulate soon.

"Have you heard from Coggins since he's been in prison?" he asked.

"He wrote once to say that he was sorry," said Sir Crispian. "Damn cheek. I burnt it."

"You say that you think Rhonda's been abducted," said Edgar. "Do you think it might be linked to Ernest Coggins?"

"Don't see how it can be," said Sir Crispian. "Fellow's in prison. Police said he was acting alone. It'll be some other commie."

But communist kidnappers were few and far between, thought Edgar. He didn't put this thought to Sir Crispian.

At twelve o'clock precisely, Bobby Hambro emerged from the front door of the Ritz, accompanied by a burly bodyguard and a slight, dark man in a pinstriped suit. As one, the girls screamed and ran forward. Meg ran

84

with them, feeling extremely foolish. She couldn't bring herself to scream but she put her fingers in her mouth and whistled. This was a great success. Even Jean looked at her with admiration and Bobby actually turned his head and waved. Over the heads of the swooning fans, Meg waved back.

Bobby and his entourage got into the waiting Rolls and it purred away. The girls looked at each other, slightly breathless with excitement.

"He waved at us!" said Veronica. "He actually waved."

"That was Meg and her whistle," said Isabel. "Can you teach me how to do that?"

"Sure," said Meg, who had learnt from her older brothers. But it proved impossible for the Bobby Soxers to reproduce the whistle. Perhaps middle-class people had softer lips? In the end they gave up and drifted away towards a nearby Wimpy bar. Meg went with them but they offered no more interesting confidences about Rhonda. The conversation was mainly about *Golden Heart*, and whether there would be any romance in it. The girls had a complicated attitude towards Bobby's love life. They were insanely jealous of any woman who was seen with him but they obviously approved of some consorts more than others. An actress called Vanessa Lee almost met with their approval for the simple reason that she was blonde like Bobby and "looked nice". But Maria Garcia, a Mexican-born singer, was cordially disliked. "They don't look right together," said a girl called Sadie. Meg thought that she was the sort of person who would have disapproved of British girls going out with black American GIs in the war.

They spent ages in the café over milkshakes and sticky buns but eventually the girls got up to leave. There was no point staying at the Ritz, they explained, because Bobby wouldn't be back until the evening. "I'll be back later," boasted Jean but Veronica and Isabel said they should be getting home. Meg walked with them to the bus stop. As they waited for the number 247, Veronica said suddenly, "You know your friend, Rhonda?"

"Yes?" said Meg.

"She said something funny once, didn't she, Izzy?"

"Yes," said Isabel, who was turning herself back into a schoolgirl by putting on a tie and placing a crumpled beret on her head. "She said that she was going to be a model."

"A model?"

"She said that she'd met this agent," said Veronica, who was unrolling her skirt so that it reached almost to her knees. "And that he was going to make her famous. Izzy and I thought it was mad. I mean, Rhonda, a model."

"It does seem odd," said Meg. She caught sight of the girls' faces and added, with a burst of inspiration, "You two are much more the type."

It was the right thing to say. Veronica and Isabel both tossed their hair complacently. "Well, yes," said Isabel. "I mean, even you, you're tall like a model."

"I'm not thin enough though," said Meg.

"No," agreed Isabel. "But Rhonda ... she's all-right-looking but she's got red hair and freckles. When did you last see a model with red hair and freckles?"

"Never," said Meg. "Did Rhonda say anything more about this agent?"

"She got talking to him here, outside the Ritz," said Veronica. "We saw her with a man once but we never thought anything about it, did we, Iz?"

"Can you remember what he looked like?"

"No," said Isabel. "He was just a man."

Their bus arrived and the two girls got on, waving cheerfully at Meg from the upper deck. She set off towards the tube station, deep in thought.

Emma didn't like to admit, even to herself, how excited she was to be going out to dinner at the Grand. She had even bought a new dress, a green shift with embroidery around the neck and cuffs. She brushed her hair until it shone. It was too long, really, but she hoped that it made her look younger and less like a mother of three. Should she put on some make-up? She never usually bothered but girls wore so much these days. Her mascara was dry so she spat on the brush and started to apply it rather gingerly.

She became aware of the fact that she was being watched from the doorway. Marianne and Sophie, already in pyjamas and matching pink dressing gowns.

"You look nicer than usual," said Marianne.

"Gosh, thanks, Mari."

"You look like a princess," said Sophie, coming to give her a hug that made her drop the mascara wand.

"Thank you, Soph." Emma hugged her back. "You two girls be good for Mavis now. I've told her that you can watch *Top of the Pops* before bed."

The girls squealed. *Top of the Pops*, the new music programme, was the highlight of their week, and often of Emma's too. Edgar said that it gave him a headache but Emma loved seeing the Disc Girl putting a record on the turntable and the studio filling with music. The singers mimed, which was often unintentionally hilarious, but there was something thrilling about the countdown at the end and the announcement of "the nation's number one". This week it was sure to be the Beatles singing "Can't Buy Me Love". They had had the top slot with various records since February.

Two floors down she heard the door open and Edgar's voice in the hall.

"Daddy!" Marianne and Sophie ran to greet him. Emma often envied the way that Edgar's homecoming was like the return of Odysseus. When she went out (which was rare enough) she was usually greeted with, "Where have you been?" and Jonathan being sick on her.

Emma finished applying her mascara, added some lipstick, brushed her hair and looked critically at her face in the mirror. Not bad but not exactly Ruby Magic or Lydia Lamont. When she got downstairs, Edgar was sitting on the sofa with Jonathan on his lap and a daughter on either side. Mavis, her ever-present knitting on her lap, watched them indulgently.

Edgar whistled when he saw her. "You look beautiful, Em."

"Thank you." She was rather pleased with the compliment, though. Ed was always nice about her appearance but it was usually along the lines of "*I* think you're gorgeous" as if this was a strange and unusual preference. And he rarely used the word "beautiful".

"Do I look pretty?" asked Marianne. She was now wearing a ballet tutu over her pyjamas.

"Exquisite," said Edgar. "A truly original ensemble."

"You look the spit of your mum," said Mavis. Emma could see Marianne trying to work out if this was a compliment.

"Should I change?" Edgar asked. He was wearing one of the suits he always wore for work, dark grey and anonymous.

"No. You look fine," said Emma.

"Max will probably be wearing a dinner jacket."

"I doubt it," said Emma. "Everything's casual now. He might be wearing jeans and a Stetson."

"Is Max a cowboy?" asked Marianne, wide-eyed.

"No, he's a magician," said Emma.

When Max stood up to greet them, Emma saw that he was wearing a dark-grey velvet smoking jacket, so much more elegant than anything she could have imagined.

"Mrs Stephens," he said. "You look absolutely stunning."

"Thank you," she said. "But do drop the Mrs thing. After all, you knew me when I was Emma."

"You're still Emma," said Edgar, sounding rather hurt.

"People in LA sometimes call me Mr Lamont," said Max. "Now that *is* insulting."

"You're as big a star as her," said Emma, accepting a martini with an olive floating in it. It was a new thought that Max, too, had moments when he felt like the invisible partner in his marriage.

"Not in LA," said Max. "To most people I'm still the odd British magician who married Lydia Lamont."

"Not here," said Emma. She was conscious of a strange desire to protect Max. Not an emotion she had ever felt before, in relation to him at least. "In England you're the famous one. You're Max Mephisto."

"Max Mephisto is old hat," said Max. "Come on, let's eat. I'm starving."

They went through into the dining room with its view over the sea. Lights shone on the piers and on the fishing boats, far out towards the horizon. Sometimes, Emma thought, Brighton seemed like an enchanted place. She had lived in the town all her life — except for a brief period when she'd been evacuated during the war — and, on evenings like this, she couldn't think of anywhere she'd rather be. But in the winter, when the sea and sky were the same cold grey, or in the height of summer when the streets were full of tourists and young men on motorbikes, then she did dream of escape. But where would she go? Edgar's job was in Brighton, her parents were nearby, the girls were happy at school. She wasn't Max Mephisto. She couldn't just run away to Hollywood.

Max told them about the film he had agreed to make, a remake of *Little Lord Fauntleroy*.

"You're far too young to play the grandfather," said Emma.

"Thank you but they've worked out that it's possible. Bobby is meant to be eighteen so, if his father was in his early twenties when he was born, then I could be a grandfather at fifty-four. After all, I've got a daughter of thirty-four. I could be a grandfather already."

"I can't believe Ruby is thirty-four," said Emma. "I'm only a year older and I feel middle-aged. She still looks twenty to me."

"I saw her last night," said Max. "And she does look well. She's got a nice flat in Kensington where she cooked me a truly inedible meal."

Edgar looked uncomfortable, as he often did when Ruby was mentioned, but Emma was interested. "Does she live on her own?"

"Yes, with a very superior cat called Cleopatra."

"How lovely."

"What's Bobby Hambro like?" asked Edgar. "I spoke to him on the telephone about this missing girl. I thought he sounded quite vacant."

"He's sharp enough," said Max. "After all, he's made a lot of money from acting the part of a simple country boy. He's not much of an actor but he's going to capitalise on his looks while he still has them. He's producing the film as well as starring in it."

"Has he got a girlfriend?" asked Emma. She was rather ashamed of herself for such a *Film Frolics* question.

"He didn't mention one," said Max, "but you can be sure that he'll have some starlet on his arm for the premiere. Preferably someone approved by his publicist."

Emma wanted to know more but was distracted by the arrival of their food. She had scallops followed by fillet steak, so tender that her knife seemed to sink into it. They drank red wine and talked about the days when Max had performed in variety shows in Brighton.

"The Hippodrome is closing at the end of the year," said Max. "I can't quite believe it."

"Nor can I," said Emma. "The Beatles played there last year."

"The Beatles are all we hear about in our house," said Edgar.

"The girls are fans then?" said Max.

"No," said Emma. "I am." She realised that she was rather drunk.

"Ruby's met them, apparently," said Max. "They've certainly got some loyal fans. So has Bobby. Screaming girls following him everywhere he goes. I saw them hanging about outside the Ritz."

"My WPC was one of them today," said Edgar. "Undercover."

"Is that the intrepid Meg Connolly?" said Emma.

"Yes," said Edgar, looking surprised. "How did you know?"

Before she could answer, Max gave an exclamation, "Talking of intrepid . . ." Emma turned and saw Bob Willis weaving through the tables towards them. She'd seen that look on his face before.

"Sir," he said to Edgar, "you'd better come. They've found a girl's body on the undercliff walk. She's wearing a Roedean cloak."

CHAPTER
ELEVEN

The body was discovered near Rottingdean and so Edgar and Bob drove to a nearby pub, the White Horse, and took the sloping path down to the undercliff walk, a raised walkway between the cliffs and the sea. The tide was out but Edgar could hear the waves rushing into the shore. A fitful moon illuminated the dark figure of a uniformed policeman with a sprawled shape at his feet. As he saw them approaching, the PC turned on his torch. In the arc of light Edgar saw Sam Collins and a photographer standing a discreet distance away.

"What are you doing here?" he asked.

"We heard that a body had been found," said Sam. Edgar couldn't see her expression but he could hear the note of excitement in her voice.

"Is it a suicide?" said the photographer, a man called Harry Payne, whom Edgar knew from various civic events.

"We don't know anything yet," he said. "Keep back. Have some respect for the poor girl's family."

"So it is a female then?" said Sam. Edgar ignored her. He approached the constable, who was talking to Bob. Edgar knelt and drew back the coat that was covering the body. The moon emerged from behind the clouds and he saw blonde hair partly covering a white face.

"It's not Rhonda," he said.

"Any ideas of cause of death?" asked Bob.

"No," said the PC, "but she didn't fall. There's no blood. Body was found by two men leaving the White Horse to walk back into town."

"Where are they now?"

"I sent them back into the pub to wait for you."

"Good work," said Edgar. "How long have the journalists been here?"

"They arrived soon after I did. Must have had a tip-off."

Edgar turned back to the body. It was a young woman, wearing a dark cloak over what was obviously a mini-dress. Long pale legs sprawled pathetically and she was barefoot.

"Shine your torch on her face," said Edgar.

Now he could clearly see bruising around the girl's neck. One hand was still clenched in a fist.

A voice behind him said, "That's Sara Henratty."

"I told you to stay back," said Edgar.

"It's Sara," said Sam, taking no notice. "I recognise her from the photo. Look at her hair."

The platinum-blonde head gleamed in the moonlight. Edgar thought that Sam was probably right. They had found one of the missing girls.

"Well, that's the evening finished then," said Emma. As soon as she said it, she realised how callous that sounded.

Max didn't seem shocked though. "Not necessarily," he said. "Would you like a pudding? Or coffee? Or brandy?"

"I don't want pudding or coffee," said Emma, "but I would like a brandy."

They took their brandies into the lounge and Emma was appalled to find herself saying, with real bitterness, "Edgar won't ask for my help on this case, you know. It'll be all 'let's not talk about work now'. He'll leave it all to Bob, who hasn't got a clue, and the amazing, resourceful Meg Connolly."

"You miss it," said Max, swilling the brandy to and fro in his glass. It wasn't a question.

"Yes, I do," said Emma. "I suppose you think that's very strange, to miss murder."

"Not at all," said Max. "I miss staying in freezing boarding houses and performing to sparse audiences in filthy provincial theatres."

"Do you?" said Emma, turning to look at him.

"Yes," said Max, his eyes meeting hers. "I miss it unbearably sometimes."

"But couldn't you still perform on stage?"

"Variety's dead," said Max, taking a hefty swig of brandy. "It's all film or TV these days. You have to do what Ruby's done, become a TV personality, as they're called now. It's not enough just to have a talent. You have to be a personality. To make the public love you."

"But you're a film star," said Emma. "That's better than being a TV personality."

Max laughed, rather harshly. "I've been fairly successful in a few films but I'm not really an actor.

Not the way that Lydia is. She's an actress to her fingertips; it's extraordinary the way she can become another person, from her walk to the way she moves her mouth. I've been lucky to have had roles that have allowed me to play a version of myself. No, I'm a magician. It's all I really know how to do."

"But do you have to go on acting?" said Emma. "I mean, you're so . . ." She was going to say "rich" but compromised with "successful".

"No," said Max. "I don't have to act or perform magic. And you don't have to go out and solve crimes. We've both got nice, comfortable lives with loving partners and beautiful children. But it's not enough, is it?"

Emma wanted to disagree but, faced with Max's sardonic gaze, she could only nod and look away. He was right; it wasn't enough.

They walked back along the seafront. The lights were still shining on the piers and they could hear laughter coming from the pubs on the edge of the beach. Brighton was getting ready for the summer. The covers were off the merry-go-round and as they wandered past it Emma could see the glint of the horses' teeth, bared in that slightly threatening carousel smile.

"It'll be the Whitsun bank holiday soon," she said. "Edgar's worried about the mods and rockers causing trouble."

"Joe Passolini is a mod, apparently," said Max. "Or he just likes the clothes. We don't have all this in LA, the tribal thing. Or rather, we have different tribes."

"When are you going back to America?" asked Emma. She noticed that he said "we".

"I'm not sure," said Max. "If Bobby gets the finance in place for the film, he wants to start shooting immediately. That would mean that I'm here for the summer. Lydia and the kids might come and join me."

"What's she like?" said Emma. "Lydia?" She would never have asked this normally but something about the night, and the fact that they were walking side by side, created an odd feeling of intimacy. Besides, she was still slightly drunk.

Max hesitated before replying, inhaling on his cigarette, the tip glowing red in the darkness. "Lydia's very bright," he said at last. "Very intense. She's had a hard life. She started out with nothing, apart from her extraordinary looks, of course. And her acting talent. But it makes her very insecure. She always has to be striving for the next thing. We fell in love on the set of *The Conjuror* when I played this Svengali figure and I'm afraid that she still has me cast in that role." Max was silent for the next hundred yards and then he said, "I'm not sure that I've ever been properly in love. Apart from that one time with Florence but that was over so soon. Who knows what would have happened?"

Florence had been murdered. Emma remembered finding her body, the dark hair brushing the floor, the macabre staging to make the scene look like the death of Cleopatra. She wished that she hadn't talked about missing murder. "That must have been awful for you," she said.

98

"Awful for her and her family," said Max. "She had so much talent. I've still got the plays and sketches that she wrote. That's something I want to do while I'm here. Try to get them played on the radio. Florence deserves to be remembered as something more than a murder victim."

Florence had died eleven years ago and Max still carried her writings round with him. Emma had never realised how deeply he felt about her.

"It's like the old stage trick," he said, as they made their way up St James's Street. "The girl is in the cabinet and, when you open the door, she's gone. Now you see her. Now you don't. The Vanishing Box. I went walking around Brighton yesterday, Mrs M's boarding house, the Hippodrome, the Royal Albion. I kept seeing Florence everywhere."

"Maybe it's being back in Brighton," said Emma.

"Maybe," said Max. "Maybe it's just because I've avoided thinking about her all these years. I should have found a shrink and poured out my emotions to them. That's what all the film stars do."

Is that what Lydia Lamont did? Emma wondered. Aloud she said, "Sometimes it's good to keep your feelings hidden."

Max stopped under a streetlight to look at her. "But you're lucky, you've got Edgar to talk to."

"Yes," said Emma. "I'm one of the lucky ones."

They had reached Emma's front door. She didn't know whether to invite Max in or to kiss him on the cheek when they parted. He solved that for her by making her a sweeping bow.

"Goodnight, Mrs Stephens."

And, as soon as she had the door open, he set off down the dark street.

CHAPTER
TWELVE

"The warden of the children's home identified the corpse as being that of Sara Henratty, aged sixteen. The body was discovered on the undercliff walk near Rottingdean at ten-thirty p.m. by two men leaving the nearby White Horse pub. Rigor mortis had not set in which indicates that decease was relatively recent. We haven't had post-mortem results yet but the police surgeon thinks that death was the result of manual strangulation. There was bruising around the deceased's neck and blood under her nails which indicate that she must have tried to fight her assailant off. Her necklace was broken and there were marks on her skin where it had dug into her neck. She was barefoot, wearing a skirt and jumper and a cloak that forms part of the Roedean uniform and which contained the nametag 'Rhonda Miles'. This supports the theory that the disappearances of Rhonda Miles and Sara Henratty are linked and may also be linked to the disappearance of Louise Dawkins."

That was the super's theory, thought Meg, and she wouldn't put it past his wife, genius detective Emma Holmes, winner of the public speaking championship 1944, to have put the thought in his mind. But the DI, who was giving the briefing in his usual deadpan style, wasn't about to deviate from his notes. There was something curiously upsetting about hearing another human's death described in these terms, "manual strangulation", "rigor mortis had not set in". She looked up at the photograph of Sara on the incident board: the blonde hair, the miniskirt, the defiant expression. Sara could have been any one of the girls that Meg had been to school with; she could have been any one of the girls camped outside the Ritz Hotel. She was only sixteen, she should have been at school today or working in a factory or a shop, longing for the weekend ahead. Instead, she was lying in a morgue, identified only by a nameless warden. Meg felt her eyelids begin to prickle. She couldn't cry, not here, not in front of O'Neill and Barker, both of whom were lounging in their chairs as if hearing about a teenager's death was the perfect way to spend a Friday morning.

DI Willis was winding up. "Our focus of investigation is on the undercliff area between Rottingdean and Brighton. It's well used by pedestrians and cyclists. I'm sending a team down there today to see if anyone saw anything suspicious last night. We will also follow up on Rhonda Miles and Louise Dawkins."

"I'm surprised Lord Snooty hasn't been in already," said O'Neill, "demanding to know why we haven't found his daughter."

"If you mean Sir Crispian Miles," said the DI, "Superintendent Stephens is driving to Surrey today to give him the news in person."

That's special treatment, if you like, thought Meg. She was pretty sure that the super wasn't in the habit of making house calls to concerned relatives.

DI Willis was talking to Sergeant O'Neill now: "What did you discover from Louise's nursing friends?"

"Nothing much," said O'Neill, with a shrug. "They all liked Louise but none of them were particularly close to her. The other nurses seemed to accept the story about her going to the West Indies although Louise had never mentioned any family there. There was apparently a doctor, a houseman, who seemed suspicious though, asked a few questions."

"Interview him," said the DI. "Was he Louise's boy-friend?"

"I don't think so," said Barker. "But he's on our list." He made it sound very sinister.

"Sara Henratty's mother is dead," said DI Willis. "No one knows where her father is but I'll put out an appeal. There's an aunt in Seaford. WPC Connolly, I'd like you to come with me to break the news to her. Any questions?"

Plenty, thought Meg. Why do I have to visit the aunt in Seaford? Is it because DI Willis is scared that she'll cry and he needs a woman to do the tea and sympathy bit? Why is the super driving all the way to Surrey? Why do O'Neill and Barker always get to do everything together? She always liked to ask a question though, just to show that she was paying attention, so she said, "What about Sara's shoes?"

"What?" The DI, who had been pinning something on the board, turned to look at her. O'Neill whispered something to Barker, who laughed.

"You said that Sara had been found without her shoes. I mean, that's strange, isn't it? She was warmly dressed, wearing a cloak and everything, why wasn't she wearing shoes?"

"It seemed that she had been wearing shoes," said DI Willis, "the soles of her feet weren't cut or dirty as they would have been if she'd been walking barefoot. It appears that the shoes were removed from the scene."

"Why?" said Meg, adding "sir" as an afterthought.

"The super thought they may have been taken by the killer as a trophy of some kind," said DI Willis. "Or else they held a clue. The pin that holds the cloak together was also missing. That might also have been kept as a trophy or keepsake."

"Fancy a new pair of shoes, Meg?" said O'Neill.

Meg ignored him.

Having caught the early train to London, Max was not amused to be kept waiting ten minutes at the Garrick Club by Bobby Hambro and his director, Wilbur Wallace. He didn't like the Garrick either, even though it had links with one of his favourite venues, the Theatre Royal on Drury Lane. But today the place seemed to have little or nothing to do with show business. In fact the decor, with its leather armchairs and flock wallpaper, reminded Max of his father's London club, where they had met once or twice for uncomfortable lunches where the then Lord Massingham had told his son quite what a disappointment he had proved to be. Max hadn't been close to his father; he supposed that, subconsciously, he had always blamed him for his mother's death. Alastair Massingham had been a distant parent, disapproving of Max's show-business career and hardly much more impressed with his wartime exploits. Though, to be fair, Max did remember his father once sending him a telegram, care of the War Office, enquiring if he was still alive, so perhaps he had cared a bit.

It was funny, he had never seen much of his father when he was alive, but now Max found himself almost missing him. The late Lord Massingham would be quite at home here, ordering tea and digestive biscuits, or perhaps a martini as it was almost midday. Max sighed and drank some of his — almost undrinkable — coffee. He'd give Bobby another ten minutes and then he'd head off to somewhere more congenial.

Bobby arrived just as Max was gathering up his things.

"Sorry, sorry." It was pronounced "sarree". "The morning just got away from me." This was hardly an excuse, in Max's book. He was also irritated to see Joe Passolini in attendance on the Hollywood star. He knew that Joe, who hated to see a profitable client slip away, would like to control his affairs again but Max was quite happy with his American agent, a quietly spoken New Yorker called Harvey Broom, who was known as the deadliest deal-maker in the business.

Wilbur Wallace, the director, didn't look the deadly type. He was a thin, bespectacled man with a slight look of John Lennon, for Max's money the only interesting Beatle. It was a surprise, when Wilbur spoke, to hear an American accent rather than a Scouse twang.

Bobby and Wilbur ordered tea but Joe asked for a Bloody Mary. The hangover drink, thought Max. Joe certainly had the slightly pasty look of someone who had been out on the tiles the night before.

"So, Max," said Bobby, flashing him the famous "golden" smile. "We have the funding. I've been searching for a big old house that we can use for Dorincourt. I was in Worcester last weekend." He pronounced it "War-cester".

"It's pronounced Wooster," said Max.

"No! That's real neat. They didn't have anything that was quite right though. But — great news — we've got Vanessa Lee to play Sandy."

"Who?"

"Fauntleroy's American girlfriend, Sandy."

"You know he didn't have a girlfriend in the book?"

"Sure." Bobby waved the book away with a careless hand. "But this is a Bobby Hambro film and the fans will want some romance. They like Vanessa too, she has mostly positive comments in the fan magazines. And there's some love interest for you too, Max."

"Really?" said Max, his heart sinking.

"Yeah. In our version the Earl of Dorincourt gets together with Dearest."

"With his own son's widow?"

"Yeah. Neat, eh?"

"Maybe they just have a warm friendship," said Wilbur Wallace, soothingly.

"I think that's preferable," said Max.

"Well, that's all up to the script guys now," said Bobby. "So, Max, when we get a location I'm thinking of renting a place. Wanna be my housemate?"

"I think I might rent somewhere of my own," said Max. "I'm hoping that Lydia and the children will join me."

"That would be great for publicity," said Joe.

"It would be rather nice for me too," said Max.

"Are you still in Brighton?" said Wilbur. "I was brought up near there. A little place called Rottingdean."

"I know it well," said Max who, in truth, usually drove as fast as he could past Rottingdean with its picturesque village pond and plethora of genteel tea rooms.

"I know Rottingdean," said Bobby unexpectedly. "I used to spend my holidays near there. In Peacehaven."

"No one goes on holiday to Peacehaven," said Wilbur.

"I did," said Bobby, with unruffled affability. "I had an aunt who lived there."

"It's the sort of place where aunts live," said Max, accepting the inevitable and ordering a dry martini.

Aunts also seemed to proliferate in Seaford, a coastal town between Brighton and Eastbourne. Meg's Auntie Maureen lived there and, she learnt in the course of the drive, so did DI Willis's Auntie Doreen.

"I wonder why," said Meg, watching out of the window as the art deco roofs of Saltdean gave way to the grey, gridlike streets of Peacehaven.

"No hills," said the DI immediately. "Not like Brighton. The beach is flat too. Auntie Doreen likes to swim in the sea from April to October."

"I don't know what Auntie Maureen likes to do," said Meg. "Drink stout and bet on the horses probably."

Unexpectedly the DI laughed. "She sounds good company anyway. When we visited as children Auntie Doreen used to read aloud to us from the Bible. We hated it."

"Oh, Catholics never read the Bible," said Maureen. "We go to the pub in the evenings instead."

Once again she'd said too much (and mentioned the C word). The DI's ears went red and he lapsed into silence.

Susan Blake, Sara Henratty's Auntie Sue, lived in a block of flats on the coast road. Today the view was enchanting — blue water topped with little white waves, a yacht with red sails on the horizon — but Meg wondered how cosy it would be on a winter's night when the wind howled in from the sea.

Susan Blake was also older than she had imagined, a white-haired woman in her seventies, at least. She must be Sara's great-aunt, Meg decided.

"Good morning," said the DI. "I'm DI Willis and this is WPC Connolly. Could we come in for a minute?"

Mrs Blake looked surprised but ushered them into a neat sitting room with a window full of the sea and sky. The DI and Meg sat side by side on an upright sofa while Susan faced them from the rocking chair which was obviously where she sat each evening, her knitting and a pair of binoculars (for birdwatching?) on a table within arm's reach.

"We're very sorry," said the DI, "but we've got bad news about your niece Sara."

"Sara?" said Susan, as if she didn't recognise the name.

"Your niece, Sara Henratty. I regret to tell you that she was found dead last night."

"We're so sorry," said Meg, before the DI could say "regret" again. "This must be such a shock."

"Sara," said Susan, this time as if it registered with her. "Bernadette's daughter. I haven't seen her since she was a child. What happened to her?"

"I'm not at liberty to say," said the DI, "but we're treating her death as suspicious."

"Suspicious? Does that mean someone killed her?"

"We don't know yet," said Meg, "but when we do you'll be the first to know."

"Born to trouble," said Susan, her eyes beginning to fill. "Just like her mother."

"Bernadette?" said Meg.

"Yes, my niece Bernadette. She was a lovely girl. So pretty, she could have been an actress or a model. But she got in with a bad sort. He left her pregnant and went off somewhere. No one knows where. Bernadette wouldn't give the baby up though. She used to take in sewing to make a living. But then she died. TB. Such an awful illness. Sara would have been eleven then, I think."

"And what happened to Sara?" said Meg, although she thought she knew.

"She went into care, as they call it," said Susan. "I couldn't take her in. I'm too old and I've got a bad heart. Sara lived with foster parents and then in a children's home."

"Did you ever visit her?" said Meg, trying not to make this sound like an accusation.

"No," said Susan. "They said, the social workers, that Sara shouldn't see anyone from her old life. It would help her adjust, they said. I used to send her cards on her birthday though."

"The children's home had you down as next-of-kin," said Meg. She wondered how true it was about the social workers telling Susan not to visit. Maybe it was just more convenient to believe that. But looking at the old lady now, sitting in her rocking chair, dabbing at her eyes, Meg felt a rush of pity. It would have been hard to take on a young girl who had just lost her mother.

"Her father's her real next-of-kin, I suppose," said Susan. "But no one knows where he is. In prison, I expect."

"What was his name?" asked the DI. "Was it Henratty?"

"Yes," said Susan. "Bernadette gave the baby his name although they never married." Her lips pursed in disapproval. "Malcolm Henratty. Malc, that's what he called himself. I met him once. Bernadette brought him here to meet me. She adored him but you could see he was a bad 'un. Charming enough but rotten inside."

DI Willis took a note of the name. "Thank you," he said, "you've been very helpful."

"Can I make you a cup of tea?" said Meg. "You've had a shock. Is there anyone who could come in and sit with you?"

"I'm all right, dear," said Susan. "At my age you get used to bad news."

CHAPTER
THIRTEEN

Edgar wasn't a fan of Surrey. He had been brought up in Esher which, to his parents, had seemed liked paradise but to Edgar had often felt like a prison, a tidy prison surrounded by privet hedges and smelling of roast lamb on Sundays. After his father died, his mother had stayed on in their house, laying the table for one every day and living a life of bravely managed disappointment. Then, unexpectedly, three years ago she had married again, to Colonel Brian Cooper-Smith, a florid gentleman she had met at the library, Rose inspecting the romances for unnecessary displays of affection and the colonel checking a recent military history for mentions of himself. Edgar had found himself liking his new stepfather. Brian was a large, noisy, generous man with no time for subtleties; Edgar sometimes imagined him as an elephant at a watering hole, the nuances of family life simply washing over him in a muddy tide. Rose seemed happy and his mother's marriage meant that Edgar no longer felt guilty about not visiting her enough. Rose had sold the family home and moved in with her new husband. They still lived in Esher, in a square twenties house on the edge of the golf course. Visits there were surprisingly jolly. Brian got on well with the girls and played cricket with them in the garden or took them for drives in his opulent pre-war Rolls Royce. Emma and Rose, after initial mutual suspicion, now maintained a fairly easy relationship, as long as Emma confined her conversation to praise of Edgar and stories about the children. Edgar liked the new house with its conservatory and view of the thirteenth hole. It had none of the depressing memories of the bungalow and even Jonathan's picture, still in pride of place on the mantelpiece, only gave him a momentary, and almost comforting, twinge of sorrow.

Crispian and Valerie Miles lived in Weybridge, only fifteen minutes away from Esher, and their house initially reminded Edgar of the colonel's hacienda. It had the same solid, complacent look, as if it had every right to take up its acreage of land. Unlike the colonel's house, though, Green Lawns was mock-Tudor in style, with mullioned windows and a lot of unnecessary timbering. The door was opened by a maid, unusual enough these days, but this one was actually wearing a uniform. She gave Edgar an unfriendly look (he didn't blame her) and asked him to wait in "the parlour". Edgar had to stop himself muttering "said the spider to the fly". There was something web-like about the shadow of the mullions on the green wallpaper. Or prison-like.

Crispian Miles entered the room like a whirlwind, the window panes rattling as he flung back the door.

"Why are you here? Have you found Rhonda?"

"Is Lady Miles in?" It was partly to see the elusive Lady Miles that he had come all this way.

"She's resting. What's this all about?"

"I'm afraid we haven't found Rhonda." Better say this straight out. "But the body of a girl has been found in the Brighton area. We think there might be a link to Rhonda's disappearance."

"A link? What do you mean?"

"The girl, Sara Henratty, was wearing a Roedean cloak with Rhonda's nametag inside."

"She was wearing Rhonda's cloak? Why?"

"I don't know. It's obviously a line of investigation. Do you know if Rhonda was acquainted with a girl named Sara Henratty?"

"Sara what?" Sir Crispian's voice rose in incredulity. Edgar was about to repeat the name when Sir Crispian suddenly raised his hand and tilted his head, as if listening. Edgar heard footsteps, light childlike footsteps, coming down the stairs and then the door opened and a voice said, "Why are you shouting, Crispian?"

Lady Miles. At last.

She was a tall woman, a head taller than her husband, but very thin, almost emaciated. She was dressed in what may have been a dressing gown or a housecoat, floor-length embroidered silk. It made her look as if she'd come from a different century altogether.

"Go back to bed, Valerie," said Crispian, but in a gentle voice. In fact, Edgar had not thought that the irascible MP could sound like that.

"But why are you shouting?" said Valerie. "Is it Rho Rho? Have you found her?" She said it in a vague way, as if Rhonda had been playing hide-and-seek.

"I'm afraid not," said Edgar. "I'm Superintendent Edgar Stephens from the Brighton Police."

"A policeman!" Valerie backed away, her hand to her throat. "What are you doing here?"

"It's nothing to be alarmed about . . ." Edgar began.

But Valerie had turned to her husband in terror. "Is he going to arrest me?"

"No, dear." Crispian moved forwards but his wife backed away further, her eyes still on Edgar.

"He's a policeman. He's going to arrest me for losing Rhonda."

For losing her? Trying to make his voice sound reassuring, Edgar said, "I'm simply here to give you some information, Lady Miles. It's nothing to be alarmed about."

Valerie Miles came closer and put her hand on Edgar's sleeve. Her fingers were almost skeletal but their grip was like a vice. "I let her walk home alone," she said. "What sort of a mother does that? She was meant to be with a friend but they quarrelled. Rhonda's quick-tempered, like her father. Then *he* took her. That man. And he's taken her again, hasn't he?"

She must be talking about the first kidnapping attempt, when Rhonda was abducted on her way home from her ballet class. "Ernest Coggins is in prison," said Edgar. "He hasn't taken Rhonda. We think this is the work of someone else entirely and we're working flat out to find them. To find Rhonda."

"Valerie . . ." Crispian put his arm round his wife. "The police will find her. Superintendent Stephens is a clever man. The very best. He'll bring her back to us."

Despite everything, Edgar wished that he could get this glowing reference in writing. Crispian was looking at his wife with tender affection — again, Edgar was surprised that the MP's features could even form themselves into such an expression — but Valerie spun round and her face was a mask of fury.

"You did this!" she screamed at her husband. "This is all your fault. You killed Rhonda."

Meg and the DI drove back in a silence, which lasted until Newhaven. The bridge was up which meant they had to wait in a line of cars, watching a tall sailing ship glide past, like an emissary from another age. Meg wondered if she ought to make some casual conversational remark (but what?) when DI Willis said, "It's sad, isn't it? A young girl has died and there's no one who really mourns her."

This was so much what Meg had been thinking earlier that she turned to look at the DI, his familiar profile serious as he stared straight ahead. Was it possible that DI Willis also had human feelings? This was a new idea altogether.

"Yes," she said. "I was thinking the same thing. I'm one of seven. If I went missing there would be plenty of people to notice. It's as if Sara just slipped out of sight and no one really cared. That woman, Susan, she wasn't a bad sort — and she'd obviously been fond of Sara's mother in her way — but she didn't really *care*, not in the way a mother would care."

She wondered if she'd said too much but the DI said, still not looking at her, "I wonder if we'll ever trace the father. Not that he seemed to bother about his daughter when she was alive."

116

"That seems wrong too," said Meg. "Imagine having a daughter and not knowing about her." Too late, she remembered that this was the story with the super's famous friend, Max Mephisto. He was the father of the TV star, Ruby Magic, and hadn't known of her existence until they were both mixed up in the Conjurer Killer case. She couldn't remember who had told her this bit of gossip. She thought it might have been Sergeant O'Neill.

"Sara was such a pretty girl too," said the DI, moving the car forward. "Not that that's significant in any way," he added hastily.

"What if it is significant?" said Meg.

"What do you mean?"

"Do you remember what Susan said about Bernadette, Sara's mother? She said she was so pretty that she could have been an actress or a model. Sara obviously took after her. Well, when I was in London, undercover with the Bobby Soxers, two of them said that Rhonda had been approached by a man who said that she should be a model. It's in my report."

"Yes," said the DI, in a way that made Meg think that he hadn't read it.

"What if there's a man going round telling young girls that they could be models? Then he lures them away and kills them. That could have happened to the nurse, Louise, too."

"You're right," said the DI, almost sounding excited. "Did you get a description of the man who spoke to Rhonda?"

"No," said Meg. "I suppose I'll have to go undercover again."

By lunchtime, Emma could bear it no longer. She had waited up for Edgar to come in last night but all he'd told her was that a girl's body had been found and they thought it was one of the missing girls, Sara Henratty. He also told her that Sara had been wearing Rhonda's cape. "So I was right," Emma couldn't help saying, "the two cases are linked." "Yes," Edgar had said heavily, "you were right." He had looked so sad and reproachful that Emma hadn't wanted to ask more.

All morning she had thought that he might ring to tell her the latest developments. She had even rung through to the station to be told that the superintendent was "away from his desk". "Where is he?" she'd asked. "Surrey," replied Rita, Edgar's secretary, in the repressive tone that she seemed to reserve for Emma.

So there was a lead important enough to be chased by the superintendent himself and Emma didn't know about it. She put the phone down and looked at Jonathan who was sitting happily in his playpen, banging a saucepan with a spoon. Edgar didn't like him to be in the pen (something to do with finding a dead body in one years ago) but it was impossible to get anything done with a baby crawling all over the place. Emma almost dreaded the day that he learnt to walk. Marianne and Sophie had done this at ten months but everyone said that boys were slower at reaching the milestones.

"Come on, Johnny," she said now. "We're going on a trip."

It was a pain bumping the pushchair down the front steps but at least it was better than the pram, which needed a turning circle bigger than the *Queen Mary*. Emma walked briskly to the seafront and caught a bus to Rottingdean. Once again, it was a palaver getting the pushchair on board but the conductor was helpful and, once installed in a seat, with Johnny on her lap, Emma enjoyed the journey, the sea on one side, Regency houses on the other, giving way to the golf course and then to Roedean itself. When they passed the school, Emma could see girls playing lacrosse on the front field. She'd hated lacrosse but now she felt a wave of nostalgia so strong that she almost felt sick. Or maybe it was the diesel fumes from the bus.

At Rottingdean the conductor helped her lift the pushchair off the bus and said goodbye with a cheery, "See you later, alligator." Why did that remind her of something? She crossed the road and pushed the buggy down the ramp beside the White Horse pub.

The tide was out, exposing chalk rocks interspersed with limpid blue pools. Johnny strained at the straps of his pushchair and Emma vowed to take him on the beach. There was nothing Jonathan liked more than getting thoroughly wet. But she had something to do first. A section of the undercliff walk was cordoned off with police tape and sitting on a wall opposite, eating chips out of newspaper, were Sam Collins and a man whom Emma vaguely recognised.

119

"Well," Sam greeted her, "if it isn't the great detective herself."

"Just out for a walk," said Emma.

"Of course," said Sam. "Of course you'd take a bus all the way to Rottingdean just to walk past the place where a body was found last night. Makes perfect sense."

Emma ignored this. She was looking at the crime scene, a square of concrete by the foot of the cliff. The chalk had been shored up with bricks which reached to about seven foot and embedded in this wall was a green wooden door, padlocked shut.

"What's behind the door?" said Emma.

"Apparently it's an old smugglers' tunnel," said the man, who was offering Johnny a chip. "But it's been locked up for years."

"Emma, you know Harry Payne, the press photographer, don't you?" said Sam.

"I think we've met before," said Emma. They shook hands. Harry was a tall man with pale blue eyes and colourless hair, receding slightly at the temples. Emma thought she recognised him but he was the sort of man who faded into the background. Perhaps that was necessary for his job.

"What do you know about the dead girl?" Emma asked Sam.

Sam gave her a rather quizzical look but answered, "Sara Henratty, aged sixteen. She was the girl I mentioned before, the one who disappeared from the children's home. I had a word with the PC who found the body and he said that it looked as if she'd been

120

strangled. Then your husband arrived and stopped us asking any more questions."

"He was only doing his job," said Harry.

"Maybe," said Sam. "But this proves that I was right. There was something sinister about Sara's disappearance. I couldn't get close to the body but it looked as if she was wearing a Roedean cloak. That's a definite link to Rhonda."

Emma wanted to tell Sam about the nametag but she knew that this was the sort of detail the police liked to keep to themselves so that it was known only to them and to the perpetrator of the crime. She contented herself with saying, "It certainly looks like there's a link."

"I'm going to do some more digging on Louise," said Sam. "I'm calling on Pete, my doctor friend, as soon as I've finished my chips. He's got a break in half an hour."

"What are you doing here anyway?" said Emma. "Surely the coroner must have taken the body hours ago."

Sam shrugged. "We wanted to get some pictures and, I know it sounds ghoulish, but sometimes people visit the scene. Relatives and friends, sometimes even the murderer comes back to have a look. You'd be surprised."

"I wouldn't," said Emma. She knew that murderers were often drawn back to the scene of their crimes. "Have you seen anyone?"

"No," said Sam. "Poor Sara. It seems that nobody cares about her. I thought I'd go to see Peanuts, the ex-boyfriend, too. He might have something more to say. I talked to him before when I was investigating

Sara's disappearance. He's a nice boy. A mad keen mod."

"I wonder if anyone's told him that Sara's dead," said Emma. She thought that it was just the sort of detail that would slip Bob's mind.

"It'll be in the papers tomorrow," said Harry.

Sam finished the last of her chips. "Today's paper," she said, "tomorrow's chip wrapping. Why don't you come with me to see Pete, Emma? Harry's got a car."

"I should take Johnny on the beach. He'd love the rock pools."

"He'd prefer a drive in Uncle Harry's Mini," said Sam in her most persuasive voice.

"Oh, all right then," said Emma. "But I have to be back in time to pick the girls up from school."

CHAPTER
FOURTEEN

"I'm sorry about that." Sir Crispian sounded as abashed as Edgar had ever heard him. Lady Miles had been taken away by the woman who — Edgar now realised — had been wearing a nurse's, rather than a maid's, uniform.

"Valerie's never been the same since Rhonda went missing that time," Sir Crispian continued, sinking heavily into a William-Morris-patterned armchair. "She blamed herself. That's why she keeps thinking that the police are coming to arrest her."

"But that was six years ago," said Edgar. "Has Lady Miles seen a . . ." He was going to say "psychiatrist" but changed it to "doctor".

"Oh, she's seen all sorts of trick cyclists," said Sir Crispian. "But they never do any good. Occasionally she has spells when she's almost . . . normal . . . but this latest thing, with Rhonda, it's set her right back. I've had to employ a full-time nurse. Valerie has moments when she's almost . . . frantic. She's attacked me, she's threatened to kill herself. She tried to throw herself out of the window the other day. Then, suddenly, she's talking about Rhonda as if she's in the other room."

"She seemed . . . angry with you," said Edgar. This was rather an understatement when Valerie Miles had actually accused her husband of killing their daughter.

"Sometimes she blames me," said Crispian, "sometimes she blames herself. It's rather hard to take."

Sir Crispian put a hand over his eyes. Edgar saw the liver spots on the back of it and felt another lurch of sympathy. No wonder Sir Crispian was so angry all the time. His daughter was missing and so, it seemed, was his wife. He said, "Don't give up hope, sir. Sara Henratty's death was a tragedy but we're hoping that it will provide clues that lead us to Rhonda. I've got every available officer working on the case."

Sir Crispian looked at him, his eyes dull. "It's too late," he said. "I've known that from the beginning."

Edgar wanted to reassure him, to tell him that Rhonda would be found, but he knew that he couldn't give that promise. It had been a week since Rhonda had disappeared and every passing day made a happy outcome less likely. Besides, there was something about the Weybridge house with its barred windows and poison-green furnishings that seemed to engender despair, to drain all hope from the situation. Valerie, locked in her upstairs room, was Mrs Rochester, the mad woman in the attic, but, like her fictional counterpart, did Lady Miles also have moments of clarity? She had accused her husband of murder. Edgar had been feeling sorry for Sir Crispian but there was no doubt that he was a hard and ruthless man. He had sent his daughter away to boarding school and claimed not to have even read her letters home. Could he conceivably be guilty of such a heinous crime? *It's too late*, Crispian had said. How could he possibly know?

It was difficult fitting the pushchair into the boot of the Mini but eventually Emma managed it. They set off along the coast road, Sam in the front, Emma in the back with Johnny on her lap. He seemed enchanted by the car and started to make happy little humming noises. Maybe this was all he needed to keep him contented, a trip in a ramshackle car with a Union Jack painted on its bonnet. Emma could drive but there was nowhere to park a car by their Kemp Town house. Edgar used a police-issue Wolseley for work and for family outings. It was years since Emma had been behind the wheel. She thought of her father teaching her to drive, risking his beloved Rolls Royce in hair-raising trips up to Ditchling Beacon, Archie yelling "brake, girl, brake" every time they came to a corner. Later on she'd had a boyfriend with a two-seater and, although she'd tired of Raymond fairly quickly, she'd never tired of bowling along the promenade, the wind whipping her hair back against her face. Picturing it now, it was as if she was describing another person.

They took the road up by the racecourse. A sea fret had blown in and the white railings loomed suddenly out of the mist. Emma remembered searching for two lost children here, years ago, when the ground had been covered in snow. The road into Brighton had changed since that time, new tower blocks dwarfing the terraced houses.

"We went to photograph one the other day," said Sam. "Twenty storeys high. You wouldn't catch me living there. It would be like being a canary in a cage."

"Apparently people agree with you," said Harry. "I read that most of them are still empty."

Emma looked back at the new buildings, solid blocks of concrete and glass, their upper storeys lost in the fog. She tried to imagine living up there, high above the town, battered by wind and rain. You might feel God-like and omniscient but you might also feel lonely so far away from the comforting hum of street-level life. She thought of the missing children again from that case over a decade ago. They had lived in terraced houses on Freshfield Road, two-up two-down, no inside toilets, exactly the sort of "slums" that were being demolished to make room for the new high-rise living, but Emma remembered that there had been a real community there, a sense of neighbours looking out for each other. She wondered whether you would ever get to know your neighbours, living in an eyrie in the sky.

They took the back road to the hospital and parked in the doctors' car park. A young man in a white coat was sitting on a wall, smoking.

"That's Pete," said Sam. "Thanks for the lift, Harry."

"Shall I wait?" said Harry. "I could drive you to collect your children, Emma."

It was the first time he'd addressed her directly and, for some reason, Emma felt herself blushing. "It's OK," she said. "The school's not far from here."

They got the pushchair out and installed Jonathan in it. He waved a sad farewell to the car as the Mini chugged away down the hill.

"Emma," said Sam. "This is Pete. Dr Peter Chambers, I should say."

"Pete is fine." Dr Chambers stubbed out his cigarette and stood up to shake Emma's hand.

"Emma's a detective," said Sam.

"I used to be one," said Emma. She gestured towards the baby in the pushchair as if this explained everything. Which perhaps it did.

"A girl's been found dead on the undercliff walk," said Sam. "We think she might be linked to Louise's disappearance."

"Oh my God," said Pete. "That's awful."

"Can you tell us anything else about Louise?" said Sam. "Anything that might help us find her."

Pete was silent for a moment, fiddling with his cigarette packet as if he wanted to light another.

"She was a nice girl," he said at last. "We worked together on my last ward. She was one of those nurses who always knows what to say to patients. Not too chatty but just knowing when they needed reassurance or cheering up. She told me once that she had always wanted to be a nurse but her parents had died when she was young and there wasn't any money for training. She paid her way by modelling."

"Modelling?" said Sam, in the same way she might have said "prostitution".

"Yes. Louise said that agencies were always looking out for coloured models. And she was very striking-looking. But she was shy really. She never went out with the other nurses. She said that she preferred to spend her evenings reading."

"Did she have a boyfriend?" asked Emma.

"Not that I know of," said Pete but his blush had revealed something. If he wasn't Louise's boyfriend, thought Emma, he had certainly wanted to be.

"Were you surprised when she suddenly disappeared?" said Sam.

"Yes," said Pete. "I mean, Louise wanted to be a nurse. It was her life's ambition. Why would she give it up when she finally had a place at a teaching hospital? And that note. Why would she go to the West Indies? She didn't have any close family there. She was born in London."

"Did she have family in London?" asked Emma.

"She mentioned an aunt once," said Pete. "Some cousins. I don't think they were close."

"Did you see the note that she left?" asked Emma.

"No. One of the other student nurses told me about it. A girl called Harriet Francis." Sam wrote down the name. "Harriet said that Matron accepted the note at face value. That's typical. Matron's a cow. She was always trying to imply that Louise didn't belong in the hospital."

"Because she was coloured?" said Sam.

"Yes," said Pete. His pleasant face suddenly looked quite fierce. "She's a bigot, pure and simple. A racist. No better than a Nazi. We've got an Indian doctor, one of the best in his field, and Matron can hardly bear to talk to him."

128

Emma had never heard the term "racist" before and it was a long time since she'd heard anyone — and an Englishwoman, no less — compared to a Nazi. But she had no trouble believing that such prejudices existed, even in nice teaching hospitals.

"Did Louise ever mention anyone hanging around the nurses' home?" said Emma. "Maybe a boyfriend of one of the other nurses?"

"No," said Pete. "We didn't talk about stuff like that. We mainly talked about books."

He sounded as if this had been a big disappointment.

Edgar arrived back at the station in time for a conference with Bob Willis. This was a grand way of saying that Edgar sent Rita out to buy chips and bottles of ginger beer and the Superintendent and DI shut themselves in Edgar's office for an hour. Edgar enjoyed these times with Bob. It reminded him of the days when he was the DI and Bob and Emma were his sergeants. They had handled some difficult, dangerous cases but there had always been the sense of working as a team, the three of them against the world. When Edgar and Emma had got married, she'd left the force and Bob had become his loyal deputy, then, when Hodges retired, Edgar was promoted to Superintendent and Bob to DI. Edgar had missed working with Emma but, for the first few years, he was still delirious with happiness that she had become his wife. It was only recently that he had begun to wonder how much Emma herself missed those days.

"How did it go in Surrey?" said Bob, selecting a chip and eating it carefully. He ate maddeningly slowly. Edgar often wondered how Betty put up with it.

"Strange," said Edgar. "I met Lady Miles and she's clearly very disturbed. Sir Crispian said that she had a breakdown when Rhonda went missing the first time. Apparently she thinks that the police are going to arrest her."

"What for?"

"For neglecting her daughter, I suppose."

"But she wasn't neglected, was she? She was just walking home from ballet class. It sounds as if Sir Crispian and Lady Miles showered her with everything: ballet lessons, expensive boarding school, the lot."

"Or they sent her away? I think that's how Lady Miles might have seen it. She actually turned on Sir Crispian and accused him of killing Rhonda."

Bob let his chip fall back onto the newspaper. "Sir Crispian's wife accused him of killing their daughter?"

"Yes, it was quite chilling. I even wondered for a moment if she could be right but it wouldn't explain the other disappearances and I just can't believe it. Sir Crispian is a bully but he does seem to love his daughter. And he was very kind to his wife. I felt sorry for him, living there with her."

"You have to watch that, feeling sorry for people," said Bob, as if he were the superior officer.

"It's part of being a good policeman," said Edgar, "showing empathy. You're pretty empathetic yourself."

He could see Bob trying to work this one out. He said, "Do you think that Rhonda thought that her parents had sent her away? Do you think she was unhappy?"

"I don't know," said Edgar. "I remember Sir Crispian saying that, after the first kidnapping, Rhonda had really wanted a dog but he sent her to Roedean instead."

"It's a fantastic school though," said Bob. "So big and grand, like a castle. I wish Betty and I could afford to send the children there."

"Except that they're boys," said Edgar.

Bob reddened, as he always did if he was teased. "You know what I mean. I wish we could send them to private school."

"Private schools aren't always the best option," said Edgar. "Max hated his."

"I bet you end up sending Marianne and Sophie to Roedean all the same," said Bob, sounding rather truculent.

"Emma would never hear of it," said Edgar. "What about Sara Henratty? Not much privilege there, I expect. You and Connolly went to see her aunt, didn't you?"

"Great-aunt. Yes. Nice old lady, living in Seaford. She hadn't seen Sara for years though. She said that Sara's mother, Bernadette, had been taken in by a thorough rotter and got pregnant by him. He deserted her so Bernadette brought up Sara on her own until she died of TB. It's a sad story."

"It certainly is. Do you know what became of Sara's father, the rotter?" Edgar was always amused when Bob used words that seemed to come from a Victorian melodrama. Where did he get them from?

But Bob was nothing if not thorough. "I checked the prison records," he said, "and sure enough he's inside, serving five years for theft at Ford Open Prison."

"Ford? That's where Ernest Coggins is. The man who abducted Rhonda."

"Well, it's the only prison round here. Except Lewes, of course, but Malcolm Henratty sounds like a petty criminal, he wouldn't need high security."

"Are you going to see him? Henratty?"

"Yes. I mean, he deserves to know that his daughter's dead, even though he never seemed to want anything to do with her when she was alive."

"Anything else about Sara? Poor girl. She doesn't seem to have had a very happy life."

"WPC Connolly had a good thought. The aunt mentioned how pretty Bernadette had been, how she could have been a model. Well, some of the girls outside the Ritz — you know, the Bobby Whatsit fans — said that Rhonda had been approached by a man saying that she should be a model. Sara was a good-looking girl. You've seen the photo of her with the mods. What if someone had approached her with the same story?"

"That *is* a good thought," said Edgar. "Connolly is obviously a bright girl."

"She is," said Bob. "A bit rough around the edges but she's got the makings of a good officer."

Edgar had known Bob long enough to understand what this meant. Meg Connolly was not someone of whom Bob's mother would approve.

132

"I've told Connolly to go back to the Ritz, undercover again, and see if she can get anything more from the fans. That could be our man's modus operandi, telling girls that they should be models, luring them away with promises of stardom."

"Tell WPC Connolly to be careful," said Edgar.

It was mid-afternoon by the time that Max got back to Brighton. It was time, he thought, to complete the Florence tour. Fortifying himself with a double whisky at the Railway Tavern, he walked up the hill (another hill!) to Montpelier Crescent, the house where she had died. This was an expensive area of Brighton, tall white houses with wrought-iron balconies looking out over a semicircle of lawn containing a may tree in full flower. Looking at the street in the soft spring sunshine, Max found it hard to believe that anything bad had ever happened there. In fact, his main memory was of calling on Florence one morning and drinking coffee in the elegant sitting room. They had faced each other across the burnished parquet floor, talking politely and knowing that they were going to end up in bed together. That room, though, was where she had died. Edgar had never described the crime scene to him but the papers had got hold of some of the details and these, now, were as clear to Max as if he had been there: Florence stretched out naked on the sofa, her dark hair touching the floor, a gold crown on her head, feather boa around her neck in morbid imitation of Cleopatra's asp.

Had Florence been the love of his life, as he had intimated to Emma? The whole experience was so vivid and sensual — their bodies on the bed, Florence's body on the sofa, rose-tinted lights, the mirrors in the apartment's opulent bathroom — that it still seemed almost like a dream. What would have happened when he'd woken up and attempted to have a future with Florence? Would they have got married and had children? He couldn't think of such things. That way madness lay. He had married Lydia and they had children. They were his life now. As Max turned away from the house he felt his heart lighten, as if something had floated away, as free and transient as the blossom on the may tree.

Emma was on time to collect the girls. They were thrilled to see Jonathan. A baby was almost as big a playground draw as a puppy. They soon had him out of his pushchair on a triumphal tour of classrooms, pupils, parents and teachers. It was a long time before Emma could corral them for the journey home. Once back at the house, Marianne instigated a game of schools with herself as a rather tyrannical teacher and Sophie and Johnny as the pupils. Jonathan's role was to sit on the floor being "naughty boy", a task he performed with ease. Emma felt that she could safely leave them and make herself a cup of tea. But as soon as she had descended to the basement kitchen and put the kettle on, the phone rang.

Marianne picked it up on the upstairs landing. As Emma made her way back up the stairs she could hear her repeating the number in the way that she had been taught at school. Emma couldn't get used to there not being letter codes any more.

"Mum! It's for you."

Emma took the receiver. "Hallo, Emma. It's Ruby."

"Ruby!" Not the last person she had expected, but very close to it.

"Listen, Emma. I'm in Brighton tomorrow. Saturday. Can we meet? I'd like to talk to you."

"Talk to me?" repeated Emma stupidly.

"Yes. It's important but I can't explain on the phone. I'm calling from the studio and there are too many people listening. Can you meet me on the Palace Pier at one o'clock tomorrow? By the gypsy caravan?"

By Emma's friend Astarte's caravan. "Yes," said Emma, "but why —"

"You're a doll," said Ruby. "Can't stop. Bye."

She rang off but, for several minutes, Emma still held the receiver to her ear. The very dialling tone seemed to have a quizzical, interrogative sound.

CHAPTER
FIFTEEN

It was difficult to escape from the family. Marianne had a ballet lesson at ten and, though Edgar offered to take her, he looked so tired that Emma took pity on him. Instead Edgar took Sophie and Johnny for a walk on the seafront. This gave Emma time to do some shopping on her way home with a pirouetting Marianne. Then she laid out a light lunch, Grosvenor pie and salad, and announced that she was going out.

"But you haven't had anything to eat," said Edgar, who was trying to wedge Jonathan into his highchair.

"I'm meeting Ruby," said Emma, her hand on the door.

"Ruby?" said Edgar. "Why?"

She didn't know why she hadn't mentioned it earlier, maybe because she still avoided talking about Ruby even after all these years. She knew that Edgar was no longer in love with Ruby but it still felt strange to think that her husband had once been engaged to that glittering creature. Now it was awkward, though, standing in the doorway, Marianne looking avidly from parent to parent, sensing a drama.

"She said she wanted to talk to me," said Emma.

"What about?"

136

"That's what I'm going to find out," said Emma. "I won't be long. Back in an hour." And she shut the door on the mingled expressions of surprise, bemusement and dismay. As she set off down the street she could hear Johnny starting to cry.

It was a lovely day. The sky was the pale blue of a duck's egg and the sea stretched out in bands of shallow turquoise, trimmed with white. The promenade was already filling up with day-trippers and a few brave souls were paddling. Next weekend, the bank holiday, it would be packed solid, especially if the good weather continued. Maybe she should take the children to the beach. On second thoughts, thinking of the threatened battle between mods and rockers, maybe they should steer clear of Brighton altogether and go to see her friend Vera's horses in Rottingdean.

Palace Pier was crowded too. Children eating candyfloss, adults caught on the hop by the sun, shirtsleeves rolled up, bald heads reddening. Astarte's caravan stood by the entrance to the penny arcade and a sign announced that Madame Zabini was in residence. Emma leant on the ornate railing by the caravan's steps and thought about the previous Madame Zabini, Astarte's grandmother, who had been thrown to her death from this very spot. From this vantage point the water looked deep and mysterious, blue-green depths. A seagull swooped in front of her and Emma jumped. Someone laughed. Emma turned around and saw a youngish man in a trilby hat looking at her.

"On your own?" His accent was South London tinged with a self-conscious American twang, reminding Emma of Joe Passolini.

"I'm waiting for my husband."

"Suit yourself." The man loped away. Emma looked at her watch. A quarter past one. Where was Ruby? She should be easy to spot, even in the crowds, with her fashionable clothes and her TV star sheen. Why did Ruby want to see Emma anyway? *It's important but I can't explain on the phone*. Edgar was still the only real point of contact between Emma and Ruby. Well, Edgar and Max. But what could Ruby have to discuss with Emma, her ex-fiancé's wife, that she couldn't raise with her own father?

A woman descended the steps of Astarte's caravan, looking shell-shocked. What had the crystal ball foretold for her? Astarte was not the kind of mystic who only gave her clients the good news. Emma was tempted to pop her head through the velvet curtain and say hallo but then she might miss Ruby. The merry-go-round on the end of the pier was playing "My Boy Lollipop", a maddeningly catchy tune that was in the charts.

Emma looked at her watch again. Twenty-five past.

My boy lollipop. You make my heart go giddy up.
Ruby wasn't coming.

Max was also looking at the Palace Pier but from within a Rolls Royce with tinted windows. Bobby Hambro sat in the front next to the chauffeur. Wilbur Wallace was next to Max, reading through a typescript.

138

"Cedric could come here with his grandfather," he said. "Go on the pier, win a coconut or two."

"I'm not sure that it's the first place that an eighteen-year-old would go," said Max. "Especially with his grandfather." However much he was told that the earl was "a handsome dissolute aristocrat" he was still depressed to be cast in the grandfather role.

"It's where they start to get to know each other," said Wilbur. "Barriers start to break down."

"Perhaps they could go swimming," said Bobby. "Fans love a little shirt-off action."

They were parked by the arches on Madeira Terrace. A tide of humanity washed past them, children with buckets and spades, girls in miniskirts, mods and rockers, flotsam and jetsam. Max felt as if he was invisible, a visitor from another planet, sent to deliver some cosmic warning. What would it be? Don't go to see *Golden Heart*, starring Bobby Hambro and Max Mephisto?

When Bobby had suggested a day "scouting for locations" in Brighton, Max had even thought that it might be rather fun — a drive in the purring Rolls, lunch at a country pub — but now he felt that if he heard one more word about Bobby's fans and what they liked or disliked, he would throw himself off the nearest cliff.

"Brighton is one hell of a town," said Wilbur. "Has it always been like this?"

"Since the late eighteenth century, I believe," said Max. "The then Prince Regent brought it into fashion.

Before that it was just a fishing village. Brighthelmstone, it was called."

"A royal connection," said Bobby. "Perhaps the prince could come into *Golden Heart*?"

"Hardly, since the film is set in the late nineteenth century," said Max.

"Who was on the throne then?" asked Bobby.

"Queen Victoria," said Max. "And she hated Brighton, apparently. Thought it was vulgar."

You could see her point, although Max had always loved the cheerful brashness of the town. As he watched, a group of youths in semi-rocker clothes — leather jackets and jeans — crossed the road by the Aquarium. A woman passed and they whistled at her, one boy turning and shouting something that made the others laugh. The woman, dressed in a short pink summer coat that barely covered her even shorter skirt, swept past without a backward glance.

"Would you look at that," said Wilbur.

But Max was already looking. The woman had been wearing a scarf and dark glasses that covered most of her face but Max was almost certain that it was Ruby.

Emma climbed the steps and called, "Astarte?"

"Come in," came a voice.

Astarte Barton (aka Madame Zabini) was sitting at a table draped in midnight-blue cloth. Draperies covered the caravan's windows too, giving the interior a mysterious and dusky glow. The only light came from candles on the table and from the glittering crystal ball that sent the motes dancing around the room. Astarte

140

herself was wearing a red velvet cloak but she shrugged this off as soon as she saw Emma. She jumped up and gave her a hug.

"Emma! This is a surprise."

"Surely you saw me coming?"

Astarte laughed and threw a cloth over the crystal ball. The room darkened immediately.

"Want some tea? I've got a kettle in the back."

Astarte pulled aside another curtain to reveal a small kitchen. She put the kettle on the hob looking, as ever, entirely unsuited to any domestic task. At nearly thirty, Astarte was as beautiful and other-worldly as she had been at nineteen, her white-blonde hair pulled back in a bun, her skin pale and flawless. But Astarte, like Ruby, had never married and didn't have children.

They drank their tea at the table. Emma asked after Astarte's father Tol who, after setting up a highly successful chain of coffee bars in Brighton, had married a rich woman and gone to live in the South of France.

"Dad's thriving," said Astarte. "He's opening a casino in Menton. Not that he needs to work. Mimi's got more than enough money for both of them."

"I can't imagine Tol not working," said Emma.

"No," said Astarte, shooting Emma one of her penetrating silvery glances. "So how are you? How are the lovely children?"

"They're fine. Marianne is growing up fast, sometimes she seems like the most sophisticated person in the house. Sophie wants to be a pirate and Johnno's an angel. When he's not being a devil, that is."

"I'd love to see them again." Astarte was a big favourite with the girls. She let them dress up in her fortune-teller's robes and showed them how to read tarot cards. Edgar hadn't been especially pleased at this last, especially when Marianne had predicted his imminent death.

"You must come to lunch," said Emma. "With Sam perhaps."

Despite — or because of — being so different, Sam and Astarte got on well. Sam thought that Astarte, beneath the draperies and incense, was a very shrewd business-woman. Astarte thought that Sam was a "pure soul".

"I was meant to meet Ruby today," said Emma, sipping her tea which, like everything prepared by Astarte, tasted musky and aromatic.

"Ruby Magic?" said Astarte, who was a big fan of the programme. "Why?"

"I don't know. She said she had something important that she wanted to discuss with me. I suppose it's about a man. At Diablo's funeral, she told me that she had a new boyfriend."

Astarte looked into her teacup before replying. Reading the leaves or just playing for time?

"It's not always about a man," she said.

CHAPTER
SIXTEEN

Max pushed open the heavy gates. It felt wrong that they weren't locked but then, even if they were, he would have the keys. The solicitor had handed them over to him on a great fob, like something from a Gothic horror story, the day that he had read Max his father's will. Now, waving the Rolls Royce through, the stone lions snarling on either side of the gates, Max felt more like the gatekeeper than the lord of the manor. But that was what he was.

He hadn't wanted to visit Massingham Hall, much less with Bobby and Wilbur in tow, but, after a day spent fruitlessly driving around stately homes in Sussex, he had felt honour bound to tell them that he knew where there was an empty house replete with sweeping staircases, suits of armour and panelled walls. There were grounds too and a lake where Little Lord Fauntleroy could frolic to his heart's content. Or, rather, where teenage Fauntleroy could canoodle with his American girlfriend, Sandy. Had he known all along that he would end up playing the lord of his own manor? Maybe. Or maybe it was just that he couldn't quite face going back to the house alone. Bobby and Wilbur were company, at least.

"Say," said Bobby, getting out of the car, "this is something like. So this is where you grew up, Max."

"Yes," said Max. He was looking up at the hall thinking, as ever, that it looked more like a school or a lunatic asylum than someone's home. Massingham Hall had been a Tudor manor, modest for the times, famous only for its knot garden and its tower, an isolated folly believed to be haunted by Mad Max Massingham, a Regency rake who had parted company with his horse in the surrounding woodland. Max had no idea why his father had chosen to name him after his accident-prone ancestor but, when he was a child, the story used to terrify him. It was Alastair's father, Max's grandfather, who had created the current monstrosity, replacing the warm Tudor bricks with monolithic Bath stone and adding two new wings bristling with turrets and cloisters in Gothic-revival style. Now, the front door was reached by a double staircase, above which loomed a multitude of mullioned windows like the thousand eyes of Argus. The roof was pitched and grooved and crenellated in a dizzying range of heights and architectural styles. Max shut his eyes but, when he opened them, the house was still there.

"It's beautiful," said Wilbur, "but not a very comfortable place to live, I imagine."

Max was grateful for this unexpected understanding.

"No," he said. "My grandfather was heavily into the Oxford Movement. He thought that we should go back to devout medieval times but he had a rather confused way of going about it. He built a chapel here too, a Catholic one. It used to be consecrated but my father

144

went back to the Church of England after my mother died."

"How old were you when she died?"

"Six."

"That's tough. Mine only passed away last year but I still can't get used to being without her." The producer took off his glasses and polished them. Max recognised the move as playing for time. He turned to Bobby who was still exclaiming about the hall's proportions.

"It's perfect for Dorincourt House. Perfect. I can just see the earl coming down those steps to greet Ceddy for the first time."

"Are you sure you won't mind us filming here?" said Wilbur, replacing his glasses.

"No," said Max. "I need to spend some time in the place while I work out what to do with it. And, if Lydia and the children come over, they can stay here too."

"They'll love it," said Bobby.

That was what Max was afraid of.

They climbed the steps and Max unlocked the double doors. The smell of the hallway — musty, woody, redolent of Sunday lunches and drawn curtains — almost sent Max reeling backwards. He must have spent years of his life here, sitting on the window seat halfway up the staircase, practising card tricks and dreaming of escape. He'd been homesick at boarding school but never for this place. Only for his mother.

"Just look at that panelling," said Bobby. "And those oil paintings. Are those your ancestors, Max?"

"Some of them."

There had been some good paintings once, including a van Dyck, but the old boy had sold them long ago. Max had been rather fond of Mad Max Massingham, whose portrait had hung in the Long Gallery. He was tall and dark, wearing a ruffled shirt and breeches and carrying a riding whip. The eyes, Max remembered, had a distinctly saturnine gaze. As a child he'd felt that it was an evil face; now he had the uneasy suspicion that the two of them would be almost identical.

How long ago was it that he'd visited the house? The solicitor had offered to drive him there after the will reading but Max had declined. He was only in England a short time, he'd said, and had to get back to London that night. He'd brought a girlfriend down before the war, Gloria something, a chorus girl from the Shepherd's Bush Empire. But that had been mainly to annoy his father. He'd brought Ruby to visit once, a happier memory. Lord Massingham had been unexpectedly enchanted by his unexpected granddaughter. He always said that she resembled his mother, reputedly the prettiest woman in five counties, and he'd left Ruby a generous bequest in his will. Suddenly Max wished that he had Ruby with him today, throwing back draperies and opening windows. He was meant to be meeting her for a meal this evening. Had it been Ruby that he'd seen in Brighton yesterday, sauntering along the promenade in her pink suit? He didn't know why but the thought made him slightly uneasy.

Bobby certainly seemed to be enjoying the place though. Max heard him opening the double doors that led into the drawing room. Then there were some

146

tinny-sounding notes as Bobby found the grand piano. A few minutes later a gong was clanging, the sound echoing and re-echoing through the empty house.

Bobby appeared again at the foot of the stairs.

"We're going to have some fun here," he said.

Max agreed, his voice sounding as hollow as the gong.

Emma's parents always came to lunch on Sundays. Edgar went to collect them in the Wolseley. He found himself looking forward to the ten-minute drive. Emma had seemed strange this weekend, ever since she had come back from the pier, having apparently been stood up by Ruby. In his mind, he kept hearing the door slam behind Emma when she had left that lunchtime, that decisive final click, signalling an end to all further discussion. Why couldn't they talk about Ruby? Or about whatever was making Emma so angry? On Saturday evening Edgar suggested asking Mavis to babysit so that he and Emma could go to the cinema but she said that she was too tired. She was always tired these days. Well, three children made a lot of work. But was there more to it than that? Was she, in fact, tired of him?

They had been so happy when they were first married, living in Edgar's flat on the seafront in Hove, feeding the seagulls from the window and watching the clouds from their bed. Edgar knew that it had been a wrench for Emma to give up work but she had become pregnant quite quickly and the new baby seemed like the biggest adventure possible. Emma's parents had helped them buy the house in Kemp Town and they had moved in just before Marianne's birth, painting the rooms themselves and sleeping with the windows open so that the fumes wouldn't harm the unborn baby. How wonderful it had felt to carry his daughter over the threshold of his own house. Neither of them had known the first thing about being parents but they had learnt together and, in those early days, married life had seemed a serene and manageable thing. When did it become more difficult? When Edgar got promoted or when Sophie was born? They'd been more proficient the second time round, which was lucky because Marianne had not been delighted to lose her only-child status and had quickly relapsed into tears and tantrums. Edgar had spent a lot of time with his eldest daughter, taking her out on long walks, or to see the cartoons at the cinema, anything to give Emma a break. But had this been the wrong thing to do? Should he have spent time with his wife instead?

He knew that Emma hadn't wanted a third child. Jonathan hadn't been planned but Edgar couldn't pretend that he wasn't delighted when he found out. And he couldn't pretend that he wasn't delighted to have a son. But, after Johnny was born, some of the light seemed to leave Emma. She seemed constantly tired and often irritable. Edgar had always talked to her about his work but, these days, Emma seemed almost competitive with him, wanting to remind him that, when they'd worked together, she had often been the better detective. He knew that she missed work but what could they do? A married woman with three children would never get a job with the police and, besides, Emma said that she wanted to bring up her children herself and not "leave it to a nanny". She wasn't attracted to the sort of charitable work that her mother enjoyed. What Emma wanted, Edgar thought, was her old life back. But that was impossible.

Edgar's parents-in-law, Archie and Sybil, were waiting for him. Archie was wearing one of his old suits that now hung loosely on his spare frame, while Sybil wore a mink coat, despite the warmth of the day. Edgar could still not get used to Archie Holmes, one-time terror of the boardroom, being reduced to a stooped old man who had to be helped up and down stairs. Sybil was older too but she still had plenty of her old style and charisma. "Hallo there, Superintendent," she greeted him gaily. "Come to arrest us?" It was an old joke. People who had never been in trouble with the law always thought that imprisonment was highly comic.

Back at the house, Sybil helped Emma prepare lunch while Edgar and his father-in-law walked to the pub. This was their tradition, a rare chance for the two men to talk. The pub was only a few streets away but now the walk seemed to take for ever because Archie had to stop every hundred yards to get his breath back. The heart attack, two years ago, had left Archie with chronic angina and it was painful to see him wheezing and mouthing at the air. But Edgar knew better than to say anything or to try to help. He waited until Archie's colour was back to normal and they continued their slow progress towards the Hand in Hand. Once settled with a half of mild, Archie became chattier and usually regaled Edgar with stories of deals done on the golf course or over double whiskies in Soho nightclubs. Today, however, Archie seemed to have something else on his mind.

"Emma seems a bit quiet," he said, looking into his glass rather than at his son-in-law.

"She's tired, I think," said Edgar. "Jonathan doesn't sleep much and the girls are quite demanding." Even as he said this, he was aware that it wasn't the whole truth. Emma's current state of dissatisfaction seemed to go much deeper than the everyday stresses of being a mother, hard though these undoubtedly were.

"You should get a nanny," said Archie. A popular refrain.

"Emma doesn't want one," said Edgar. "She says that she wants the children to grow up with our hang-ups, not a stranger's."

This was meant to be a joke but it didn't go down well with Archie who, after all, had hired a full-time nanny for his only child.

"I know my daughter," he said stubbornly. "And she doesn't look happy to me."

And, secretly, Edgar agreed with him.

It wasn't as bad as Max had feared. The house was monstrous, of course, all stone fireplaces, oak panelling and fading wallpaper, but it was now just a shell, an architectural curiosity, it didn't seem like a place where anyone had ever actually lived. The furniture was shrouded in dust sheets and there were lighter patches

150

on many of the walls where more paintings had been taken down. Obviously money had been short in recent years. Max had enough money to restore the Hall but was that what he wanted? Wouldn't it be better to sell it to some American millionaire, like Bobby Hambro, who was exclaiming over the tapestries in the gallery?

The chapel, cleared of pews and of the mysterious red light that used to glow on the altar, was now just a room with odd-shaped windows. There were gaps on the library shelves where the most valuable books had been removed. Max didn't think that his father would have minded this too much. He couldn't remember ever seeing him read a book. The bedrooms were mostly empty apart from his father's suite with the parrot wallpaper and the four-poster bed. Bobby and Wilbur were very taken with this last.

"Say," said Bobby, "we'll have to have the earl waking up in here, pulling back the curtains, taking off his night-cap, all that."

"As long as he wakes up alone," said Max. He felt oddly reluctant to sleep in his father's bed. His own room was at the end of the passage, the single bed covered with a sheet as if a corpse lay underneath. The wardrobe and the chest of drawers were both empty but, stuck in the skirting board behind the curtain, he found a single playing card. The four of hearts. Max put it in his pocket.

They descended the stairs, the Americans in high spirits now, putting on what they believed to be British accents. "After you, Lord Wilbur." "Be my guest, Sir

Bobby." Max followed, absent-mindedly making the card appear and disappear.

"I'd like to have a quick look in the grounds," said Wilbur. "Is that all right, Max?"

"Of course," said Max. "There's one more room I want to see."

It was the room that he had dreaded entering. His father had called it his study but he never seemed to do any studying in there. It was his place though, somewhere he went after lunch and supper, shutting the door firmly behind him. Perhaps he just went there to get away from Max. Well, now it was Max who was sitting at the desk, looking out at the garden, a view his father must have regarded every day of his life. What did he think when he sat here, surrounded by books that he never read? There was a large wireless in the corner of the room; perhaps Alastair came here to listen to *Mrs Dale's Diary*? Max couldn't imagine it somehow. He opened one of the desk drawers. A pile of papers, neatly tied together with string. Estate Accounts 1945-55. Alastair had died in 1959 but didn't seem to have kept such careful records in his final years. Perhaps that was why he had ended up selling all those books and paintings. Max opened the drawer below and his own face stared up at him. "Max Mephisto and Lydia Lamont, at home in Beverly Hills."

Max remembered posing for this article shortly after his marriage. There had been the usual guff about the handsome Englishman and the beautiful Hollywood star, the tone still managing to convey surprise that Lydia Lamont, with the whole of screen royalty to choose from, should settle on a man almost twenty years her senior and a foreigner to boot. The pictures showed Max and Lydia side by side on a sofa and at their "breakfast nook", a bowl of oranges glowing in the background. One particularly embarrassing example had them with their backs to the camera, staring into each other's eyes. Lydia was wearing a bright-red evening dress — perfect attire for a cosy evening at home — and Max was in a dark suit. "The newlyweds only have eyes for each other" read the caption.

Alastair had always nagged Max to get married. "Can't let the name die out and all that." But Max had been Mephisto since his first proper theatrical booking at the age of eighteen. And he didn't imagine that his father would have viewed any of his subsequent girlfriends as Lady Massingham material. Even Ruby's mother, Emerald, had been a snake-charmer, something which Alastair had tried hard to forget. But, when Max had telephoned to say that he was marrying Lydia, Lord Massingham had seemed genuinely pleased. He'd been too frail to come to America for the wedding but had sent a telegram. *Congratulations. Stop. Massingham.* "Is that your dad?" said Lydia. "Why didn't he send his love?" "He's not really that sort of father," Max had said. Lydia understood this. She hadn't seen her own male parent since he abandoned her mother when Lydia was three. But Alastair had been interested enough to purchase and keep this newspaper article. Where on earth had he got hold of a copy of *Film Frolics*? Max supposed that even his father hadn't been entirely immune to the lure of celebrity. There was a

153

television set in the small drawing room and Lord Massingham had never missed an episode of *Ruby Magic*.

"Max?" Wilbur was standing at the door. He was, rather incongruously, holding a bunch of dog roses. "I hope you don't mind," he said, when he saw Max looking, "they seemed to be growing wild."

"Help yourself," said Max. "I don't suppose anyone has seen to the gardens for years."

"I've just been talking to Robbins," said Wilbur. "He says we need to leave now if we're heading back to Brighton. Apparently the drive will take three hours and Bobby wants to stop somewhere for lunch."

"You're right." Max stood up. "I need to get back. I'm seeing my daughter this evening." He shut the desk drawer. He had a strange compulsion to take something from the room and, as he stood up, expertly palmed a paperweight, a small blue stone in the shape of a cat.

"Is your daughter Ruby French, Ruby Magic?" asked Wilbur as Max followed him out of the room.

"Yes." Max was surprised although his relationship with Ruby wasn't exactly secret. They had even once performed on stage together as "Magician and Daughter". It was just that he hadn't thought that Wilbur was particularly interested in him or his private life.

"Will Ruby inherit all this one day?" asked Wilbur. They were walking back through the empty rooms, their footsteps echoing on the parquet. Bobby had joined them; he was wearing a straw hat that he had discovered somewhere and looked like a farmhand, or, rather, a Hollywood actor pretending to be a farmhand.

This, together with Wilbur's bouquet, made Max think of an amateur production of *Oklahoma!*

"The estate's entailed on the male heir," said Max, "so, as it stands, my son Rocco will inherit it after me. I'd like to break the entail if I can though. I can just imagine Ruby as the lady of the manor."

"So can I," said Bobby although, to Max's knowledge, he had never met Ruby.

After lunch Emma and her mother took the children to Queen's Park. Edgar washed up while Archie dozed on the sofa. Then it was time for tea, crumpets and cake ("bought cake" Emma called it, as if there was something shameful about buying things from a shop rather than making them yourself). After tea, Edgar drove his parents-in-law home. "Thank you for a lovely day, darling," said Sybil, when she kissed him goodbye in the hall. The art deco house, which had once intimidated Edgar, now seemed too big for the two elderly people. He knew that, after he left, they would settle down in what had once been called the breakfast room. This was how they spent most of their evenings, huddled in front of the television with the gas fire on and cups of cocoa on trays. "Bye, Edgar." Archie extended a hand. "Take care of my daughter."

Was this a friendly injunction or a warning? thought Edgar as he drove back along the coast road. Emma was the apple of Archie's eye, he didn't think she was happy and he blamed Edgar for that. And surely it must, on some level, be his fault. Well, he would make her happy, he'd suggest a weekend away, just the two of them, he'd buy her flowers, make love to her. Full of good intentions, he parked the car in the police station garage and set off towards home. But, as he approached the house, he could hear the telephone ringing.

"Dad!" Marianne sang out, as soon as she heard his key in the lock. "It's for you."

It was Bob. "You'd better come, sir. Ernest Coggins, the man who abducted Rhonda when she was ten, he's escaped from prison."

CHAPTER
SEVENTEEN

It was Monday morning by the time that Edgar got to the prison. When he arrived at the station on Sunday night, Bob and his men were already searching the grounds and surrounding countryside. The hunt went on all night but there was no sign of Ernest Coggins. Edgar had called in reinforcements and they were there today, a slow-moving blue line edging its way across the yellow spring fields. Edgar had the feeling, though, that Coggins would be miles away by now. Edgar had also informed Sir Crispian who had, predictably, been furious. "I said at the time that Coggins should be kept in a secure prison. Don't hold with all this open nonsense. Hanging's too good for criminals, in my opinion." Edgar had promised Sir Crispian that he would visit the prison personally.

Ford Open Prison had once been an ex-RAF base and the sight of the Nissen huts and overgrown runways always brought back the mixed feelings of fear and boredom that Edgar associated with the war. Despite the open spaces, the prison was secure, surrounded by high fences and with a modern alarm system. Edgar couldn't remember another break-out.

He showed his warrant card at the main door and was ushered into a waiting room before another door was unlocked and an orderly was escorting him to the prison governor's office.

The governor, a nervous-looking man called Francis West, who looked more like a vicar than someone in charge of a prison, offered Edgar tea or coffee, made by a "trustee". The window looked out over outhouses where glum inmates were feeding two smug-looking pigs.

Edgar asked for coffee because he didn't want to look as if he distrusted drinks made by the prisoners.

"I'm so shocked," said West, as soon as the door had shut behind the trustee. "I never thought that Coggins was the type."

"You know that the girl Coggins abducted has gone missing again?"

"Yes, I read about it in the papers."

"Would Coggins have known about it?"

"Well, inmates aren't allowed newspapers but word always gets round somehow. They make these ham radio sets, you see. It's against the rules but some always slip through the net."

Edgar wondered how many other things had slipped through the net.

"Did Coggins seem agitated recently?" he asked.

West took a sip of his coffee. Edgar admired the way he could drink it without gagging. His own cup, with a kind of scum floating on top of the liquid, sat untouched in front of him.

"Not agitated as such," said West. "But I spoke to him yesterday. He worked at the prison farm. He loved animals and was very good with them. We were talking about the hens and he said that he thought they should have more light and air. We shouldn't keep innocent things caged up, he said."

"Do you think he could have been talking about Rhonda? Or himself?"

"I didn't think so at the time. He was quite a sensitive chap. Very concerned about animal welfare. It distressed him that we ate the pigs." He waved towards the window. The animals could be heard oinking, even through the reinforced glass. On second thoughts, maybe they shouldn't be looking so smug.

"Can you tell me what happened yesterday?" said Edgar. "I know you've already given a statement to DI Willis."

"Coggins was loading the egg van," said West. "It was one of his regular jobs. The gates were open to let the van through and he made a dash for it. The guards gave chase, of course, but Coggins had vanished. He must have had an accomplice waiting for him."

"Any idea who the accomplice could have been?"

"He was good friends with another inmate called Davies, Howell Davies, an ex-actor who was in for fraud. Davies was released last year and I know they kept in touch."

"Did you tell this to DI Willis?"

"Yes. He took down the last address we had for Davies."

"Thank you," said Edgar, standing up. "If anything else occurs to you, let me know. While I'm here, could I possibly have a word with an inmate called Malcolm Henratty?"

"Henratty? Someone came to see him the other day. About his daughter."

"Yes," said Edgar. "I'd like to speak to him too, if I may."

"Of course," said West. "I feel terrible about this whole business." He took another sip of his disgusting coffee while, outside, the pigs oinked miserably.

Meg was pleased to see Veronica, Isabel and a couple of other Bobby Soxers in place outside the Ritz. She was afraid that, as it was Monday and a school day, they might not be there. But Isabel told her that Monday morning was set aside for something called Domestic Science and no one bothered if you didn't attend. "It's all about ironing your husband's shirts," said Veronica, "and when I marry Bobby we'll have servants to do that." "When I marry Bobby" was a common theme amongst the Bobby Soxers. They never seemed to wonder how, barring polygamy or a swift change in religion, they were all going to achieve this ambition.

"If I get married," she said, "which I don't think I will because the men I meet are all two foot tall, I'll make my husband iron his own shirts."

"You do make me laugh, Meg," said Isabel. Which was friendly at least, if slightly worrying.

They settled in a café opposite which had a view of the famous arches. The owner, a friendly, sardonic

160

Italian, also seemed relaxed about the girls sitting for hours over their milkshakes.

"You know the other day," said Meg, "when you said that Rhonda had met a man outside the Ritz who said that she should be a model?"

"Yes," said Veronica, using her straw to hoover up the final bubbles.

"Did Rhonda say anything else about this man? She thought he was an agent, didn't she?"

"Why?" said Jean, who had been watching them silently up until now. She hadn't ordered a drink and Meg wondered if she was short of money. She didn't live at home like Veronica and Isabel and so presumably didn't have the same access to parental handouts. Meg had never had pocket money herself, in a family of nine the concept was as alien as space travel, but she could spot middle-class girls a mile off. And Jean wasn't one.

"Rhonda's missing, isn't she?" Jean went on. "I read it in the paper. Why are you asking all these questions? Are you a policewoman?"

Meg took a deep breath. She hadn't been planning to break disguise quite so soon. She remembered what Jean had said about hating the "pigs". But the girls would have to know sooner or later and, besides, it felt wrong to lie in answer to a direct question.

"Yes," she said. "I am. We're investigating Rhonda's disappearance and I was asked to go undercover. Look, here's my identification card."

Veronica and Isabel gasped as if she had performed one of Max Mephisto's magic tricks.

"That's so cool." Veronica.

"Amazing." Isabel.

"Do you have a gun?" Sadie.

Jean stood up. "Get out," she said, pointing towards the door with a trembling finger. "You're not one of us. You're not a Bobby Soxer. You're a grown-up."

This last sounded so ridiculous that Meg could not stop herself laughing, despite the genuine anger in Jean's voice.

"I'm only nineteen," she said. "I'm a girl just like you. Just like Rhonda. Her family are worried about her. Imagine if it was your sister who'd gone missing."

"I haven't got a sister," said Jean, but she lowered the accusatory arm.

"Nor has Rhonda. She's an only child. Just think how worried her parents must be."

"Why should we help the pigs?" said Jean.

"Don't think of helping the police," said Meg. "Think of it as helping Rhonda. She's a real Bobby Soxer, after all. She loved Bobby. I've seen her room at school. It's full of pictures of him. The man who asked about modelling might be a suspect. That's why I came up here to talk to you again. It's torture squeezing into this skirt, I can tell you."

This made Isabel laugh and the ghost of a smile even flitted across Jean's face.

"Do you remember anything about the man?" said Meg. "Anything at all?"

"No," said Isabel. "Like I said, he was just a man. Tallish, oldish, in a suit."

"Did Rhonda say anything about him?"

Veronica and Isabel looked at each other.

162

"Just one thing," said Isabel. "She said he was American. That's what made her think that he must be the real thing."

Malcolm Henratty was a wiry, dark-haired man with a rather piratical air, although that could just have been the gold earring in his right ear. He was short with receding hair but there was something about him that made Edgar understand how he could have seduced Sara's mother, Bernadette. Henratty reminded him of Emma's friend Tol Barton, whose Romany charm Edgar had always slightly distrusted.

"I know an officer came to see you on Friday," said Edgar. "I'm very sorry about your daughter."

"Thank you," said Henratty; he had a London accent with an odd, transatlantic twang. "I'd never even seen Sara but, even so, it was a shock."

"Do you mind me asking why you'd never seen her?" asked Edgar. "I mean, you knew she existed, didn't you? You knew that Bernadette was pregnant."

Henratty paused before replying. He had bright, dark eyes, like those of a blackbird or a magpie.

"It was easier that way," he said. "I knew that I wouldn't be much of a father to her. I thought that Bernie and Sara would be better off without me. I've always been a bad boy, Superintendent."

This was said almost mockingly but Edgar didn't return the smile. He didn't find Henratty very endearing and, besides, at nearly forty he really should stop referring to himself as a "boy".

"Did you keep in touch with Bernadette at all?" he asked.

"No," said Henratty. "I didn't even know she was dead until that policeman told me. Poor Bernie. She was such a pretty girl too. They tell me Sara looked like her."

"I believe so," said Edgar. "Can you think of any reason why anyone would have abducted and killed Sara?"

Henratty's face darkened, making him look more piratical still. "No," he said. "The scum. To kill an innocent girl like that. If I ever see him . . ."

Petty criminals were always the most judgemental about their more hardened brethren. That was why child killers got such a hard time in prison. Edgar understood this but there was something rather disingenuous about it at the same time, a self-righteous unloading of guilt.

"You're in for theft, aren't you?" he said.

"Yeah. Robbed an off-licence. The things a man will do to get a drink." The smile flickered again. Edgar stared stonily back.

"Did you know a man in here called Coggins, Ernest Coggins?"

"He's the chap who escaped, isn't he? Everyone's talking about it."

"Did you know Coggins?"

"Not really. I might have exchanged the odd word with him, that's all. Odd fellow. Always feeding the birds or staring at the pigs. I thought that he might be a bit simple, to tell you the truth."

But Coggins had been clever enough to escape while cocksure Henratty was still in prison. There was nothing more to be gained from the interview. Edgar signalled to the guard that he was about to leave. But, as he moved towards the door, Henratty said, "Superintendent. Have you got a photograph of Sara?"

"There's one at the station, yes."

"Could I have it? After you've finished with it, I mean."

And Edgar found himself agreeing.

Driving back to Brighton, Edgar thought about Malcolm Henratty and about Ernest Coggins, the man who had loved animals and worried about their welfare. He'd had a dog called Lenin, a dog that Rhonda had apparently cared about. Where was Lenin now? Probably dead, like his namesake. Coggins couldn't have abducted Rhonda this time. He'd been in prison until yesterday. But, all the same, his escape was a coincidence too far. Coggins was apparently coming up for a sentence review and, as a prisoner with a previously unblemished record, he stood a good chance of an early release. What had happened to make him throw this chance away?

At the station, Bob was on the telephone to the search team.

"Nothing doing," he said, when he put the receiver down. "Man seems to have vanished into thin air. We checked on his friend Davies though. He hasn't been seen at his digs for over a week. I think we should assume that they're working together."

"I agree," said Edgar. "We should warn the Surrey police. It's not inconceivable that Coggins might approach Rhonda's family. Like I said, her mother's in a very frail state of health."

"Did you see Henratty?" asked Bob.

"Yes. Not a very pleasant character. Did you interview him?"

"No. I sent O'Neill. Thought he might be more intimidating."

"Henratty didn't strike me as easily intimidated. Said he'd never even seen Sara. Had never even bothered to ask after her, much less send her mother any money."

"He sounds like a bad lot," said Bob. "Did he have any links with Coggins?"

"He claimed not to know him very well. Said he'd always thought of Coggins as slightly simple."

"He managed to escape from prison though."

"My thoughts exactly. I think we should get some protection for Rhonda's family."

"I'll speak to Surrey now," said Bob. He put his hand on the telephone but, before he could dial, Edgar's secretary Rita appeared. "Please, sir, Max Mephisto's on the line for you."

Edgar took the call in his office. "Max. What's up?"

"Probably nothing." But Edgar could hear a note of concern in Max's voice. "It's just, I was due to meet Ruby at the Grand for dinner yesterday and she didn't turn up. I didn't think much of it. She's got a busy life, maybe she forgot. But I rang her flat last night and there was no answer. So I tried the TV studio today and apparently she didn't turn up this morning."

"She hasn't turned up for work?" Edgar could imagine Ruby missing dinner with her father, or even a date with a boyfriend, but never a rehearsal.

"I know. It's very unlike her."

"Ruby was meant to be meeting Emma on Saturday," said Edgar. "Ruby said she had something to tell her but she never arrived."

"On Saturday?" Now Max's voice was sharp with anxiety. "I thought I saw Ruby on Saturday. Walking along the prom, towards the Palace Pier."

"Emma was meeting her on the pier."

"Can you check this out, Ed? Send someone round to her flat?"

"I will," said Edgar. "I'm sure she's fine but I'll get the Met onto it." As he said this, Edgar remembered the last time Ruby had gone missing. That time she had been the bait, a trap to catch Max. Who was the intended target this time?

CHAPTER
EIGHTEEN

Emma started Monday with the best intentions. She would stop wishing that she was involved in the investigation and get on with her day-to-day life, trying to be the best wife and mother she could be. After dropping the girls at school she walked, with Johnny in the pushchair, to Brompton's Butchers in Kemp Town to buy steak and kidney for Edgar's favourite supper. Then she walked back, stopping at Mavis's on the way to ask if she needed anything from the shops. Mavis was enchanted to see Jonathan, easily her favourite of the three children, and, if Emma was forced to drink sweetened tea and look at hundreds of photographs of Mavis's dead relations, then at least she felt as if she'd done a good deed.

Back home, she gave Johnny rice pudding and rusks for lunch and ate some herself in an absent-minded way. Then, while Johnny had his nap, she tidied the house and did some hand-washing. By two o'clock, though, her resolve was waning. She wanted to know what was happening in the case. She wanted to know why Ruby hadn't turned up on Saturday. Yesterday her mother had said that she was looking tired. "You need some more help around the house, darling. Then you can have some time to yourself." But time to do what? The activities on which her mother had always lavished such care and attention — her personal appearance, socialising, charity work — seemed, to Emma, even worse than housework and childminding. What she wanted, she had to admit it, was a job. Specifically, a job as a detective.

She telephoned the newspaper but was told that Sam was out "chasing up the hatches, matches and dispatches". Emma knew that this referred to the paper's column of births, marriages and deaths and that interviewing bereaved relatives (or mothers-of-the-brides) was Sam's least favourite journalistic task. Next she tried to get Ruby's number from directory enquiries but it was, unsurprisingly, ex-directory. Emma was just wondering if she dared to ring Edgar at the station and risk hearing Rita's scornful voice saying, "Mrs Stephens for you, sir", when the phone rang.

"Hallo. What's going on down on the ranch?"

It was Edgar.

"Hi," said Emma. "It's the usual never-ending round of gaiety. What about you?"

"The same, of course. I spent the morning in a prison. The thing is, Em, you know you were meant to meet Ruby this weekend?"

"Yes?"

"Well, Max was meant to meet her for dinner on Sunday and she didn't turn up. She hasn't turned up for work this morning either."

"Oh my God. You don't think anything's happened to her?"

"I got the Met to send a man round to her flat. He heard a cat meowing inside. Max says that Ruby's devoted to her cat, she'd never go away without asking someone to look after it."

"Did the PC manage to rescue the cat?"

"Yes, the warden of the flats had a key and she's looking after it now. But Max is worried. I just wondered if you had any ideas. Did Ruby say anything to you?"

Despite her own genuine concern for Ruby, Emma felt the familiar lift of spirits at the thought of having her opinion sought. "She just said that she had something important to tell me," she said. "Something she couldn't discuss on the phone."

"Did you have any idea what it was?"

"I assumed it was about a man. At Diablo's funeral Ruby said that she was seeing a delicious new man."

"She didn't give you a name?"

"No."

"Do you think she wanted your advice about the new man?"

"That's what I thought at the time but now I'm thinking — why would Ruby want to talk to me about a new boyfriend? It doesn't make sense."

"Perhaps it was someone Max wouldn't approve of. You must be one of the few people she knows who also knows Max."

"But why would she care about Max's approval? Ruby's a grown woman with a successful career and her own money." She hoped that Edgar couldn't hear the note of envy in her voice.

170

"I know," said Edgar, and Emma could almost hear him thinking, a flashback to the days when they would be discussing the latest case and Emma, a keen young DS, would hang on Edgar's every word and inflection. "Ruby doesn't fit the pattern of the missing girls," said Edgar. "She's older, for one thing, and, as you say, she's independent. It's hard to see her falling for the 'I can make you a model' line."

"Is that your theory?"

"It's one of them. WPC Connolly, you know, the policewoman I was telling you about, she came up with it. Apparently Rhonda was approached by a man outside the Ritz who said that she should be a model."

"WPC Connolly is obviously a good detective."

"Bob thinks so," said Edgar. "Are you OK, Em? Your voice sounds a bit odd."

"I'm fine. I went with Sam to talk to Pete, Louise Dawkins' doctor friend. He said that Louise had done some modelling in the past."

"Really? That's very helpful. I'll get Bob to send someone to talk to Pete. What's his full name?"

Emma had, of course, remembered the name. Dr Peter Chambers. She told Edgar, unable to stop herself from adding, "Why not send WPC Connolly to interview him?"

"That's up to Bob," said Edgar. "He does seem to rate her though. Thanks, Em, you're a wonder."

I might be a wonder, thought Emma, as she went wearily upstairs to collect a now wailing Jonathan, but I'm a wonder who's got to cook steak and kidney pie later. She bet that Meg Connolly had never cut up a kidney in her life.

Max couldn't just sit around in Brighton doing nothing, especially after hearing about the empty flat with the cat meowing inside, so he set out to call on Emerald, the ex-snake-charmer who had, unbeknownst to him at the time, given birth to Ruby after a brief fling with a young magician called Max Mephisto. When Ruby was a year old Emerald had married a plasterer and they went on to have two more children. They lived in Hove and Ruby had been brought up in a close, loving home. Ruby called her stepfather Dad. Max had to admit that, if she were in trouble, Ruby would go to Emerald and — what was his name? Tom? — before she confided in him.

Emerald and Tom lived in one of the wide boulevards leading up from the seafront: Grand Avenue, First, Second and Third Avenues. The houses were handsome and well-proportioned but Max always found them rather depressing, perhaps because of their uniformity, endless white stucco frontages turned grey by the wind and the rain. There was none of the uneven charm of Brighton.

Ruby had told him that her parents now lived on the top floor of their Second Avenue house and rented the rest out to lodgers. What else had she told him? Tom was now retired and Emerald did a lot of charity work. Max couldn't imagine it somehow. He had seen Emerald a few times after he found out about Ruby's existence but to him she was still a dimly remembered presence from that summer season in Worthing, a golden shape accessorised by a poison-green python.

Anything less like a showgirl than the woman who answered the door would have been hard to imagine. Emerald was still an attractive woman, her dark hair well-styled and only lightly streaked with grey, but she now looked the epitome of respectability. Max thought of Betty, Bob's wife, who had once been part of a tableaux act, even less respectable than being a snake-charmer. Betty was now a solid citizen in tweeds and twinsets. Emerald was slightly more stylish but she still looked like the sort of woman who proposed the guest speaker's health at a WI meeting. She was even wearing a pony club brooch.

"Max," she said, when she saw him at the door. "This is a surprise." She didn't look as if it was an entirely welcome one.

"Hallo, Emerald," said Max. "You look well. Could I have a word?"

"Well I'm just out to a Distressed Gentlewoman's meeting."

"It won't take long."

They ascended a handsome, but extremely steep, staircase. Max was breathing heavily by the time they reached the top. It was as bad as the Brighton Alps. Emerald opened the door to a sunny flat, decorated in comfortable good taste. The only unusual object was a painting, hanging in an obscure corner, showing a large green snake lying coiled on a beach.

Emerald saw Max looking at it. "Is that George?" he said.

"Yes." Emerald smiled properly for the first time and he saw a trace of the girl he had once known. "He was a treasure. The best co-star I ever had."

Max's best co-star was probably Ruby but he thought it was better not to say this. Emerald had not been pleased when Ruby had followed her newly discovered father into show business.

"Have you seen Ruby lately?" he asked.

"Not for a week or so," said Emerald, sitting down and smoothing her skirt over her knees. "But we talk on the telephone a lot. Why?"

"When did you last speak to her?"

Emerald paused before replying. "It must be a week ago. She usually calls me on Sundays but she didn't yesterday."

"She didn't call you?"

"No, but that's nothing to worry about. Ruby has a busy life."

This was said with pride and a little sadness. On the surfaces of the room Max had noticed many photographs of Emerald's sons, who must both be now in their late twenties or early thirties: weddings, christenings, family days out. There were also several pictures of Ruby, studio portraits showing her in full-glamour mode, peering over a shoulder or gazing mistily into the distance. The juxtaposition made Ruby seem like a star but it also effectively put her outside the family circle. Max wondered whether Emerald would have liked to have just one photo of Ruby in white at a church gate or cuddling an infant.

174

"Emerald," he said, "has Ruby talked to you about her new boyfriend?"

Again, a slight pause. "She has mentioned someone," said Emerald, "but it was quite vague and she didn't give a name. Max, what is all this about?"

"Probably nothing," said Max, "but she was meant to meet me for dinner last night and she didn't turn up."

He thought he saw Emerald relax.

"You know what she's like," she said, "something more exciting probably came her way. Or Joe wanted her to attend a function in London."

"That's what I thought," said Max. "But I rang the studio. She didn't turn up for work this morning."

Emerald looked at him and he saw his fear reflected in her eyes.

Edgar ended up seeing Dr Pete Chambers himself. WPC Connolly was still in London and Bob was busy with the Sara Henratty enquiry. Chambers met him in the car park, saying he needed a cigarette. Edgar thought that the young doctor looked exhausted, eyes shadowed, a muscle twitching in his cheek.

"I've been on call for twenty-four hours," said Chambers, lighting up the moment they were outside.

"Isn't that dangerous?" said Edgar. "For you as much as for the patients?"

Chambers laughed hollowly. "Of course it's danger-ous but the consultants did it when they were housemen so they don't see why we shouldn't suffer too. And, when I'm a consultant — if I don't die of a heart attack first — I can spend all day on the golf course. Trouble is, I don't like golf."

"Nor do I," said Edgar. "I had a boss who was always telling me that I should learn because it was good for my career but it's hard to see what swinging a club has to do with solving crimes."

"A good walk ruined," said Chambers. "Isn't that what someone said about golf?"

"Probably," said Edgar. "I do appreciate you taking the time to talk to me. I'm investigating the disappearance of Louise Dawkins."

"About time too," said Chambers.

"Yes," said Edgar, slightly discomforted. "I understand that you were never satisfied that Louise had gone to the Caribbean."

"For God's sake!" Chambers started to pace to and fro as if he couldn't bear to stay still. Edgar could see what he meant about the heart attack. "Louise had no family in the West Indies. She was born and brought up in Hackney. Both her parents were dead and she had no close relatives. The Caribbean story was just useful for the hospital, to stop them wondering why one of their best student nurses had suddenly disappeared. I never believed it for a minute."

"When did you last see her?" asked Edgar.

"It was on the ward. I'd given her a book. An Ernest Hemingway. We talked about that."

"Did she seem unhappy? Perturbed?"

"I've thought about that a lot," said Chambers. "And, in retrospect, she was probably a little quiet, as if

176

she had something on her mind. But Louise was a quiet girl. She wasn't one to talk about her feelings."

"I understand that she had done some modelling in the past," said Edgar.

"Yes. How do you know about that?"

"You met my wife, Emma, with the reporter, Sam Collins."

"Oh, that was your wife." Chambers gave Edgar rather an appraising look, as if wondering what Emma could possibly see in him.

"Do you know any details about the modelling work?" said Edgar. "Was it with an agency?"

"I don't know," said Chambers. "Like I say, Louise was quite reticent about her private life. She only mentioned it because we once talked about strange jobs we had done to pay for our studies. I was a dustman for a time, Louise said that she'd been a model. She didn't like it much but it paid well. And, as I say, she had no family, no means of support. She must have needed money badly. Why are you interested?"

"It's a line of enquiry," said Edgar. "Is there anyone who would know more about the modelling?"

"Maybe Louise's friend Harriet. They were quite close. It was Harriet who showed me Louise's note."

"Could I talk to Harriet?"

"She'd be on duty now. You might be able to get a few minutes with her. Come with me. I need to be back on the ward anyhow."

Pete Chambers led the way through endless corridors, painted cream on top and green under the dado rail, and through a maze of swing doors. Eventually he came to a door marked "Isaac Goldsmid".

"It's a men's surgical ward," said Chambers. "A bit grim. Wait here. I'll get Harriet to come out to you."

Edgar waited, thinking how alien the hospital environment seemed. He'd been here for the birth of his children (not present at the actual birth, of course, that was strongly discouraged) and on many occasions as a policeman. He remembered visiting Emma after various accidents in the course of her intrepid career. He had first declared his love for her in this hospital, as she lay recovering from an encounter with a killer. A romantically inclined sister had let him visit again that night and he and Emma had sat out on a covered balcony and looked down on the lights of Brighton. He'd thought then that, if Emma would agree to marry him, he would be perfectly happy for the rest of his life. He had to fix things with Emma. He had to.

The door opened and a nurse appeared. She had smooth blonde hair under a winged cap and a round, pleasant face.

"Are you Harriet Francis?" said Edgar.

"Yes. I can only be a minute. The ward sister's a real dragon." Harriet's voice was distinctly upper-class; Edgar guessed that she wouldn't have had to resort to odd jobs to pay her bills.

"I'm Superintendent Edgar Stephens. I'm investigating the disappearance of Louise Dawkins. I'm interested in some modelling work that she might have done prior to becoming a nurse."

"Oh." Harriet looked surprised. "Why are you interested in that? It was a while ago. I don't think Louise enjoyed it very much."

"Did she work for an agency?"

"Oh yes." Harriet sounded quite affronted on her friend's behalf. "It was all above board. The agency had an office and everything."

"Can you remember the name of the agency?"

"Yes. It was called Angels. I remember because sometimes nurses get called angels. Some angels!" But she smiled when she said this. Edgar thought that Harriet was the sort of person who passed easily through life. She didn't seem insensitive — she would hardly be a nurse if she was — but she was somehow serene. Edgar was glad that Louise had had her as a friend.

"Do you know where it was? The agency? Angels?"

"London somewhere. Sorry, that's all I know."

"It's very helpful. Thank you."

"You will find her, won't you?" said Harriet. "I'm sure she wouldn't just go off like that. I tried to tell Matron but she wouldn't listen."

"We'll do everything we can," said Edgar. It sounded like a lukewarm promise but it seemed to comfort Harriet.

"Good," she said. "I've got to go now." With a last, slightly nervous smile, Harriet dived back into Isaac Goldsmid Ward.

Max left Emerald and caught the first train to London. He took a tube to Kensington High Street and walked up the hill to Ruby's flat. On the way he passed a woman with a toddler, a little girl pulling a toy dog on wheels. It made a comforting clackety sound and Max found himself smiling. The woman smiled back. For some reason Max thought of Ruby. He had never known her as a little girl, going shopping with her mother, inseparable from a favourite toy. He'd been lucky enough to have that time with Rocco and Elena but it didn't make up for missing those years with Ruby.

Ruby's block had an entry phone but Max remembered the number from his first visit. He keyed in the digits and climbed the steps to Ruby's apartment. Even though he knew that she wouldn't answer, he still knocked on the door. The sound reverberated through the lobby and he imagined the egg-shaped chair, the unused kitchen, the bed with the zebra-skin cover, silent and listening. Where was Ruby, his enigmatic but much-loved daughter? Was she missing or did she simply not want to be found?

He went downstairs to the warden's flat, prepared to use all his old stage charm to discover the secrets of Ruby's life. He needn't have worried. The warden (she preferred the title concierge) was an ex-actress called Celia Ward who was thrilled to find Max Mephisto on her door-step and was fully prepared to tell him everything she knew. Cleopatra the Siamese, enthroned on Celia's best armchair, was less delighted to see him. Max wondered suddenly why Ruby had given her cat a name that was, to Max — and Ruby too, surely? — forever associated with Florence.

180

"Ruby's such a lovely girl," said Celia, placing a tray containing tea and scones in front of Max. "I hope nothing's happened to her."

"So do I," said Max. Ruby was thirty-four but she still looked young enough to be called a girl. Max felt a sudden fear. Had Ruby been abducted by whoever was kidnapping girls in Brighton, because she still looked like a teenager?

"I don't want to pry into Ruby's personal life," said Max, accepting a rather dry-looking scone. "She's an adult, after all. But it's very unlike her to miss work and I'm a bit worried. I just wondered whether you'd seen anything unusual in recent weeks. Someone visiting, perhaps?"

"Well . . ." Celia settled herself in the chair opposite. Despite being well over sixty, she was still attractive, with dyed red hair and a gravelly voice. She had actress's eyes too, large and expressive, accentuated with false eyelashes, and these were in full play now.

"She's had a few boyfriends over the years. Well, haven't we all, darling? The stories I could tell you about when I was in rep . . . But recently there's been someone new. He usually calls quite late at night and I haven't been able to get a good look at him." This was said regretfully, as if she'd had a damn good try.

"Can you remember when he last came round?"

"Last week," said Celia promptly. "The day you came for supper. Ruby said she was cooking you something nice. I did wonder because she wasn't much of a cook. I could smell burning if she so much as made toast. Anyway, that night, after you left, *he* arrived."

"Can you remember anything about him?"

"Not much, I'm afraid. It was dark and he had his hat pulled down over his face. It looked like he had a balaclava on too."

"A balaclava?"

"Yes, I could see something black. Otherwise, he was tall, I can tell you that. And he was carrying a case."

"A case?"

"Yes, the kind musicians have."

With a chill, Max remembered Edgar standing outside a boarding house in Eastbourne and telling him about a woman's body cut into three and placed into boxes that had once housed musical instruments. It had reminded Edgar of a trick of Max's called the Zig Zag Girl. That was the case that had reunited him with Edgar, and it was a horrific memory for all sorts of reasons.

Celia couldn't remember anything else about the man apart from the obvious fact that anyone who wore a balaclava on a dark night was clearly someone who needed to keep their identity hidden. Max left the mansion block feeling more anxious than ever.

His next stop was Joe Passolini. Although Joe had once been his agent, Max had never visited his office. Joe preferred to do business over drinks in bars or meals in dark little Italian restaurants where he knew the owners. When Max saw the premises, he understood why. The tall house in Notting Hill had seen better days, and there were a number of doorbells by the once-grand front door, most of them sounding like made-up businesses: R. Porter Bespoke Garments; B.

Price and Co; Angels Modelling; Tommy's Travel You Trust; Henry Oberman, Notary. J. Passolini, Theatrical Agent, was on the top floor. Max rang the bell.

"Max!" Joe sounded positively shocked over the entry phone but, by the time Max had climbed the stairs, he had recovered his equanimity. "Come in, come in. I don't get many visitors." Joe was clearing old newspapers off the visitor's chair. This, apart from the desk and Joe's own swivel chair, was the only piece of furniture in the tiny room. A picture of the Bay of Naples, cut out of a magazine and stuck to the musty yellow striped wallpaper, was the only decoration.

"I wasn't expecting you," said Joe, wiping the seat with his cuff. Unlike his surroundings, Joe was as smart as ever, even in his shirtsleeves. His white collar gleamed and his hair shone with brilliantine.

"Weren't you?" said Max. "Didn't you think that I might be concerned about Ruby?"

"Hasn't she contacted you either?" Joe took his seat on the other side of the desk. He looked more in control now but his shiny black eyes were unusually troubled.

"No. And she didn't turn up for work this morning."

"I know. The producer rang me. It's not like Ruby. She's a real pro."

"Didn't that ring any alarm bells with you?"

"I was surprised, yes. But I thought she must be off with her new man."

"Ah, yes. This new man. Tell me about him. I remember you mentioning him, that evening in the bar at the Grand, the day of Diablo's funeral. You said that

Ruby had gone back to London because she had a hot date."

"I don't know anything about him," said Joe. "Ruby keeps her private life to herself."

Except when it's in the gossip columns, thought Max. But it occurred to him that he hadn't read anything about Ruby's new love interest.

"You must know his name," he said.

Joe shook his head. "Ruby told me that she was seeing someone new. Obviously I asked if there was a publicity angle for me. She said, 'If you knew who it was, you'd be shocked.'"

"'You'd be shocked.' What did that mean?"

"I don't know. I thought, maybe a royal or a pop star, maybe even one of the Beatles."

"Shocked, though. Not surprised. Or impressed."

"Yes," said Joe, as if this had only just occurred to him. "You don't think something could have happened to Ruby?"

"She was meant to meet Emma Stephens on Saturday and didn't turn up. She was meant to meet me on Sunday. She didn't arrive for work this morning. Either she's run off with this mystery man or something's happened to her. You know about the other girls who've disappeared?"

"I thought there was only one of them. The Roedean girl."

"Edgar thinks there are others. It's hard to see how they connect to Ruby though. They're all teenagers, two of them without any family ties."

"Ruby hasn't got many family ties."

"She's got me," said Max sharply. "And her mother and stepfather. I went to see Emerald this morning. She's worried too. Apparently Ruby usually telephones her on a Sunday night." He didn't add that this information had given him a sharp pang of jealousy.

"If she's gone missing," said Joe, "we have to keep it out of the papers."

"Why?" said Max. "Worried it will affect her career? Or yours?" It had been a long time since he had hit a man but that might be about to change.

But Joe sounded genuinely aggrieved. "No!" he said. "What do you think I am? But, if someone's taken Ruby, it'll be because they want to be in the papers. Mark my words."

CHAPTER
NINETEEN

"Ruby French has gone missing," said Edgar. "We can't discount the theory that she was taken by the same person who abducted Rhonda, Sara and Louise."

"Ruby French?" said Sergeant O'Neill. "Ruby Magic?"

"Yes," said Edgar. "We're trying to keep this out of the papers for now so discretion is needed."

O'Neill looked as if this was a foreign word. Or concept. He nudged his partner, the brainless Chubby Barker, and whispered something.

"Rhonda was approached outside the Ritz Hotel in London by a man who said that she should be a model," said Edgar. "Louise Dawkins used to do some modelling. It's possible that Sara was approached too. The only clue we have about this man is that he had an American accent. Thanks to WPC Connolly for this lead."

Meg, who was standing by the door, blushed bright red.

"I spoke to Dr Peter Chambers, a junior doctor at the hospital," said Edgar. "He confirmed that Louise had done some modelling work in the past. One of the nurses gave the name of the agency, Angels."

Edgar gestured to Bob, indicating that he should take over the briefing. He stood up, still awkward even after nearly five years in this role.

"We're trying to trace the agency," said Bob, apparently addressing the light fitting. "They're not in the London directory. We don't know if Sara Henratty had any links to modelling agencies but WPC Connolly and I are interviewing Percy McDonald, known as Peanuts, Sara's ex-boyfriend, later this morning. WPC Connolly is also maintaining contact with the Bobby Hambro fans. We've warned them to be on their guard too."

"What about you, Meg?" said O'Neill. "Fancy being a centrefold?"

Meg blushed redder than ever. Edgar waited for Bob to reprimand O'Neill and, when he didn't, said, "That's no way to speak to a colleague and fellow police officer, O'Neill. WPC Connolly is a valued member of the investigation team."

O'Neill muttered something that might have been an apology. Bob looked as if he was about to say something but then coughed and looked back at his notes. Edgar wondered if he was angry that his boss had stepped in or just embarrassed by O'Neill's behaviour. Bob continued, in his usual monotone, "Ernest Coggins, the man who abducted Rhonda six years ago, has escaped from Ford Open Prison. It's hard to see how he could have had any involvement with the other girls but it's still a link and one that should be investigated. We think that Coggins had an accomplice, a released fraudster called Howell Davies. We need to track him down."

Edgar waited for O'Neill to comment but the sergeant was staring straight ahead.

"Time is of the essence," he said. "Rhonda has been missing for a week now, Louise for longer. We have to find them. Brighton will be chock-a-block this weekend for the bank holiday. Easy for people to go unnoticed in the crowds. The last thing we want is for another girl to go missing."

Emma had thought long and hard about what to serve for lunch. Sam never minded what she ate but Astarte favoured exotic food, salad made from garden herbs, soups full of ginger and spices. In the end she settled for ham and salad but she boiled some eggs and scooped out the yolks and mixed them with mustard and mayonnaise, the way Cook used to do.

"Devilled eggs," said Sam when she saw them. "Very fancy."

"Is that what they're called?" said Emma, who was putting Johnny in his high chair. The name suddenly struck her as ill-omened.

"They look like little suns," said Astarte. As she spoke, the actual sun seemed to break into the basement kitchen, blazing on Astarte's golden hair and Johnny's ruddy cheeks. The baby laughed and tried to grab Astarte's necklace as she bent over to kiss him.

"You can't have that," she said, "but you can have this."

188

She got a toy out of her bag. It was a wooden soldier that divided into three blocks. Johnny was enchanted, took it apart, looked at the pieces and put one in his mouth, then took it out to inspect it further. Emma tried not to think about the Zig Zag Girl, the woman cut into three. She hadn't worked on the Conjuror Killer case but it had achieved mythical status with the Brighton police.

Over lunch they talked about the children, about Tol in the South of France, about Sam's unsympathetic editor. They could have been three housewives meeting for a gossip apart from the moment when Astarte reached into her bag and brought out her crystal ball.

"Do you have anything that belonged to the three girls?" she asked.

"I've got Rhonda's school hat," said Emma. "I asked Ed to bring it home so I could look at it. All I've got from the others are the newspaper cuttings that Sam gave me."

Astarte took the felt hat and placed it on the table in front of her. Jonathan watched her, fascinated, the toy halfway to his mouth. Then she put the three newspaper articles in a circle around it and placed her hands over them. There was silence apart from Johnny's appreciative grunts as he gnawed on the wooden block.

Astarte turned the crystal ball so that it caught the sun, the rays flashing around the room, illuminating the china on the dresser, the cobwebs on the ceiling that Emma hadn't been able to reach. Astarte took a deep breath and stared into the orb. What could she see, Emma wondered for the hundredth time. Were there really images in the cloudy depths, things that had happened and events yet to come? Or did Astarte just dream it all up and present her clients with vague platitudes that they wanted to believe? Astarte had once told Emma that occasionally she looked at a person's palm and saw nothing. "Does that mean they're dead?" Emma had asked, facetiously. "Sometimes," Astarte had replied.

Now Astarte raised her head. She looked at Sam and Emma, her eyes unfocused and distant.

"He hasn't got a blonde," she said.

Percy "Peanuts" McDonald lived in Southwick, a small town to the west of Brighton. He was seventeen and worked as an apprentice plumber.

"During the week," he explained to Meg and the DI.

"And at the weekends?" asked Meg.

"At the weekends I'm a mod."

He said this with real fervour. Up to this point, Peanuts had been an uncommunicative, almost sullen interviewee. As he was only seventeen, the DI had asked if an adult could be present so Percy's father, Alf, also a plumber, sat glumly on the sofa, dressed in his overalls as if to emphasise how ill he could afford to take any time off work.

"Two of my brothers are mods," said Meg. "They spend hours attaching things to their bikes."

"Ah, well." Peanuts leant back in his chair, properly relaxing for the first time. "Your scooter's your calling card, isn't it? My Lambretta's got chrome on the rear rack, side guards and front wheels, spotlights, a two-tone air horn and fifteen wing mirrors."

"He spends all his wages on that thing," said Alf McDonald. "And on the clothes. Ask him about the clothes."

Peanuts shot his father a look. Unlike McDonald Senior, Peanuts was not in overalls but neatly dressed in slim-fitting trousers and a Fred Perry shirt. Meg instantly recognised the look as off-duty mod.

"We're investigating the murder of Sara Henratty," said the DI, obviously feeling that the fashion chat had gone on too long. "I know you've already spoken to one of my officers, Percy, but we've just got a few more questions about Sara. I'm sorry. I know this must be upsetting for you."

"Yeah," said Peanuts, reaching up to pat his hair into place. This too was carefully arranged and gleaming with oil. But Meg thought that the gesture was more for reassurance than anything. "I didn't know Sara that well but I was upset. I mean, she was so young. It's not what you expect, is it?"

Meg agreed that it wasn't. "How did you meet her?" she asked.

"It was at the youth club," said Peanuts. "It's run by the church but it's not too God-squaddy and they've got a pool table. Sara was there with a friend. We got talking and we went for a walk the next day."

"Did you see her often after that?"

"Just once or twice." Peanuts looked at his father. "Just to the cinema and that. It wasn't anything serious."

191

"He brought her here once," said Alf. "Pretty little thing. The wife and I were really shocked when we heard the news."

"Mum didn't like her," said Peanuts. "She thought Sara stole one of her necklaces."

"It wasn't that Mum didn't like her," said Alf. He turned to Meg as if appealing for her support. "We felt sorry for Sara. She lived in a children's home. She didn't have much. If she took the necklace, then she was welcome to it. Like I said, we were very upset when we heard the news."

Sara had been wearing a necklace when she died, Meg remembered. Had it once belonged to her boyfriend's mother? The chain had been broken when her killer put his hands round Sara's neck. Meg hoped that Sara had managed to get some pleasure out of the stolen jewellery but she doubted it somehow.

"Peanuts," she said. Percy had asked them to use his nickname ("everyone does, except my mum") although the DI was obviously finding it difficult. Meg sympathised. Her mother still called her Margaret. "Peanuts, I saw a picture of Sara in the papers. She was dressed in mod clothes. Do you remember that photograph being taken?"

Peanuts shook his head. "No, but I heard about it. Sara was really proud of that photo. She had all the mod gear, the dresses and the boots, and she looked really good in it. And she had that blonde hair. Mum said it was dyed but it still looked great. Like a film star. Like Marilyn Monroe."

Hardly a happy comparison, given that the film star had killed herself two years earlier. Meg's brother

Patrick had been inconsolable. She exchanged a glance with the DI and leant forward. "Do you remember anyone approaching Sara and saying that she should be a model? Did she ever mention anyone who had said something like that to her?"

"Yes," said Peanuts immediately. "She told me that a man had stopped her in the street and said that she should be a model. I didn't know whether to believe her. Sara . . . well, she didn't lie." Another look at his father. "But she made things up sometimes. She said this man stopped her in Western Road and said that she could make a fortune as a model."

"Did she say anything more about the man?" said Meg. "How old was he? What did he look like?"

"I can only remember one thing," said Peanuts. "She said that he was American. That's what made me think it wasn't true. I mean, how many Americans do you get in Brighton?"

"What do you mean?" said Emma.

Astarte put her hands on the newspaper cuttings. "Rhonda's a redhead, Louise has black hair. He had a blonde but he lost her. He wants another."

Emma felt her skin prickle. The sun disappeared behind a cloud and the room seemed suddenly to be full of shadows.

"How did you know that Rhonda has red hair? The picture's in black and white."

"I saw her in the crystal ball," said Astarte. "She's alive but she's in danger. He's looking. He's looking for another girl to add to his collection. He has a brunette now. All he needs is a blonde."

"A brunette? Do you mean Ruby?"

"I can't see Ruby," said Astarte. "She's behind a veil. But he has another girl. He has them in a cage."

For some reason, Emma thought of Edgar's description of the playpen where he had found a woman's body behind the bars. She remembered now what the killer had called it. The wolf trap.

CHAPTER
TWENTY

Meg was alone in the incident room when the call came through. The sergeant, McGuire, put his head round the door.

"Where's DI Willis?"

"District strategy meeting with the super," said Meg. "In Hove." She was typing up her notes from the interview with Peanuts McDonald and was glad of a break. She'd never really learnt to touch-type although all the male officers seemed to believe that this was her forte. Well, that and making the tea.

"Got this man on the phone," said McGuire. "He says he's found some shoes in a tunnel. In Rottingdean. Could be a nutter but he's asking for the DI."

As clearly as if he were in the room, Meg heard the DI's voice. "It appears that the shoes were removed from the scene." Sara Henratty's shoes had been taken away. Sara's body had been found on the undercliff at Rottingdean.

"I'll go and check it out," she said, standing up.

"You?" said McGuire.

"I'm a member of the investigation team," said Meg, quoting the super. "And I'll investigate."

"On your own?" McGuire was smiling now. Meg wanted to slap him.

"I'll get PC Black to drive me," she said. She'd seen Danny in the rest room. She was pretty sure that he'd jump at the chance of escaping from the station for an hour.

"What shall I tell the DI when he gets back?"

"Tell him I'm on the case," said Meg grandly. She attempted to sweep out of the room but spoilt the effect by almost falling over a chair.

She was right, though. Danny was only too happy to drive her to Rottingdean.

"We're on a mission," he said, as they bowled past Roedean, high on the cliff, the seagulls circling around the clock tower.

"Connolly and Black. Secret Agents."

"Black and Connolly. Alphabetical order."

"It sounds better my way round."

They parked by the village green which was complete with duck pond, ancient stone church and various grand-looking houses.

"It's like a picture postcard," said Meg. She found some crumbs in her pocket and threw them into the water.

"It's full of nobs," said Danny gloomily, watching the ducks fight over the specks of bread.

The call had come from a man called Tony Peters, who ran a gift shop on the High Street. Its name was The Smugglers' Cave and it was the sort of place that Meg usually avoided because of her propensity to knock things off shelves. She entered sideways, trying to keep her limbs in check. Danny looked at her oddly.

Tony Peters was a tall man with a rubbery, humorous face. "I didn't know what to make of it," he said. "I never normally go into that tunnel."

"Are there lots of tunnels then?" asked Meg, keeping well away from a display of glass animals.

"Yes," said Tony. "Rottingdean's famous for smugglers. The gentlemen, they used to call them. You know the windmill on the hill by the golf course?"

"Yes," said Meg. She'd seen it many times, the stocky black shape against the sky.

"Well, the villagers used it to send messages. When the windmill's sails made a cross, it was safe for the smugglers to land. When they made an X-shape, it meant that the excise men were around. The whole village was in on it. Even the vicar, apparently."

"Did the smugglers use the tunnels to hide stolen goods?" Meg only had a vague idea of what the goods might have been. Brandy? Tobacco?

"That's right. The smugglers used to land here, you see, because there's a natural gap in the cliffs and they used the tunnels to bring the goods from the beach into the village. There were loads of them at one time but most are blocked up now."

"Where does this tunnel lead? The one where you found the shoes?"

"I'll show you." Tony took a torch from a shelf and opened a door by the till. "You'll have to duck," he said to Meg. "It's not made for people our height." Danny, who was shorter than Meg, did one of his cross-eyed looks.

Tony led them down stone stairs into a brick-lined passage. "This leads down to the beach," he said, "but the end is blocked up by rubble. Or so I thought. I brew my own beer and I keep the barrels down here. There's another tunnel that leads off at right-angles. I don't usually go in there but this morning I thought I'd just check that the ceiling hadn't fallen in. That happens sometimes. So many buses and lorries on the High Street these days. It dislodges the chalk."

They had reached what seemed to be a dead end but Meg saw that there were actually two archways, one leading left and one right, like Sister Angela's story about the fork in the road. In that version, one road led to heaven and the other to hell. She hoped that Tony was going to choose wisely. They took the left-hand entrance and immediately found themselves in a new tunnel, more roughly hewn than the one before, with walls and ceiling made from chalk. It was cold and uncomfortably narrow.

"We're almost at sea level now," said Tony. "Like I say, I thought the end was blocked but I was wrong."

He stopped suddenly, causing Meg to bump into him and Danny to cannon into her.

"Sorry," he said. He was laughing though. Meg could see his teeth gleaming in the darkness.

"We're at the end," said Tony. He shone the torch to show a low door. "That leads directly onto the

198

undercliff walk. There's a sort of niche here and that's where I found the shoes."

They were in a semicircular space, almost a cave. There was a concrete floor here and alcoves carved out of the chalk. In one of these were eight shoes, neatly placed together in pairs: schoolgirl's brogues, nurse's rubber-soled flats, tatty white stilettos that needed heeling and a pair of black-and-white slingbacks, so shiny and new that they could have been part of an avant-garde fashion shoot.

"It seemed so odd," Tony was saying. "That's why I called the police. I asked for DI Willis because I heard him on the radio, talking about that poor girl who was found near here."

Near here. Where were they exactly? There was a distinct smell in the air, something unpleasant but also familiar.

"Is the door locked?" asked Meg.

"I assumed so," said Tony, "but look." He pulled at the door, the wood scraping against the concrete. Sunlight streamed in. Shielding her eyes, Meg stepped out onto the paving stones of the undercliff walk. She looked around. The White Horse pub was directly above them, the beach opposite. They were in the exact spot where Sara Henratty's body was found.

Meg telephoned from the shop and the DI was there in twenty minutes. Meg was disappointed to see that he had Sergeant O'Neill with him.

"Been doing some digging, Meg?" That was O'Neill's first comment.

Meg ignored him. "Mr Peters telephoned to say that he'd found some shoes in a tunnel under his shop," she said, addressing the DI. "I drove out here with PC Black to investigate."

"Why didn't you call a DS?" said O'Neill. "Someone senior?"

"There was no one available," said Meg. "And I thought it was urgent."

She was relieved that the DI seemed satisfied with this.

"Where's this tunnel then?"

"We can get in from the undercliff walk," said Meg, looking at the DI and O'Neill, neither of whom were exactly sylphlike.

"Lead the way," said the DI.

They walked down the ramp towards the sea. It was almost midday and the sun was bright overhead. The tide was out and the beach was deserted apart from a man throwing stones for his dog. Meg led the way to the wooden door and pushed it open. The DI switched on his torch and stepped inside.

"The shoes are there, in that alcove," said Meg.

The DI continued to shine his torch around the cave, the chalk walls, the concrete floor. The shoes were in one corner and for the first time Meg saw some sacking in another alcove alongside a plastic bucket.

"Someone's been living here," said the DI. He moved closer, followed by O'Neill. Meg was glad that Danny and Tony Peters had stayed outside. It meant that there was just room for her to peer over the DI's shoulder.

He picked up the bucket and put it down again quickly. "Stinks of urine."

That was the smell that Meg had noticed earlier.

"There are some cigarette butts on the floor," said O'Neill. "And some breadcrumbs. Jesus. Is this where he's been keeping them?"

"Well, they're not here any more," said the DI. "Where does this tunnel go, WPC Connolly?"

"Back to the shop," said Meg. "The other end is blocked. But Tony, Mr Peters, says that there are lots of tunnels in Rottingdean. The smugglers used to use them, apparently."

The DI sighed. "We'll have to search them all. But it's a definite lead. The first we've had. Well done, WPC Connolly. It's proof that the girls were together too. Those look like a schoolgirl's shoes to me."

"And those look like they belong to a TV star," said Meg.

"But why did he leave them here?" said O'Neill.

"Like the super said, they could be trophies of some kind. Or else he's leaving us a clue, trying to mislead us. Like the hat in the Roedean tunnel."

Meg had discovered that too. Was the kidnapper, the killer, deliberately leaving things for her to find? It was a disconcerting thought. She took out her own torch and shone it slowly round the claustrophobic space, thick with the smell of ammonia and the sea.

"Look," she said.

On the wooden door, someone had made a number of marks with a piece of chalk. Vertical lines, all of similar length. There were twenty or thirty of them.

"What's that?" said O'Neill.

"I think it's the number of days that they were kept here," said Meg.

CHAPTER
TWENTY-ONE

"It's hers," said Emma. "She was wearing them at Diablo's funeral."

She'd been surprised when Edgar turned up at lunchtime. Pleased but also slightly embarrassed because she'd bought all the papers to see if any of them mentioned Ruby's disappearance and they were spread out on the kitchen table. When Edgar's feet started descending the basement steps, she shoved the newspapers to one side and tried to look as if she was concentrating on her son and heir, who was absorbed in rubbing jam into his hair.

"Hallo, Em. Hallo, Jonathan. You look very jammy."

Emma dabbed at Johnny with a cloth. "He always gets food everywhere," she said. "What are you doing here?"

"Came to see my wife." Edgar came round the table to kiss her, avoiding Johnny's outstretched hands. "Actually, I wanted your opinion on this." He held up a paper bag and, with a slightly theatrical air, shook its contents out on the table. Emma stared at a single high-heeled sling-back shoe.

"Do you recognise it?" asked Edgar.

And of course she did. Ruby had been wearing these shoes with her black-and-white outfit at Diablo's funeral. She said as much and then the significance of the find struck her. Suddenly the single shoe seemed ominous, a sinister Cinderella. And wasn't it bad luck to put shoes on a table?

"Where did you find it?" she said.

"In a tunnel under a Rottingdean shop," said Edgar. "The owner telephoned the station this morning. WPC Connolly visited on her own initiative. It's a real breakthrough. The tunnel comes out at the exact place where Sara Henratty's body was found."

Emma bit back the words "bully for WPC Connolly". "So this proves that Ruby has been abducted," she said.

"I think so," said Edgar. "I've left a message for Max. There are signs that someone — several people — have been living in the tunnel but there's no one there now. Bob's organising a search of all the tunnels. There are loads of them in Rottingdean, apparently."

"Of course there are," said Emma. "Kipling lived in Rottingdean and it's where he wrote that poem. 'A Smuggler's Song'. Haven't you ever read it? 'Watch the wall, my darling, while the gentlemen go by.'"

"I haven't read much Kipling," said Edgar. "I can never forgive him for 'If'. But, if we can find the girls in one of these smugglers' hideouts, that would be terrific. I'm worried that it's escalating. First he murders Sara and now he's kidnapped Ruby, someone in the public eye. It's almost as if he wants to be noticed."

"Are you going to tell the press about Ruby?" said Emma.

"We'll have to think it through very carefully," said Edgar. "On one hand, Ruby's so high-profile the public will get involved and that might be helpful. On the other, it might panic the kidnapper into harming one of the girls. He has already killed Sara, perhaps because she tried to escape."

"Maybe publicity's what the kidnapper wants," said Emma. "It struck me just now. All the girls have been in the papers. Rhonda because of the chess competition. Louise in that picture with the other nurses. Sara in the mod photo. And Ruby's in the papers all the time." She thought of Astarte's hands hovering over the news cuttings. *He has them in a cage.*

"That's a very interesting theory," said Edgar, looking at her as if she was still DS Holmes, his brightest sergeant.

"It just came to me," said Emma. She could feel herself blushing.

"You're the cleverest blonde I know," said Edgar. This was an old joke between them, going back to the time when Superintendent Hodges had told Emma that she was quite intelligent "for a blonde". "I must be getting back," said Edgar, kissing her again. "I might be late tonight. Bye, Johnny. Give my love to the girls." He dropped a kiss on his son's head, avoiding the jam, and made for the door.

"Bye," said Emma. She hardly noticed that Johnny had started to cry. An idea was starting to take shape in the Holmes brain.

Watch the wall, my darling, while the gentlemen go by.

Edgar was not surprised to see Max waiting for him at the police station. His friend was as smartly dressed as ever but his habitual air of sang-froid was missing as he accosted Edgar.

"I got your message. Is it Ruby?"

"We haven't found her and it's not bad news," said Edgar, steering Max towards the doors. He'd spotted two reporters hovering. "But it is a lead. Come into my office."

In the basement room with the painting of Henry Solomon looming over them, Edgar explained about finding the shoes in the tunnel.

"Rottingdean," said Max. "Why on earth would they be there?"

"There's a network of tunnels under the village," said Edgar. "I've got men searching them now. They're all over the place. Under the church, under the village hall, under most of the shops. If the shoes are there, it's possible the girls are there."

Once more, Edgar put the shoe on the table. Max immediately recognised it from the funeral. Edgar remembered that Max had an unerring ability to recall what people were wearing. It helped with magic tricks, apparently.

"So this proves that Ruby's with the other girls," said Max. "Rhonda and the others."

"Rhonda and Louise, we think," said Edgar. He didn't remind Max what had happened to the third girl.

Max covered his face with his hand. Edgar noticed, with surprise, that Max was wearing a wedding ring. Also that the hand was shaking. He wondered if his friend was crying but, when Max looked up, his eyes were dry and had the fierce, determined look that Edgar remembered from their Magic Men days.

"Why have they been taken?" he said. "There hasn't been a ransom note for Ruby. Have there been for the others? The Roedean girl must be well-off."

"No," said Edgar. "There's been no contact from the kidnapper at all. Rhonda's father was sure that she had been abducted for money. It's happened before." Briefly he told Max about Ernest Coggins.

"But what can this Coggins person have to do with Ruby?"

"Nothing as far as I can see," said Edgar. "But it is an odd coincidence, him escaping from prison like that."

"Is there anything that links the girls?" asked Max.

"We've following up a lead about modelling," said Edgar. "It's tentative as yet but Rhonda and Sara were both approached and told that they could be models. Louise had once done some modelling for an agency called Angels."

"Angels," said Max. "Angels. Why does that ring a bell? But Ruby doesn't seem to fit the pattern. She wouldn't be interested if someone offered her modelling work. She doesn't exactly need the money. I mean, she's famous. Since I've been back in England I've been surprised how famous she is. People recognise her in the street."

"Emma's got a theory that it's all linked to press coverage," said Edgar. "Ruby's always in the papers but Rhonda was featured because she won a chess competition and Louise was in a group photo of nurses from the hospital."

"If Emma thinks that then we should consider it," said Max. "Funnily enough, Joe said something similar. He said that whoever had taken Ruby had done it so that they could be in the papers."

"But, in that case, why haven't they contacted us? Raised the stakes?"

"Maybe that's what the shoes were all about. A clue for you to find. Misdirection."

"We'll have to say something to the press about Ruby's disappearance. Maybe we should try to start a conversation with the kidnapper."

Max was silent, thinking. Then he said, "That's a good idea. Appeal to his vanity. Say that it's a brilliantly conceived trick."

"Trick?" This seemed an odd way for Max to refer to the kidnapping of his daughter.

"It's a trick all right," said Max. "I'm sure of it. Making a woman disappear is a classic stage illusion. Of course, it's bringing her back that's the difficult part."

Max was silent for a moment and, when he spoke, his voice wasn't entirely steady. "We have to find her, Ed. I've been a rotten father to Ruby. I can't help thinking that, if it wasn't for me, she wouldn't have been in the public eye at all. It's not what Emerald wanted for her. If Ruby hadn't tracked me down and become my assistant, she'd probably be happily married to a bank manager by now. I've done nothing for her except put her in danger."

"We'll find her," said Edgar. He had reasons of his own for feeling guilty about Ruby.

"You must be mad," said Sam.

They were sitting in a café near the *Argus* offices. The Roma was one of Tol's original coffee bars and was the first establishment in Brighton to possess an Italian coffee machine, a stylish chrome affair that produced clouds of aromatic steam. There were stools at the bar and discreet booths where you could sit for hours over a cappuccino. Today the place seemed to be full of art students, long-haired and confident, their portfolios lying on the floor beside guitar cases and army surplus rucksacks. Emma and Sam were the only customers over thirty and Emma was certainly the only person with a baby in a pushchair.

Emma took a sip of coffee and handed Jonathan a rusk. "It's bait," she said. "I'm bait. Remember what Astarte said? *He hasn't got a blonde.* Well, I've got blonde hair." She pulled a lock from behind her ear and dangled it for Sam's inspection. "If there's an article about me in the paper, he might see it and . . ."

"And what? Kidnap you? Well, that's a great idea, Emma, I must say. One of your best."

"We'll say in the article that I'm always in a certain place at a certain time and we'll see if he turns up."

"And what if he does?"

"You can be there. Hidden behind a tree or something. We can confront him. Or at least get a description. It'll be flushing him out into the open."

209

"If he reads the article. If he's in Brighton. That's a lot of ifs."

Emma thought of Edgar's dislike of the poem "If". "He must be local," she said. "What about the shoes in the tunnel? He must know Rottingdean really well. He knew about the Roedean tunnel too."

Sam knew about the discovery in Rottingdean. She had been there that morning with Harry, taking photographs of the police search parties. That's why, when Emma had rung her, saying that she had news about the case, Sam had been keen to meet. Now, she didn't look so happy. She was frowning as she stirred milk into her coffee.

"Look," said Emma. "If he doesn't come, then we haven't lost anything. I just think it's worth a try. Think of Rhonda and Louise. Think of Ruby."

"I didn't know you were so fond of Ruby."

"I think I have grown . . . well, fond's not the word . . . used to her over the years. She's part of our lives. She's Max's daughter. He'd be devastated if anything happened to her."

As Emma expected, the mention of Max made Sam look thoughtful. "Why would we publish an article about you anyway?" she said. "I don't want to be rude but you're not exactly a household name. My editor's not going to jump at the idea."

"There must be something," said Emma. "I was the first woman detective sergeant in Sussex."

"A long time ago," said Sam. She fiddled with her spoon for a few minutes before breaking into one of her rare grins. "Come to think of it, there is a piece we could do on you. You'd hate it though. Every month we publish a feature on the wives of prominent men in the community."

Emma winced. "What's it called?"

" 'Behind every famous man'."

CHAPTER
TWENTY-TWO

Max was on his way back to London. It had come to him in a flash when he was shaving that morning. *R. Porter Bespoke Garments; B. Price and Co; Angels Modelling; Tommy's Travel You Trust; Henry Oberman, Notary; J. Passolini, Theatrical Agent.* The modelling agency was in the same Notting Hill house that Joe used as his business headquarters. Should he tell Edgar? No, Edgar would only send Bob and the rest of the flat-footed bobbies charging in. He'd go himself and see what he could discover. It was better than sitting in his hotel room, waiting and worrying.

The street was as shabby as ever, its only occupants some slouching teens who looked as if they might be some of Joe's mod friends. Max pressed the bell beside Angels. There was a crude drawing beside the name, just a triangle with a circle on top and a halo around the circle. Not exactly a high-class outfit. He rang again. No answer. He was just wondering what to do when the door opened.

"Maxie!"

If Joe had been surprised to see Max on Monday, now he looked positively astounded. He backed away, like someone who has discovered a rabbit in their top hat.

"Hallo, Joe."

"What is it? Is it Ruby? Have you had any news?"

Joe really did look genuinely concerned. Max took pity on him. "There have been a few developments. Can we talk inside?"

"Sure," said Joe. "I was just going to the barber's." Max noticed that the agent's hair, rather than being greased back as usual, fell limply to his collar. It made him look much younger.

They climbed the stairs to Joe's office where the Bay of Naples looked down on them. Max told Joe about the shoes in the tunnel.

"Bloody hell. You don't think he's got Ruby shut up in there?"

"I don't know," said Max, "but I'm afraid it looks like she might be with the other abducted girls. Joe, what do you know about the modelling agency downstairs? Angels?"

"Lou and Sally? They're OK. They've taken a few pictures of Ruby over the years."

"What?"

"They've done some photoshoots with Ruby. They did one in her flat for *Vogue*. Why? What's the matter?"

"Do you know where they are today, this Lou and Sally? They're not answering the door."

Joe gave a sly smile. "Well, none of us answer the door if we don't know who's on the other side of it."

"You did when I called round before."

"Yes, but I'm a risk-taker, like all Italians. Lou and Sally are a bit more cautious. They're in, I'm sure of it. I saw Sally making coffee in the kitchen earlier. Come on."

On the floor below there was a door with the same triangular angel painted on it. Joe knocked and, sure enough, it opened cautiously.

"Sally, my little darling. I've brought a friend to see you."

Sally wasn't what Max had imagined. She was grey-haired and middle-aged, wearing a trouser suit with glasses on a chain round her neck. Lou was a heavily built American with white hair and battered features.

"Max has got a few questions for you," said Joe, insinuating them both into the room.

"Say," said Lou. "You're that actor. I saw you in *The Conjuror*."

It still felt odd to be called an actor rather than a magician. Max owned up to the film.

"You're married to Lydia Lamont," said Sally. She was as stereotypically English as her husband was American.

"Yes, I am," said Max. They were in a very strange room, bigger than Joe's and retaining some of the elegant dimensions of the original house, but with blackout curtains covering the sash windows. The high walls were covered with a variety of materials; one corner was wallpapered, another was tiled, a fur rug was tacked up on one wall and what looked like artificial grass stuck on another. On another wall was a

214

collage of photographs: the Taj Mahal, the Colosseum, Brighton Pavilion, the Eiffel Tower.

"What's the grass for?" said Max.

"It's for glamour shots," said Sally. "If the models stand against the wall it looks like they're lying down." The rest of the room was filled with cameras, trolleys and tripods. Max imagined a woman, naked or half dressed, standing against the grass-covered wall with the cameras trained on her like guns. It must be desperation that brought people to studios like this, even if it was only desperation to be famous.

"Max is Ruby's father," said Joe. "You remember Ruby Magic? You took the pictures for that *Vogue* article."

"Of course I remember," said Lou. "A very classy-looking dame."

"I loved her flat," said Sally. "Especially the egg chair."

"It's very uncomfortable," said Max. He wanted them to know that he'd been in his daughter's apartment and sat in her chair.

"I just wanted to ask you about some other girls you might have photographed," he said. "Do you remember a Louise Dawkins? She was saving up to be a nurse."

"Coloured girl?" said Sally. "Yes, I remember her. She was a real beauty. Lovely skin."

"Do you remember a Rhonda Miles or a Sara Henratty?" Max had got the names from Edgar and committed them to memory. He was still good at learning lines. "Rhonda's a redhead and Sara's got dyed blonde hair. Both aged about sixteen."

"Can't say I do," said Lou. "And sixteen's too young for us. Unless they've got their parents' permission."

"You'd be surprised how many of them do have their parents' permission," said Sally. "Mothers coming along asking us to take topless pictures of their daughters."

"Do you take topless pictures?" asked Max.

"Sometimes," Sally answered coolly.

"How do you get your models?" Do you scout for them in the street?"

"We don't need to," said Sally. "You just put pictures in the right magazines and the girls come running. Celebrities are different. We only got Ruby because of Joe."

Joe looked down modestly but Max was struck by the words "we only got Ruby". Who else had got Ruby? Lou seemed impatient with the conversation. He reached out and turned on the radio.

"The television actress Ruby French has been reported missing." The words reverberated against the wallpaper, tiles and fake grass.

It felt very strange hearing Bob's voice coming out of the wireless. Emma had, by and large, got used to her former colleague's promotion. Part of her was actually pleased for him; she'd got on well with Bob when they worked together and they had been through a lot, one way or another. But another smaller, meaner voice said, "What's Bob done to deserve being the DI? All he's done is stay around all these years, plodding along, keeping his nose clean. It should have been you."

Emma tried to silence the voice by turning up the volume.

"We are investigating the possibility that the disappearance of Ruby French is connected to the earlier abductions of Rhonda Miles, a sixteen-year-old schoolgirl, and Louise Dawkins, a nineteen-year-old student nurse. We believe that we are dealing with an extremely clever individual, one who is capable of planning and executing an audacious kidnap."

Edgar had told her of his plan to "open a dialogue" with the kidnapper, to flatter him and force him to show his hand. Emma could see the logic of this but it still felt wrong to hear the words coming out of Bob's mouth, or rather out of their transistor radio, a recent and much-prized purchase. For one thing, Bob would never use the word "audacious".

Emma gave the transistor a cursory sweep with her feather duster. She was tidying up because Sam and Harry, the photographer, were coming later that afternoon to interview her. "The editor likes readers to see the wife at home," Sam had told her, putting aural quotation marks around the word "wife". "He says it gives the piece an intimate feel." Emma looked around the sitting room. It looked intimate all right, Sophie's colouring things all over the floor, Edgar's newspaper open by his chair, Johnny's playpen with its weird collection of objects including a saucepan and the spare back-door keys. The girls would be home when Sam arrived which meant that they'd hang around asking silly questions and getting overexcited. Marianne would be sure that the photographer would want myriad pictures of her in her ballet dress.

She hadn't told Edgar about the interview or about her own plan to flush the kidnapper out into the open. She was sure that he'd be embarrassed by the first and would disapprove violently of the second. So why was she doing it? Emma asked herself this question sternly as she pushed the carpet sweeper up and down. It was partly because she wanted to do *something*. She couldn't just sit at home being the supportive wife behind a successful man. But she had to admit (and Emma was as good at examining her own motives as she was at guessing those of criminals) that she also wanted to prove that she was a better detective than Bob, better than the entire Brighton force, in fact. Certainly better than Meg Connolly who had made such an important breakthrough with the tunnels and was, in Edgar's words, "heading for great things".

Maybe you are, Meg, thought Emma, as she carefully ranked Sophie's crayons in colour order, dark cyan to palest pink. Just make sure you don't get married first because then your career will be over before you can say "wife and mother". She must have spoken the words aloud because Johnny laughed and said something that sounded remarkably like "Mama".

"It's OK for you," said Emma, picking him up and cuddling him. "When you grow up you can be anything you want. Policeman, doctor, journalist, actor, prime minister. Anything."

She thought suddenly of Jonathan, Edgar's brother, for whom the baby was named. What would he have done with his life if he hadn't died at nineteen, on the beach at Dunkirk? Being a man did have its drawbacks after all. She held her son tightly while he meditatively wiped his sticky fingers in her hair.

Meg and DI Willis were on their way to Crawley. They had found an address for Howell Davies's ex-wife, Beryl. Meg was glad to have another chance to interview someone. Maybe the DI was starting to appreciate her skills after all. On the other hand, it was still quite a strain making conversation with him. Maybe she shouldn't even be trying. Maybe she should just be sitting in subservient silence. She wished there was a radio like in American cars.

Crawley was a new town between Brighton and Gatwick Airport. The development had started after the war and new streets were still being added, rows and rows of identical houses all with their own neat strip of garden. Meg, who was meant to be map-reading, kept sending them down one-way streets.

"Little boxes," said the DI contemptuously, executing what felt like a twenty-five-point turn. "There's no soul in places like this."

Meg thought it looked rather nice.

Mrs Davies's house, when they finally located it, was in a road by the park, very clean and quiet, smelling of privet hedges and newly cut grass. Meg thought of how much her parents would love this, instead of their terraced house in Whitehawk with its view of the gas station. You could almost be in the country, apart from the distant, and rather soothing, sound of traffic.

Beryl Davies's first words were, "I don't want any trouble. People round here don't know about Howell."

"There won't be any trouble," said the DI. "We'd just like a few words."

"What do you think you're doing? Turning up on my doorstep with a woman dressed up as a policeman."

"I am a policeman," said Meg. Beryl looked like she wanted to refuse them entry but maybe she thought it was better to get them out of sight because she reluctantly ushered them into the house.

"I haven't got long," she said. "I work at the new Sainsbury's on the high street. My shift starts in an hour."

"It won't take long," said the DI, taking a seat in the immaculately tidy sitting room. Meg perched on the edge of a chair, feeling as if she was taking up too much space.

"We're anxious to speak to Mr Davies," said the DI. "He's no longer at his boarding house and doesn't seem to have left a forwarding address."

"I don't know where he is," said Beryl, sitting up very straight. "I divorced Howell as soon as he went into prison. I haven't seen him since. We've never had anything like that in my family."

"He went into prison for fraud, didn't he?" said Meg.

"Trying to dodge his creditors by giving different names," said Beryl. "I didn't know anything about it. He lied to me too. Said his father was a lord when he really worked down a mine in Wales. A fantasist, that's what they said in court. I should have known. He was an actor and that's what they are, isn't it? Liars. Always pretending to be someone else, putting on different voices, making up stories."

220

"It must have been hard for you," said Meg.

"It was," said Beryl. She didn't relax exactly but some of the stiffness seemed to leave her body. She leant back slightly in her chair. "I come from a respectable family. My mother refused to talk to me when Howell was arrested."

That was friendly, thought Meg. She couldn't imagine her own family disowning her in similar circumstances, although her mother would say that she'd seen it coming, because that's what she always said.

"And you've no idea where Howell could be now?" said the DI, obviously wanting to get back on track. "Have you got an address for the family in Wales?"

"I've got it somewhere," said Beryl. "But I don't think he's there. His father's dead now and his mother's a bit doolally."

"What about other friends?" asked Meg.

"I don't think he kept in touch with anyone after he went inside," said Beryl. "All his actor friends dropped him. His agent wouldn't even return his calls."

"Well, if he does get in touch," said the DI, "can you telephone us on this number?" He scribbled on a card. "We're anxious to talk to him."

"What's he done?" said Beryl, with only a flicker of interest.

"We're not sure yet," said the DI.

"You shouldn't have gone on your own," said Edgar.

"I wasn't sure that they were the right people," said Max. "In fact, I only had a vague memory of seeing the name." He smiled blandly at Edgar but could see that his friend wasn't convinced.

"Well, what did you make of them, these Angels?"

"They seem legitimate enough, a husband and wife team. She's English, he's American. They didn't seem sinister to me, for all that they take naked, or nearly naked, pictures of women. But there is a link with Ruby. They photographed her for a feature in *Vogue*. And they took pictures of Louise. They remembered her well."

"And Rhonda and Sara?"

"They said they'd never heard the names. And they said they'd never tout for business in the street."

"You say the man is American?"

"Yes. Why?"

"Rhonda and Sara were both approached by a man with an American accent, saying that they should be models."

"Well, maybe you should talk to this Lou."

"I will," said Edgar. "If you haven't put him on his guard."

"I'm sorry," said Max. "It's just that I'm so worried about Ruby."

Edgar softened immediately. He put a hand on his friend's arm. "We'll find her," he said.

"I hope so," said Max. He looked at the clock over Edgar's desk. Like everything else in the police station it looked like a prop from the Hammer House of Horror, a carved wooden thing with a sinister, ponderous tick.

"I'd better go back," he said. "I've got my weekly telephone call with Lydia in an hour."

222

"Transatlantic?" said Edgar.

"Yes," said Max. "It's early morning in Beverley Hills."

The interview was even more of an ordeal than Emma had expected. The questions from Sam were all right. She had to ask the ones about "how do you support your husband?" but at least she did them in a soppy voice accompanied by an eloquent eye-roll. It was the photographs that were excruciating. First Harry wanted her to pose on the sofa clutching a photograph of Edgar. "It's as if he's dead," said Emma. The only photograph she had of Edgar on his own was one that she'd been given by her mother-in-law, Rose. It showed Edgar in his brief student days, standing outside his Oxford college, stick thin and holding the handlebars of a bicycle. Then Harry wanted her with her children grouped around her. Marianne loved this, of course. She'd taken her hair out of its plaits and it stood out in a Pre-Raphaelite cloud. But Sophie was embarrassed and hid behind her mother. Johnny was teething, so alternately drooling or crying.

"Perhaps it's better on your own," said Harry. He was sweating profusely.

"Harry seems very nervous," whispered Emma to Sam as she stopped in the hallway to apply more lipstick.

"He's just shy around you," said Sam. "You should see him letting his hair down in the pub, singing Frank Sinatra songs and chatting up the girls."

Emma looked at herself in the mirror. The lipstick seemed too bright for her pale face. She didn't think she'd ever looked less alluring. "I find that hard to believe," she said.

Sam laughed. "Come on, let's get some more pictures taken."

Harry wanted a photo in the kitchen, so Emma posed by the stove, pretending to stir something in a saucepan. "Our readers will love the domestic touch," said Sam. "Have you got an apron?"

"No," said Emma. The only one she possessed had been a present from the girls. It had "World's Best Mummy" printed across the pockets.

"This will have to do then," said Sam. "Smile!"

"I am smiling."

"You look beautiful," said Harry.

At this, Marianne and Sophie laughed so much that they could hardly stand.

CHAPTER
TWENTY-THREE

Max left the telephone room feeling thoughtful. The weekly call with Lydia had run along familiar lines. Lydia had said that she missed him and kissed his photograph every night. She said that the children and the dog missed him too. She asked about *Golden Heart* and said that she'd never been to England. Then she mentioned all the film offers that she'd received and hinted at the hordes of men who were besieging her in the absence of her husband. When Max refused to rise to this last she had grown tearful and accused him of having a mistress in England. When he said that he was distracted by worry over Ruby she said that Ruby was able to look after herself and had, clearly, "gone off with a beau".

Max stopped in the lounge to light a cigarette. The silver case seemed to wink at him mockingly. *For MM with love, LL.* Standing by the house in Montpelier Crescent, he'd vowed to forget Florence and concentrate on his marriage to Lydia. Visiting Massingham Hall, he had even been able to imagine himself there with his wife and children. But, after a conversation like this, the crackling and delays only heightening the distance between them, he wondered whether he'd ever really loved Lydia.

Had he just been dazzled by her beauty, as he had by Florence's? How could he stay with someone who so clearly disliked his eldest daughter? But he had to stay with her, she was Rocco and Elena's mother. He wasn't going to be the one to break up his hard-won family.

Max put the cigarette case back in his pocket and his hand closed around the little blue cat that he'd taken from his father's desk. A whimsical object for the prosaic Alastair to possess. It felt as though it should be a lucky charm. Max always liked to say that, unlike most pros, he had no pet superstitions. But he always walked in an anticlockwise circle before going on stage and had never knowingly said the word "Macbeth" within a theatre. Now he turned the cat over in his hand. *Find Ruby*, he told it.

Could Lydia possibly be right? thought Max, leaving the lounge and heading towards the lobby. Could Ruby have run away with a lover? They were her shoes in the tunnel but, as every magician knows, the girl's clothing does not equal the girl herself. He'd lost count of the times that he'd used that particular bit of misdirection; a robe that resembled the body that had once filled it, shoes sticking out from the end of the cabinet shortly to be sawn in two. It was possible, in theory, for someone to have stolen Ruby's shoes, or even purchased an identical pair, and put them in the tunnel so that everyone would jump to the easiest, and also most shocking, conclusion. But why? So that the kidnapper would gain the news coverage that Joe, and Emma, thought he wanted?

226

On a table by the reception desk, the day's papers were laid out. Ruby's face stared up at him from most of them: Ruby as a chorus girl in a skimpy Red Indian outfit, Ruby in her early TV days, all smiles and dimples, an older Ruby in evening dress holding an award. One picture on the front of the *Daily Mirror* jumped out at him: Max and Ruby in front of a playbill advertising *Magician and Daughter*, she radiant, he looking slightly bored. That was the Christmas season of 1953, the year that he'd met Florence. He remembered staggering through the act the night that she died, Ruby carrying him every step of the way. Ruby was a great magician. Could she possibly have masterminded this whole illusion?

"Mr Mephisto!" It was the receptionist, raising her voice as loudly as she dared.

"Sorry. I was miles away." Max came over to the desk.

"Telephone message for you."

Max took the note which had the Grand's logo on the top, golden crown against a sea-blue background. The writing was rounded and rather childish.

Mr Hambro called. Could you meet him at this address tonight at 7?

Dean Court Road, Rottingdean. Max looked at the words as a vague memory came back to him. Bobby sipping orange juice in the Garrick Club.

I know Rottingdean. I used to spend my holidays near there.

★ ★ ★

Dean Court Road was a street of handsome mock-Tudor houses that started by the village church and continued steeply upwards until it reached the Downs. At the bottom of the hill was a hotel called Dean Court Lodge, a strange collection of low-lying timbered buildings that seemed almost to be cut into the earth, reminding Max of Bag End in *The Hobbit* (a book he had read, under protest, to Rocco and Elena). He seemed to remember that the hotel had once been popular with ex-music-hall artistes. What a place to end your days.

The address given to him by Bobby was halfway up the hill, a solid-looking house with smooth lawns and a double garage. It looked like it belonged to a doctor or a dentist, possessor of a charming wife, two well-behaved children and a Labrador. It did not look like the hideout of a Hollywood star.

Max paid the taxi driver and made his way up the neatly paved garden path. The door opened before he could knock. Bobby stayed back in the shadows, presumably to avoid being recognised by passing seagulls.

"Max. Good of you to come." Even his voice sounded subdued.

Bobby looked even more incongruous sitting on the comfortable over-stuffed sofa with a fringed standard lamp looming over him and the Sussex Downs, now fading into the early twilight, visible through the French windows.

"This is Wilbur's house," he explained. "It used to belong to his parents. His mom died last year and he

228

inherited it. I don't think he likes being here without her, to be honest. He's letting me stay for a few days. Do you want a drink? The liquor cabinet's pretty well stocked."

Max asked for a whisky and was pleased when Bobby went to the kitchen to add ice. The film star himself, he noted, was still sticking to orange juice.

"Why are you staying here?" asked Max, taking a gulp of whisky and feeling it burning its way down his throat. "And why did you want to see me?"

"I just needed some downtime," said Bobby, once again speaking a foreign language. "It's very stressful, heading up a film like this. All those meetings with backers and financial people. Wilbur's great but it's me they want to see. I'm the face of this film."

"Are you having trouble raising the money?" asked Max. Maybe there was a chance that he could escape after all. But how could he return to America when Ruby was still missing?

"No," said Bobby. "That's all fixed. Having Massingham Hall helped a whole heap. Everyone's real excited to start photography there."

"Glad I could help," said Max but he felt his heart sink. He hadn't told Lydia that they would be filming in his family home. She'd want to come over immediately and start shopping for tiaras.

"The film's going to be a smash," said Bobby. Max thought how violent show-business language was sometimes: smash hits, making a killing, dying on your feet. He wondered why, if funding was secured, Bobby didn't look happier.

They were silent for a few minutes as, outside, the twilight deepened and swallows swooped into the fish pond. "The thing is," said Bobby, at last, "I wanted to explain about Ruby."

"Ruby?" Suddenly the room seemed a shade darker.

"I didn't realise she was your daughter until you mentioned it that day at Massingham Hall."

"Didn't you?" It was Wilbur who had mentioned Ruby, Max seemed to recall. He had asked if she would inherit the house.

"No. I mean, she never talked about you."

"So you know Ruby?" This, certainly, had not been discussed.

Bobby shifted so that his face was in shadow. There was no sound apart from the ice clinking in Max's drink.

"I came to England last year," said Bobby. "Kind of incognito, scoping out this film, meeting with Wilbur and the rest of the guys. I met Ruby at a party and we went out a few times. I know she's a bit older than me but she's got such a young spirit. And she's a beautiful woman."

"She is," Max agreed grimly.

"So, when I came to London this time, we met up for a couple of dates."

Had it been Bobby who was visiting Ruby that night at her flat? thought Max. Bobby, carrying a dark case? Containing what?

"I was so shocked when I found out she was missing," said Bobby. He pronounced it "sharked". "And then I got this letter. It was delivered to the Ritz on Monday and forwarded to me. I got it this morning."

Wordlessly, Max took the sheet of paper.

Dear Bobby,

I'm sorry, I think it's best if we don't see each other any more. There's no easy way to say this but I've met someone else. And, Bobby, I think you'd be happier with someone else too.

I hope we can still be friends.

Yours,
Ruby

It was, unmistakably, Ruby's writing, bold and black with curly tails and flamboyant capitals. Max recognised it from her infrequent letters to him.

"She finished with me." Bobby sounded extremely sharked. "Can you believe that?"

"She says that she's met someone else," said Max. "Do you know who that could be?"

"No. She always had lots of admirers." Bobby's tone was now positively sulky. "I thought I should tell you," he said. "The papers are saying that Ruby's been kidnapped but this proves that she's really just gone off with a man, doesn't it?"

Was that what it proved? Max's brain was in overdrive. If this letter was delivered on Monday then Ruby must have posted it on Saturday, the day that she was meant to be meeting Emma on the pier. Had she really just disappeared with her new boyfriend? But then he remembered. The other missing girls had all left notes, handwritten missives with plausible reasons for their absence.

"Can I have the letter?" he said.

"Why?" Bobby picked up the sheet of notepaper, which was lying on the coffee table, and held it close to his chest. Perhaps he thought that Max was going to sell it to the papers.

"I've got a friend who's a detective," said Max. "I'd like to show it to him. Don't worry, he'll be very discreet."

"OK," said Bobby, at last. "Just keep my name out of it, will you?"

"Of course," said Max. He didn't care if Bobby's name was emblazoned on a banner between the piers if it meant that he got Ruby back.

It wasn't possible to get a taxi in Rottingdean. The village looked like it went to bed very early and the High Street was deserted. A mist had blown in from the sea making the place seem even spookier, still and grey, a no-man's land where the occasional landmark appeared with terrifying suddenness. Crossing the coast road was like walking into the unknown. Max was pretty sure that there was a bus stop somewhere about. He loathed buses. Even in London he liked to walk or catch taxis. He didn't even mind the underground, at least it was quick and anonymous. But bus travel seemed to combine hours of waiting with slow, tedious journeys in the company of people who talked to themselves or, in worst-case scenarios, to you. But he didn't fancy walking back by the sea, especially in this fog. The undercliff walk was where the poor girl's body had been found, of course. Sara Henratty. Had she been killed by the same man who had abducted Ruby? *Had* Ruby been abducted or had she simply run off with this new man, the "someone else" mentioned in her letter to Bobby?

The bus stop appeared in front of him. In fact he nearly walked straight into it. He was outside a pub, the White Horse. Should he go in and have a whisky, something to keep the chill out? No, he needed his wits about him. Max lit a cigarette and waited, tapping his foot. It was nearly eight o'clock. Maybe Southdown buses had stopped running. No, there it was at last, a lumbering green shape appearing out of the mist.

The bus creaked its way along the clifftop. Max sat on the top deck and could see nothing on either side of him, but the knowledge that there was a sheer drop on his left didn't make him feel comfortable exactly.

"Do they stop the buses if the fog gets too thick?" he asked the conductor.

"No," said the man, sounding shocked. "Sometimes we don't run the double-deckers if the wind's very strong. But this? This is nothing. A sea fret, that's all."

And it was true that the mist had almost vanished by the time they reached Brighton. The bus stopped on the seafront and Max turned towards Kemp Town, the air clearing as he got further inland. He walked past Mrs M's house, refusing to indulge in the nostalgia game any more. The only thing that mattered now was finding Ruby.

Emma was putting the children to bed but Edgar greeted him warmly and offered tea or "something stronger". Max asked for coffee, feeling virtuous at resisting spirits for a second time. "I think I've got some somewhere," said Edgar, opening cupboards in a rather helpless way. What was it with English people and coffee? How hard would it be to keep a pot on the hob? Mind you, American coffee was even worse. Max thought wistfully of drinking espresso in Italy, dense black with a golden swirl of cream. Edgar eventually found a pot of instant coffee which, from the way he was digging at it with a spoon, hadn't been used for some time. Oh well, it was better than nothing.

It was the first time that Max had seen Edgar in his domestic setting. It suited him, the kitchen table still strewn with the remains of a family supper, the sitting room with the playpen and children's toys on the floor. Edgar was born to be a family man, thought Max. He had an uneasy feeling that he himself was most at home in hotels or boarding houses, places where he could spend a few days and then move on. In variety, Sunday was changeover day, all the pros moving around the country, from one theatre to another. There were places, like the tea room on Crewe railway station, where you could always be sure of bumping into someone you knew. "*What are your digs like?*" "*Not too bad, we had bedbugs in Rochdale.*" "*That's nothing, I had fleas in my dressing room at Great Yarmouth.*"

Emma came downstairs when they moved into the sitting room. Edgar had made her a cup of tea and she took it gratefully.

"If I have to read one more chapter of *What Katy Bloody Well Did*," she said, "I'll go mad. She's such an insufferable girl too. After she becomes good, that is. She's all right when she's a rebel in the beginning."

"I read *The Hobbit* to my children," said Max. "It's a very strange book. Not a single woman character. It would never run on Broadway."

"I can't imagine you reading to your children," said Edgar.

"Edgar's very good at it," said Emma. "Better than me. He does all the voices."

"Clearly you have hidden theatrical talents," said Max. "But it's one of my children that I've come to talk about."

He told them about Ruby's dates with Bobby and showed them the letter.

"It's her handwriting," said Edgar immediately.

"I know," said Max, "and it sounds like her too. That old line about hoping they'll still be friends. She's obviously hoping that she'll never see him again. Bobby was astounded. I don't think he's ever been dumped before."

"The other girls all wrote letters too," said Emma. "Rhonda, Louise and Sara."

"Exactly," said Max.

"She doesn't say she's going away though," said Edgar. "All the other letters do. Rhonda said she was going to London, Louise to the Caribbean. Sara said that she was going off with her boyfriend. What was his name? Peanuts."

"Bobby obviously assumes that Ruby's gone off with the new man," said Max, "and I suppose it could be true. You've only found her shoes, after all. They could just be misdirection."

"Or this could be misdirection," said Emma, pointing at the letter.

"That's true. It could."

"I think we have to assume that Ruby's been abducted," said Edgar. "No one's heard from her since Friday and she's missed work, which isn't like her. Then we find her shoes in the tunnel. We have to take this very seriously. A girl has been killed, after all." His words had a sobering effect on all three of them. On the way there, Max had almost persuaded himself that Ruby had performed a skilful vanishing trick, that she was in the South of France with her new man, laughing at their gullibility. Now he felt that he was the dupe, the stooge.

A girl has been killed, after all.

CHAPTER
TWENTY-FOUR

The article appeared in Friday's *Evening Argus*.

Emma Stephens, the wife of Superintendent Edgar Stephens of the Brighton Police, is never happier than when in her kitchen cooking up a batch of cakes for her children Marianne (8), Sophie (6) and Baby Jonathan (10 months).

"Edgar works so hard," said Emma, speaking from her sunny Kemp Town home. "I always have a hot meal waiting when he comes in. He loves my cakes too. Chocolate's his favourite."

Emma knows something about the pressures of working in the police force. Before her marriage she was a policewoman, one of the first woman detective sergeants in the country. Now she provides a listening ear when husband Edgar talks about his cases.

"Edgar's very discreet," says Emma. "He'd never tell me anything confidential but sometimes it does help just to talk something through. And, having been in the force, I do understand some of the issues."

In Emma's view marriage is a "partnership" and she and her husband share domestic chores as well as spending as much time as possible with their children. "Edgar's a wonderful father," says Emma. "He loves reading to the girls and playing games with them. And he dotes on the baby." She does admit, though, that Superintendent Stephens is "not much of a cook". And he certainly can't make chocolate cake!

Emma, thirty-five, is the daughter of businessman Archie Holmes and his ex-socialite wife, Sybil, both of Roedean Drive. Emma attended Roedean School where she is remembered for her skills in debating and public speaking. To relax, Emma likes to read mystery novels and to take baby Jonathan for walks by the sea or in Queen's Park.

"I usually visit Queen's Park before picking the girls up from school," says Emma. "Johnny loves feeding the ducks."

Little do the ducks know that they are being fed breadcrumbs by an ex-detective!

Edgar always received an early copy of the *Argus* at work and he rang Emma as soon as it appeared on his desk.

"Why didn't you tell me about this?"

"It's so embarrassing," said Emma, with truth. She had been cringing all morning about "never happier than when in the kitchen" and "I always have a hot meal waiting".

238

"I'm sorry," Sam had said when she rang earlier, "the editor changed it to make it sound 'more wholesome'. And the bloody sub put quote marks round 'partnership'. I'd put in much more about your work as a detective but the ed just blue-pencilled it."

"That's OK," said Emma. "At least he left the bit about Queen's Park."

"I thought you hated this sort of thing," said Edgar.

"I do. It was Sam's idea."

"Nice picture of you."

It was rather a flattering photograph, Emma smiling sweetly, holding a saucepan and looking saintly. There was another picture of her with the children; Marianne sitting like an angel, her golden hair loose about her face, Sophie with her eyes shut and Jonathan in mid howl.

"They were determined to go on about the cooking," said Emma. "I don't think I've ever made you chocolate cake in my life."

"Well, I'll expect one tonight," said Edgar, "as well as a hot meal and a nice chat about work." He was laughing but Emma thought that he still sounded rather put out. Perhaps he thought that the article wasn't the right sort of publicity for a superintendent.

"How's the case going?" she asked. "Did you find anything else in the smugglers' tunnels?"

"There are signs that people have been in some of them, a few cigarette butts and some empty bottles. That sort of thing. But local kids sneak in sometimes so they might not have anything to do with the kidnapper.

No other real clues. I was hoping the abductor might try to make contact after all the publicity about Ruby."

But you don't know what bait to use, thought Emma.

"Telephone for Connolly."

"For me?"

Meg wasn't in the habit of getting telephone calls. Her parents didn't own a phone and, when calls came through at work, they were almost always for the DI. She approached cautiously, half expecting a practical joke from O'Neill and Barker. On April Fool's Day they'd had her going round the station telling people that someone called I. P. Knightly was on the phone.

"This is WPC Connolly."

"Is that Meg? I couldn't remember your surname. I just asked for the tall policewoman."

It was Isabel, the blonde Bobby Soxer from outside the Ritz.

"That's me," said Meg. "What is it?" She'd given the girls the number of the station and told them to call if they had any information for her. She never expected it to happen though.

"You remember the man?" Isabel was saying. "The one who told Rhonda that she should be a model? Well, I think I saw him again."

"You think you saw him? Where?"

"Here," said Isabel, as if Meg would instantly know where that was. "Outside my house."

Meg grabbed a piece of paper. "What's your address?"

"Forty-five Bletchley Road, Dollis Hill."

"Dollis Hill. Where's that?"

"It's near Willesden Green," said Isabel, as if this explained everything.

"And you saw this man outside your house? How did you recognise him?"

"Well, I didn't at first. But I knew I knew him from somewhere. I've seen him here a few times, walking up and down the road, like he was lost. Then, this morning, when I was leaving to go to school, he was sitting at the bus stop outside the house. And I realised where I'd seen him before."

"Did he talk to you?"

"No. But he raised his hat and sort of smiled."

"Where are you now? Why aren't you in school?"

"School's finished," said Isabel. Looking at the clock on the wall, Meg was surprised to see that it was three-forty-five. School finishes so early but, when you're there, it seems as if the day goes on for ever.

"Are you at home?"

"In the phone box at the end of the street."

"Well, go home and don't go out again on your own. Are you still skiving off to go to the Ritz?"

"No. Bobby's gone away for a few days. Pat the doorman says he's in Sussex. Maybe he's in Brighton."

"Look, Isabel. Izzy. This is important. Don't leave the house on your own. Do you walk to school by yourself?"

"No, worse luck. With my annoying little sister."

"Well, stick to your annoying little sister like glue. This man might be dangerous. I'm going to have to tell the local police."

"I won't get into trouble, will I?" Isabel sounded worried for the first time.

"No. You haven't done anything wrong." Apart from truanting from school, thought Meg. But she hoped that Isabel's parents would understand if the whole story came out. "Thank you very much for letting me know. You may have helped solve the case."

"Really?" Now the buoyant note was back in Isabel's voice. Maybe Meg could convert her from super fan to super sleuth. She hoped so.

Meg knocked on the super's door, feeling rather daring. She should tell the DI but he was out on another case. O'Neill and Barker were also out and, besides, she didn't want to share her news with them. The super had said she was a valued member of the team and here was another chance to show her worth.

"Come in."

Superintendent Stephens was at his desk, an open copy of the *Evening Argus* in front of him. He shut the paper when he saw Meg, as if he was ashamed of being caught reading it.

"I've had a phone call, sir," said Meg, thinking how grand the words sounded. "I think it might be important."

The super obviously did think it was important. He didn't jump up and start issuing orders because he wasn't that sort of man. But he listened to her very seriously and wrote down what she said in his notebook.

"Well done," he said, when she'd finished. "That could be a very important lead. Shows how valuable it was to win the trust of those girls."

242

"Do you think Isabel could be in danger?"

"She needs to be very careful. I'm glad you told her not to leave the house on her own. I've got a friend in London, an inspector at Scotland Yard. I'll get him to check it out. We need to have the Met on the lookout for this man. It's a pity we don't have a better description of him."

"'He was just a man', that's what Isabel said at first. Later on she said he was 'tallish and oldish'. And she's so short that anyone looks tall to her."

The super didn't laugh at this, as she'd hoped. Instead he said, "And he had an American accent. Is that right?"

"That's what the girls said. It's what made Rhonda think he was genuine. And Peanuts, Percy McDonald, he said that Sara had been approached by a man who said that she should be a model. He had an American accent too."

"Half the young people in England put on American accents these days," said the super, sounding about a hundred. "Just like the singers on *Top of the Pops*."

"Do you watch *Top of the Pops*?" Meg didn't have a television set but she often listened to Radio Caroline with Aisling. The thought of actually watching the Beatles, rather than just hearing them, seemed almost unbelievably exciting.

"When I can't avoid it," said the super. He drummed his fingers on the table. "It's a shame that we'll be so busy this weekend, with the bank holiday and the mods and rockers. Otherwise I'd send you up to London to guard the girl."

"I could still go," said Meg. She loved the idea of being a bodyguard.

"No, I need you here. We've got reports of thousands of youths converging on Brighton. It'll be utter madness."

Meg thought it sounded quite exciting.

"Maybe I should go to London," she said. "I could be the bait. Maybe he'd try to abduct me." She didn't really think that the super would fall for this. After all, as she'd said to Isabel when they'd first met, Meg wasn't exactly the sort of girl who would be scouted as a model. The super was staring at her oddly as if he was thinking the same thing.

"That's a no then, is it?" she said, aware that this wasn't quite the tone to take with her ultimate boss.

"Yes," said the super. "No. Just . . . get on with your work."

"Yes, sir," said Meg. Even she could see that it was time to go.

Emma sat on the park bench looking at the ducks on the pond. She'd been there for half an hour already. But Mavis was collecting the girls for once so she had all the time in the world to set her trap. She'd placed herself in a conspicuous spot and, to make her identity doubly obvious, was reading the *Evening Argus*. Unfortunately, it was a cold spring day and she was already frozen. There was a sharp wind blowing, it rippled over the water and flapped at the paper whenever Emma tried to turn the pages. And, far from loving the visit to his feathered friends, Johnny was teething again and grizzled constantly. Emma tried to ignore him, stamping her feet to get the circulation back and keeping a weather eye on the undergrowth around the pond. She knew that Sam was there somewhere, she kept getting a glimpse of her red jacket as she walked slowly round the perimeter. There were lots of mothers with children too, a few of whom Emma recognised from the school gates. Maybe she wasn't isolated enough to make a good target. She got up, walked slowly round the water's edge and took the path up towards the tennis courts. Apart from two men in white shorts who looked as if they were training for Wimbledon, this part of the park was deserted. Looking back, she saw Sam's red jacket making its way through the Japanese rock garden.

Emma walked past the courts and sat down on another bench. It was more sheltered here and there was no sound apart from the *pock pock* of tennis balls whizzing over the net.

"Excuse me?" It was a woman with an Eton crop and a monocle. "Weren't you in the paper today? The one who's married to the policeman?"

She started to tell Emma how she would improve law and order in Brighton. Emma listened dispiritedly while Johnny grumbled in the background. Eventually the woman got up and trundled away. Emma sat on the bench feeling cold and fed up. The trap had failed. She folded up the paper and stooped to put it in the basket under the pushchair. As she did so, Jonathan stopped whining and gave a sharp cry of delight. Emma straightened up to find herself looking into her husband's face.

"Ed," she said. "What are you doing here?"

"I knew you'd be here," said Edgar, "because I read about it in the paper." His voice sounded strange and there was an expression in his eyes that Emma had never seen before. It made him momentarily, and terrifyingly, look like a stranger.

"That's right," said Emma, trying for a light, casual tone to dilute the atmosphere that seemed to be gathering around them like their own private storm cloud. "Creature of habit, that's me."

"Feeding the ducks?" said Edgar.

"Well, we were." Emma held up the bag of bread as if she needed an alibi.

"It wasn't bait then?"

"What?" Emma looked at her husband, one hand on the handle of the buggy. Even Jonathan had fallen silent.

"I thought this was bait," said Edgar. "This whole thing." He gestured angrily at the park and the tennis players and the hurrying families. "You thought that the killer might read the paper and that he'd come after you and you'd catch him."

Emma opened her mouth to deny it but then something made her say, in a voice that came out louder and more wobbly than she had intended, "Well, what if I did? It's a better idea than any you've had, or Bob, the wonderful DI, or the intrepid Meg Connolly."

"This man is a murderer," said Edgar. "He killed Sara Henratty. Don't you realise how dangerous it is? All on your own."

"Sam's here somewhere." But Emma had lost sight of the red jacket a long time ago.

"Sam! I might have known that she'd be mixed up in this. Was it her idea? I'll get her sacked."

"No," said Emma. "It was all my idea. Sam wasn't keen at first."

"I don't understand it," said Edgar. "You were a detective. How could you be so stupid?"

"Don't you ever," said Emma, "call me stupid." And she jerked the buggy forward so violently that Jonathan cried out.

"Emma," said Edgar. "Come back."

But Emma was heading towards home, blinded by tears.

CHAPTER
TWENTY-FIVE

The row went on all evening. Emma managed to go through the motions of making the children's supper, putting Jonathan to bed and reading to the girls. Then she descended to the sitting room. By now she was almost looking forward to the argument. Edgar was sitting in his usual chair, reading the paper. Was he going to be conciliatory, to tell her he loved her, that he understood? No, when he looked up, his eyes still had that cold, hard glitter to them.

"What would happen to the children," he said, "if you'd been abducted? Dear God, you had Jonathan with you."

"Oh, nothing must ever harm your precious son."

"Emma!" Edgar stood up and his voice made the windows rattle. "How can you say that?"

"It's true," said Emma, now perilously near tears. "You don't care about me, except as the mother of your children and as . . . as a housewife."

"A housewife! I don't think of you as a housewife."

"Yes, you do. You expect me to keep everything clean and tidy, iron your shirts, put food on the table. Make bloody steak and kidney pie. I used to be a detective sergeant. I solved cases. And I had to stop. Because I married you." She was crying properly now.

"You wanted to get married," said Edgar.

"Yes," said Emma. "I wanted to be your wife. Not the house's."

"We could get a cleaner. A nanny."

"That wouldn't solve anything," said Emma, "because I still wouldn't be a detective."

She thought that Edgar would come across the room to comfort her, as he always did when she was crying, but instead he said, in that cold superintendent's voice, "No, you're not a detective and you shouldn't try to be one. You could have been killed today. By your own arrogance and stupidity."

Edgar slept badly, the quarrel running round and round in his head. He wanted to make up with Emma but he was still furious. They had had very few arguments in the course of their married life and it was as if they had been storing everything up for this one. Edgar could not believe that he could feel so angry with Emma, his wife, the woman he had loved steadily for over eleven years, probably since the moment he first saw her. Even the sound of her quiet breathing infuriated him. How could she sleep after the things she'd said to him? After the things he'd said to her? It was a relief when the alarm went off at six.

"Don't bother to get up," he said to Emma, who had sat up, bleary-eyed. "I'm going into work. Don't take the children onto the beach today. We think that's where the mods and rockers will congregate."

"You don't have to tell me how to look after our children," said Emma.

"It seems as if I do," said Edgar. "It might be dangerous. If you care about their safety, that is." He left the room before she could answer.

Edgar argued silently with Emma all the way to the station. Despite everything, though, he was pleased to see the station full when he arrived. He'd asked for volunteers to work at the weekend and it seemed that everyone had come in. He sent a panda car down to Madeira Terrace on the seafront and the report came back that there were a few groups of mods and rockers but no trouble as yet. It was a sunny day and the beaches were full of holidaymakers. Edgar had increased the numbers of officers on the beat but, apart from the usual incidents (lost children, missing purses, an attempt to break into the penny arcade on the West Pier) Brighton was fairly peaceful. Edgar began to feel guilty that he'd made so many people miss their bank holiday weekend. Should he ring Emma, say that she could take the children out? But he heard her voice saying, *You don't have to tell me how to look after our children*. He didn't want to have another row with her, on the phone at work. They could make it up that evening.

He was glad when his phone rang. It was an old friend, Inspector Fred Jarvis from Scotland Yard.

"Are you getting ready for the great invasion?" said Jarvis. He had a laconic delivery that made everything sound like the build-up to a joke. "The battle of the mods and rockers."

"I'm ready," said Edgar. "But the invaders aren't here yet."

"They'll come," said Jarvis. "I'd heard that Monday was going to be the big day."

"Have you got secret intelligence?"

"Yeah. I'm a rocker in my spare time. But that's not why I called. We checked out Angels Modelling Agency."

"You did? What did you think?"

"Seems legit. They do a lot of glamour work, which seems to mean girls taking their clothes off, but there's no law against that. Lou Abrahams is quite a respected photographer. He's published books." Jarvis managed to make this last sound very sinister.

"You know we're looking for an American who might have been approaching girls offering them modelling work?"

"Yeah," said Jarvis, and Edgar thought he could hear him lighting a cigarette. Edgar hadn't smoked for years, since the war, but suddenly his soul ached for nicotine. "I don't think Lou is your man. He's quite distinctive-looking, for one thing, and he's no youngster."

"Tallish, oldish, that's the description we have from the girls."

"Pure poetry," said Jarvis. "But everyone over thirty's old to these kids. You and I are old, Edgar."

"Don't I know it," said Edgar. "Did you send someone round to talk to the girl in Dollis Hill, Isabel Rowlands?"

"Yeah. Do you remember Alan Deacon?"

The name brought back a memory. A memory and a smell: a neat little house in Wembley, a woman dead in a playpen, Deacon in policeman's uniform, Edgar holding a spectacularly smelly baby.

"I remember Deacon. A good man."

"One of the best. Dollis Hill's his patch. He's going to call on the family this morning."

"Thank you," said Edgar. "I think it's possible that our man might be stalking Isabel."

"I've got Lou Abrahams under surveillance just in case it's him. But I don't think it is. Doesn't feel right."

"I need a break on this case," said Edgar. "Four girls abducted, one girl dead."

"And now he's got Ruby Magic too. Now that is a tragedy. Ruby's a real favourite with me and Mrs Jarvis." Jarvis always referred to his wife like this, again with a slightly ironical note in his voice. Edgar had never met her. And Jarvis had no idea of his own history with Ruby.

"Ruby's vanished into thin air," said Edgar. And he thought of the times that he'd seen Ruby on stage, her turn at the cabinet door, waving and smiling, but then, when the door was opened again . . . the girl had disappeared.

"Look at me, Mummy!"

"I am looking," said Emma. She wondered how much harder she could be staring at Marianne. But her daughter did look adorable, perched on top of a skewbald cob called Toby. Emma wished that she'd brought a camera.

252

"My turn," said Sophie. Jonathan strained at the straps on his pushchair, wanting to touch the horse's glossy brown-and-white leg.

"Marianne's got to go round the field first," said Emma. "Then it's your turn." Toby belonged to Emma's old school-friend Vera, who also owned a highly strung chestnut called Tempest. Vera had invited Emma and the children over to Rottingdean where the horses were stabled and Emma was glad that she had accepted. At least it stopped her obsessing over the row with Edgar. She couldn't believe that he had woken up still angry with her, still in that maddeningly superior state of mind. *It might be dangerous. If you care about their safety, that is.* How dare he talk to her like that? She would never put her children at risk. The trouble was that Edgar had got used to being the boss at work, everyone doing what he said. Bob would never argue with him and she imagined Meg Connolly and the rest hanging on his every word. He hadn't even been right about the mods and rockers on the beach. They'd had a good view of the promenade from the bus and all they could see were holidaymakers and deckchairs. The sun was shining, the sea was sparkling. A perfect day.

Vera led Toby round the field. Emma had ridden the horse once and she remembered that Toby's main interest was eating. How awful for him to have to walk on grass, like a hungry human walking on bread and butter. "Come on Toby." Vera pulled him away from a tasty hedge.

"Look at me, Mummy!"

"I am looking."

Now Vera urged Toby into a reluctant trot. "Remember what I told you, Marianne. Up down, up down."

Marianne's slim body rose in the saddle, perfectly in time.

"She's a natural," shouted Vera to Emma, as she stood by the fence with Jonathan in her arms. Sophie watched enviously from her perch on the top of the gate.

"Why are you crying, Mummy?" said Sophie.

"I'm not," said Emma.

But she was.

Max was walking along the promenade at Brighton but he was not in the mood to enjoy the view. The whole scene: the sun, the sea, the holidaymakers (the English at their worst, sunburnt and noisy), seemed almost an insult when Ruby was still missing. He thought of the day that he'd seen her from the Rolls Royce, walking along this very stretch of road in her pink suit. Where had she been going? Was she on her way to see Emma? If so, she had never turned up.

Max walked past the Palace Pier, a blaring cacophony of pop music, the shouts of stallholders and screams of thrill-seekers on the Ghost Train. He could see the gypsy caravan by the railings. Should he go and ask Astarte where Ruby was? He'd met the famous medium once and had been impressed by her ethereal good looks, less so by her professed ability to see into the future. Lydia read her horoscope every morning (she was Virgo, Max was Scorpio; a clash of opposites apparently) but, as far as Max could see, it always said the same thing: you are special and wonderful, special and wonderful things will happen to you at some unspecified point in your life. All very nice, but hardly the basis for informed decision making.

He was at the arches now, the place where he'd last seen Ruby. A gaggle of mods went by on their scooters, all chrome and khaki. Like Joe, Max could see the attraction of the suits but he'd never had any desire to go round in a pack. At school he'd been described as "lacking team spirit", something he took as a compliment. Were these spotty youngsters really about to destroy the town, as Edgar feared? It didn't seem very likely. The rockers were slightly more threatening, they were older for one thing and had more horsepower. But he only saw one rocker on his walk, an overweight man in a leather jacket eating chips by the Volks Railway. As stand-offs went, this one was proving very dull.

Max had reached Black Rock without his mood improving. What should he do now? He didn't want to go back to the hotel. There were too many hours to worry and think about Ruby. Should he call on Edgar, find out if he'd made any progress with the Angels Modelling Agency? No, Edgar would be preoccupied with his non-existent riot. There was a good Italian restaurant at the Montpelier Hotel. He'd go there. It would pass a few hours, at least.

After Sophie had had her ride and even Jonathan had sat on patient Toby's back, it was Emma's turn. Vera gave her a leg-up. Toby felt much higher and more unstable than she had remembered. She was glad that she had worn trousers but, even so, her thin slacks rode up so that her calves were pinched by the stirrup leathers. Vera mounted Tempest and led the way to the field. Tempest was doing his usual curvetting, head-tossing thing but Toby plodded along stolidly, only stopping to take a chunk out of the hedge. Once on the grass, Tempest immediately started to canter and Toby followed, though at a more sober pace. Emma held on to his variegated mane as well as to the reins and hoped for the best. But it was really lovely to be on horseback with the Downs all around and the village at the foot of the hill. As they passed the gate — Sophie on the top bar and Marianne holding Jonathan — the children cheered. Emma felt her spirits lift. At least the children still loved her.

Afterwards, Emma and the girls helped Vera rub Toby down and stood for a while in his stable, breathing in the wonderful, bosky horsy smell. Jonathan had fallen asleep in his pushchair, worn out by all the excitement. They thanked Vera ("No problem. Come any time") and walked back down Steyning Road. Emma took the girls to see the pond and Rudyard Kipling's house but they weren't particularly impressed.

"I've seen ponds before," said Sophie. Emma thought of her abortive wait by the ducks at Queen's Park and she felt herself growing angry again. But this time it was with herself.

Marianne wasn't interested in Kipling or Emma's smuggling tales.

"Why didn't they just buy the brandy and stuff from the shops?"

"It's more complicated than that," said Emma. "Complicated and dangerous."

Watch the wall, my darling, while the gentlemen go by.

"Can we get some chips on the beach?" said Marianne. "Please, Mummy."

"All right," said Emma, although her legs ached and she wanted to go home.

On the High Street, Marianne stopped by the window of a shop called The Smugglers' Cave.

"Can we go in, Mummy? They've got lovely little glass animals."

Jonathan had just woken up and Emma dreaded the idea of letting him loose in a shop containing glass animals.

"Not this time," she said. "We need to hurry or there won't be any chips left."

She thought of the last time she'd been on the beach at Rottingdean, the police tape guarding the place where Sara's body had lain. Suddenly, she wanted to go home and bolt the doors. But she marched on towards the sea, pushing Johnno and holding Sophie by the hand. Marianne dawdled behind, brooding on the unfairness of life.

CHAPTER
TWENTY-SIX

The invasion started in earnest on Sunday. The mods were three abreast as they passed the Brighton gates, a phalanx like fighter planes in the war, parkas flying, multiple wing mirrors glistening. The rockers appeared in ones and twos, motorbikes roaring in side streets, leather-clad giants slouching through the Old Steine. Many of the mods had badges down the arms of their parkas which made them look like soldiers in some ersatz army. Even though it was the bank holiday weekend, pubs and restaurants started to close. Only the rocker hang-outs like the Daygo and the Little Chef stayed open, full of cigarette smoke and leather jackets, the bikes outside like horses tied to the railings of a Wild West saloon.

On Saturday night Edgar and Emma had had a chilly reconciliation. They had both apologised and had managed to get through a fairly amicable evening meal. But they hadn't kissed or even touched. Edgar went into work early on Sunday and told Emma to avoid the centre of town. Emma's parents had already decided against their usual visit, hunkering down in their Roedean mansion with poached eggs on toast and a murder mystery on the wireless. But Marianne and

258

Sophie had been invited to a morning birthday party near Queen's Park and Emma thought that would be safe enough. At least it would get them out of the house. Walking back, the girls over-excited by sugar and party games, Jonathan in his pushchair clutching a red balloon, she was struck by how empty the streets were. She could hear her footsteps as they walked along St George's Road. The shops were shut, of course, the shutters down outside the butcher, greengrocer and hardware store, but usually there were people walking down to the sea or visiting the pubs, cheerful and self-conscious in their Sunday best. Now the High Street was silent. As they passed St John the Baptist, though, Emma could hear Latin chanting. It would take more than a few mods and rockers to put Catholics off going to mass. But the singing had a mournful, almost sinister, sound. Emma remembered attending a Romany funeral in that church, more than ten years ago. It was the first time that she had seen Astarte, then only nineteen, an ethereal figure in black, walking up to the altar to sing a strange, haunting song about spirits and willow trees. It had been as if she was casting a spell with her voice.

"Where is everyone?" said Marianne.

The answer was clear when they reached the top of Burlington Street. There was a sound coming from the beach, a kind of subdued roar, unlike anything Emma had heard before. It sounded, she thought, like an army preparing to charge. Like a lot of children who'd lived through the war she had very clear images of what a battle would be like, no less violent for being second-hand.

"Can we look?" said Marianne.

Emma hesitated. They were high above the beach and very near home. Surely it would be safe? It's almost my duty to see what's going on, she thought. She was *dying* to look.

They crossed the road and looked down on the promenade. Below was a battle scene. Mods on one side, rockers on the other, Brighton policemen, wearing their white summer helmets, in the middle. As they watched, Emma saw a rocker throw a deckchair so that it hit one of the mods. With another roar the mods advanced, hurling stones and other missiles.

"Let's go home," said Emma.

By midday only the WPCs were left at the station. Was this why the super had said he needed her? thought Meg. Was it just so that she could man (or woman) the reception desk? She wanted to be out there where the action was. She had a feeling that people would be talking about the Battle of the Mods and Rockers for years to come. She didn't want to miss out.

Reception was quiet today. Everyone was obviously at home, hiding from the violent youths. Meg answered one phone query about a missing cat and told a tourist the way to the Pavilion. She felt sorry for people who had come to Brighton for the bank holiday weekend. The beach was cordoned off and most of the tourist attractions were closed. And, as if to mock them, it was

260

another beautiful day, the sky cloudless and the sun properly warm for the first time that year.

She was just wondering if she dared to leave her post to get a cup of tea and a book when a man appeared in front of her. He was middle-aged, middle height, middle everything really. But his words were anything but middle-of-the-road.

"I've come to give myself up," he said.

"Pardon?" Meg was sure that she hadn't heard right.

"I'm Howell Davies. I've heard that you were looking for me. I've come to give myself up."

Howell . . . Oh, yes. The man who might have helped Ernest Coggins escape from prison. The ex-actor and convicted conman. The man with an embittered ex-wife in Crawley. The miner's son who had claimed to be a lord. The man opposite didn't look like an actor or a fraudster. He looked like a bank manager on his day off.

"You'd better come into the interview room."

Meg had never interrogated a suspect on her own before. It felt very strange to be in the little suite, dark and dank like all the rooms at Bartholomew Square, lit only by a central bulb swinging in the underground breeze. It was Howell Davies who seemed almost to be putting her at her ease, smiling encouragingly as he took his seat — the suspect's chair — opposite her.

Meg found a notepad and wrote, "Interview with Howell Davies 17th May 1964" in large, round letters. The DI liked to record interviews but she wasn't quite sure how to work the tape recorder. This would have to do. She'd asked Liz, a new WPC, to take over on reception. That left only Denise and Angela who were Specials and not really meant to be working on cases. Meg was on her own. She sat up very straight and looked Davies in the eye.

"Address?"

"Nine, the High Street, Rottingdean."

So Davies had been in Sussex all along. What's more, he had been in Rottingdean, where the Brighton police had spent the last few days tramping up and down the High Street looking for secret tunnels. Meg and Danny might have walked past him when they visited The Smugglers' Cave.

"Occupation?"

"Retired actor. This is like one of those quiz shows on the wireless, isn't it?"

Meg, who had been thinking the same, scowled. "You said you had come to give yourself up."

"Yes." Davies recrossed his legs and leaned back comfortably in his chair. "I know you think that I might have been involved with Ernie's escape from choky. Well, I wasn't. I was in Wales that day and at least five family members can verify that. In fact, half the town can probably vouch for me. When the black sheep turns up, it's big news in Maesteg, I can tell you."

"Can I have an address for these people?" said Meg. "And a telephone number too, if possible."

Howell obliged, helpfully spelling out the Welsh words.

"Beryl told me that you'd called on her," he said. "Poor love, she lives in fear of the neighbours finding out about her jailbird husband."

262

So Beryl had known where Davies was to be found. Meg had thought as much. "Have you any information about Ernest Coggins that might help us find him?" she asked.

"Ernie was a gentle soul," said Davies. "All he really cared about were the animals. He loved looking after the pigs but he suffered so much when they were taken away for slaughter. He used to feed the birds. He made a bird table in Crafts. There was one robin that was so tame it used to sit on his hand."

Coggins was sounding a bit like St Francis of Assisi, thought Meg. She thought that she'd better remind Davies why he was in prison in the first place.

"What about the girl he kidnapped, Rhonda Miles? Did he ever talk about her?"

"Yes. I think he cared deeply for her."

"Cared deeply?" This sounded rather sinister to Meg.

"Oh, not in that way." Davies waved a disdainful hand. "What filthy minds the police have. He was sorry for the girl. He was worried when he heard that she'd gone missing. He said he thought he knew why she'd run away."

"He did?" Meg was listening properly now. "Why?"

"It was to do with her father. Ernie was a mild-mannered man but he hated Crispian Miles. *Sir* Crispian. He said that he had blood on his hands. The blood of millions of innocents."

"Blood on his hands? What do you mean?"

Davies looked at her with mild surprise. "Oh, I thought you knew. Crispian Miles is a butcher."

"A butcher?"

"He got rich through the misery of animals, that's what Ernie said. Ernie loathed the whole food industry. He used to read all these leaflets about how badly animals were treated, how they were herded into tiny crates with no food or water and driven to the slaughterhouse. They could smell the blood, Ernie said, and knew that they were going to die. It fair put me off my food, I can tell you. Which was a shame because it wasn't bad at Ford."

"You said that Ernest thought that Rhonda had run away. Why did he think that?"

But now Davies became irritatingly vague. "I can't remember. Something to do with a dog. Have you finished with me now? I want to go and see the fun and games on the promenade."

Isabel hated Sundays. The mornings were all right. Mum cooked a nice breakfast with bacon and eggs and then they usually had a walk to Gladstone Park. They didn't go to church but it was quite nice seeing all the other families on their way there, the Catholic women with their veils, the Caribbean families all dressed up in colourful clothes. Some of the neighbours didn't like the Caribbeans but Isabel's dad said that it took all sorts to make a world.

As she walked between Dad and Lucinda, Isabel looked out for The Man, the one she had told Meg about. A police officer had visited the house yesterday and told them that he was a suspect in a kidnapping case. Mum and Dad were shocked, of course, but luckily nothing came out about truanting or the Ritz. Isabel just said that all the girls had been given the police phone number at school, in case they saw anything suspicious. The policeman, DI Deacon, had even praised her initiative. Isabel thought that Dad was twitchy this morning too, scanning the faces of people at the park as they innocently walked their dogs or played with their children. But The Man would be on his own, of course. At any rate, they didn't see him.

For lunch Mum usually did roast beef or lamb with mint sauce. Sometimes Grandma and Grandad came over from Willesden, which was nice because they brought Smarties for Isabel and Lucinda but it did make lunch go on and on because Gran chewed everything about a hundred times and Gramps told long stories about the war. But, when lunch had been cleared away and washed up, that's when the Dread started. Isabel thought of it with a capital D. Mum and Dad would doze in the front room while she and Lucinda were meant to get on with their homework, sitting at either end of the dining room table. Lucinda had just started at the grammar school so she didn't have much work but Isabel seemed to have more and more. At night she dreamt about exercise books rising up and throttling her, drowning her in a sea of French verbs, history dates, Latin declensions and algebra. She wasn't stupid, she knew that, but somehow the answers seemed to be getting further and further away and sometimes the letters tied themselves in knots that she didn't know how to undo. When she'd started at Dollis Hill Girls she'd been about the same standard as her friend Veronica, comfortably in the middle of the form, but somehow Isabel had slipped down so that she was now on a level with Dorcas, who always spelled Wednesday wrong and had only got into the school because her mother was the cook.

It was Bobby who got her through Sundays. Isabel knew that, if she got through her homework after a fashion, she could, after cold meat for supper, bath and hair wash, get into bed and read *Film Frolics*. These days there was always something about Bobby in the magazine, even if it was just his horoscope or his favourite Thanksgiving meal (what was Thanksgiving anyway?). Then, when Lucinda had gone to sleep, Isabel would get out her Bobby Book. Very carefully, by torchlight under the covers, she would look through the photos, mostly cut out from magazines but one, thrillingly, taken outside the Ritz with Veronica's Box Brownie. It showed Bobby pausing to wave at them before getting into the Rolls. It was black and white, of course, but you could see the gleam of Bobby's golden hair and the flash of his smile. Then, if she was lucky, Isabel would go to sleep and dream about him rather than maths and Latin.

This evening seemed to drag on for ever. At least it was a bank holiday tomorrow so she didn't have to go to school but it was still, unmistakably and unbearably, Sunday. The page of Latin danced and metamorphosed in front of her; now the letters looked all different sizes like a ransom note. Isabel's head pounded. Maybe she should ask Mum for an aspirin. She went out into the hall. She could hear Mum and Dad listening to the

266

news, something about mods and rockers in Brighton. "Society is collapsing," someone was saying, "these young people have no respect for law and order." She was about to push open the sitting room door when she noticed something on the mat. There was no post on a Sunday so it must have been hand-delivered. What's more it was addressed to her. just "Isabel", nothing else. Was it from Veronica or one of her friends? But it didn't look like them somehow. All the girls at her school had the same handwriting. This was small and cramped, backward sloping. An adult's handwriting.

She opened the envelope. Inside was a single sheet of paper with a few words written on it.

Isabel. You are beautiful. You should be a model.

There was a telephone number underneath.

Sir Crispian Miles had a list of chores to be completed before bedtime. This was his routine, something that could be achieved even on the darkest of days. Check that Valerie had taken her medicine and was sleeping peacefully. Check on the nurse (he just tapped on her door and said "Good night", he didn't go in, of course). Check that the doors were safely locked and bolted. Do the crossword. Watch TV until they played the National Anthem. Sometimes he stood up for this. Since Rhonda had disappeared, he added another item. Look at her picture and allow himself to cry. He allotted himself five minutes for this, strictly rationed. He looked at her school photograph, grinning gap-toothed smile, lovely hair smoothly brushed, and sobbed dryly. Sometimes Rho seemed to look at him and say, "Don't cry, Daddy. I'm fine. You'll see me again." But sometimes she was as distant as an oil painting, her eyes unreadable. After he'd finished his cry, Crispian replaced the picture on the shelf and poured himself a glass of brandy. Just one glass. He didn't want to start down that path, thank you very much.

Tonight, though, as he took the empty glass through to the kitchen, there was something different about the house. He could sense it, even though there was no sound apart from the grandfather clock wheezing in the hall. Crispian rinsed the glass under the tap and, as he did so, he thought he saw something through the window, a fleeting glimpse of white, a movement somewhere out there in the carefully tended shrubbery. Crispian fetched a poker from the drawing room and went to the front door. He flung it open and shouted, "Who's there?" Silence. A dog barked a few houses along. "I'm armed," shouted Sir Crispian, although the First World War Enfield rifle over the fireplace hadn't been fired since Crispian's father had fought desperately in his Ypres trench nearly fifty years ago.

His words echoed through the dark street. But Crispian knew that someone was listening.

268

CHAPTER
TWENTY-SEVEN

On Bank Holiday Monday the reinforcements came. More Vespas on the Brighton Road, more motorbikes outside the Daygo and the Little Chef.

"We're bringing in police horses today," said Edgar, as he snatched a quick breakfast. "Hopefully just the sight of them will put some of the rioters off."

"I want to see the horses," said Marianne, her bottom lip starting to protrude.

"Another time," said Edgar, getting up and putting on his jacket. "Anyway, you saw some horses on Saturday, Mari. You went riding. Mummy said that you were really good. You'd better play it safe again today," he said to Emma. "Keep indoors. Trouble was mostly restricted to the area around the Palace Pier and the arches yesterday but there are some pretty nasty customers in town."

"Was anyone hurt?" asked Emma. Officially, she and Edgar had made up but she still found herself talking to him as if he was a stranger. She knew that Marianne had noticed something and was acting up accordingly.

"Some minor injuries but it was mostly damage to property," said Edgar. "The windows of the Savoy

Cinema were smashed and hundreds of deckchairs were broken."

"It's hardly the Battle of the Alamo," said Emma. She still thought that Edgar was exaggerating about the threat posed by the mods and rockers and was not looking forward to another day trapped in the house with the children.

"Could be worse today," said Edgar. "I've got every man out. There are rumours of another thousand mods coming down from London."

"I like the mods best," said Marianne, "because they've got nice clothes."

"They're both as bad as each other," said Edgar. "Bye." He kissed Emma politely on the cheek, patted Jonathan on the head and hugged both girls. "Stay safe."

"Bye," said Emma. She wasn't going to add "you too".

Edgar reached the station to find the place in ordered chaos. The new officers had been bussed in and were being briefed by Bob in the incident room. There was a palpable sense of excitement and tension. In his office Edgar got out his map of Madeira Terrace and the area around the Palace Pier. He marked the places where the police should be stationed, blue for the first wave, red for the second. The plan was to keep the mods on the shingle and the rockers on the promenade and prevent the twain from ever meeting. It was like a battle, he thought, and enjoyable while the forces were just different colours on paper. The reality might prove

270

very different. He checked the list of equipment provided for each constable: truncheon, whistle, rattle, torch, handcuffs. There weren't quite enough truncheons to go round and tempers in the changing room were apparently getting frayed. Edgar picked up his pocket wireless. The Brighton police had been one of the first forces to use these radio sets but the quality of transmission was notoriously poor. Edgar tested his now: "One, two, one, two . . ."

When his phone rang he thought at first that the noise was coming from his radio. But it was Rita saying, "Inspector Jarvis on the line."

"Hi, Fred," said Edgar. "What's up?"

"Sorry to bother you when you've got the barbarians at the gate," said Jarvis, "but there's been a development with the Isabel Rowlands case."

"Who?" At first Edgar didn't recognise the name.

"The girl in Dollis Hill who saw a man hanging round her house."

"Oh yes. The Bobby Hambro fan."

"Well, last night a note was pushed through her door. It said, 'You are beautiful. You should be a model.' There was a telephone number too. A Brighton number. I rang but no answer as yet."

Edgar exhaled. "Do you think that was our man?"

"It sounds like him from what you've told me."

"Did Isabel see anything?"

"No. She just found the note on the mat. I've got officers at the house now. I'll check the paper for fingerprints but, of course, that won't help unless our chap's on file somewhere."

"No," said Edgar. "Thanks, Fred. Keep me informed, will you?"

He put down the phone. The imminent arrival of the mods and rockers, not to mention the row with Emma, had almost taken his mind off the biggest danger of all. There was someone out there threatening women. A man was waiting outside a young girl's house. He had posted a sinister little note through her door. He felt another surge of anger against Emma. What had she been doing trying to tempt this creature out of hiding? He had already killed a girl. He would almost certainly kill again.

He was so deep in thought that he didn't, at first, hear the tap on the door. It was only when a face appeared that he realised that the knocking had been going on for a while.

"Excuse me, sir?"

It was WPC Connolly, wearing a duty band and a rather martyred expression.

"What is it, WPC Connolly?"

"Sir, will you be needing WPCs on the seafront today?"

"The plan is for you to stay back at the base," said Edgar. "We'll need officers here if there are multiple arrests."

"There are girl mods," said Connolly. "Sara Henratty was one. They might need a woman constable to go to if they get into trouble."

Edgar was irritated. He thought that WPC Connolly saw her job primarily as an opportunity to have adventures. Well it wasn't like that. Policing was hard slog, endless paperwork, pounding the beat. The memory of Emma, always eager for new experiences, further hardened his heart towards this new, keen woman officer. He was tempted to tell Meg to stay behind and sort out the filing. But he stopped himself just in time. WPC Connolly had done good work on this case. She had infiltrated the Bobby Hambro fans, she'd found the shoes in the tunnel and she had acted well on her own initiative. She was also the person who had raised the possibility of a threat to Isabel Rowlands. Besides, she made a good point about the mods. He had seen women — girls really — in the crowd yesterday. It might be good if there were some WPCs around.

"All right," he said, "but check with DI Willis first and don't get involved in any of the scuffles."

"I won't," said WPC Connolly. "Sir, did you send someone to see Isabel Rowlands?"

"Yes," said Edgar. "An officer visited her house yesterday. Isabel gave him a description of the man but it wasn't really any more detailed than the one she gave you. There has been another incident though. A note was pushed through Isabel's door yesterday evening. It said that she was beautiful and should be a model."

"Blimey," said WPC Connolly. "Sorry," she added quickly. "It's just, that must be the same man. The one who told Rhonda and Sara that they could be models."

"It's possible," said Edgar repressively. "The local police are at the house now."

"Good," said Meg. "I was worried. Those girls are nice but they're awfully silly. They'd go off with the devil himself if he said he'd introduce them to Bobby Hambro."

Edgar didn't smile. He thought that the remark was in bad taste. He nodded a dismissal and turned back to his map but Meg was still standing in the doorway.

"Sir," she said, "Howell Davies came into the station yesterday."

"Who?"

"The man who was suspected of being Ernest Coggins's accomplice. He came in to give himself up, he said. Davies claimed to have an alibi for the day of Coggins's escape. He was in Wales visiting his family. I followed it up and it checks out."

"Good," said Edgar. "Fact checking is very important. Did you get it all down on the file?"

"Yes, sir. It's just . . . Davies said something about Coggins hating Sir Crispian Miles because he was a butcher."

"A butcher?" This rang a faint bell. Oh, yes. Emma's research in *Who's Who*. "I believe Sir Crispian used to own a chain of butcher's shops," he said. "But he sold them when he became a member of parliament."

"But what if Coggins has a vendetta against him?" said Connolly. "He's still very involved with animals. I read the report about the work he'd done in prison, with the pigs and chickens and all that. What if Coggins broke out of prison to get revenge on the Miles family?"

"I don't think that's very likely," said Edgar. "If you're going to the seafront, you should be getting ready. Don't forget your whistle."

274

Marianne was inclined to be sulky after Edgar had left. She didn't want to play with Sophie, she didn't want to read a book and the suggestion of starting on her homework was met with the contempt it deserved.

"Let's make a cake," said Emma. If Edgar was going to hold the newspaper article against her, she might as well play up to the stereotype. She quite liked the thought of herself as the beating heart of the home, dispensing delicious meals as well as pithy advice.

The girls were immediately excited by the idea, tying tea-towels round their waists and helping to get mixing bowls and cake tins out of the cupboard. Jonathan watched from his high chair, occasionally beating the tray with a wooden spoon. But, when Emma got out her Mrs Beeton and started searching the larder, she found that she was missing half the ingredients. She hadn't got any baking powder or vanilla essence and there was only one egg in the ceramic hen by the cooker.

"Will Mrs Minton have them in the Little Shop?" said Marianne.

The Little Shop was on the corner of their road. It was a chaotic space filled with cardboard boxes and old packing cases but it mysteriously seemed to stock most things.

"I don't know if it's open on a bank holiday," said Emma.

"It is," said Marianne. "I saw a sign outside. Open until midday. What time is it now?"

It was half past ten. Emma started to hunt for her handbag. "Will you watch Johnno?" she said to the girls. "I'll only be five minutes."

"Can I go?" said Marianne. "You promised I could go to shops by myself when I was eight. And I'm nearly nine now and I never have."

Emma hesitated. It was true that she had made that promise. Edgar had told them to stay inside but the streets hardly seemed to be teeming with violent hooligans. She looked out of the window. Their road was utterly deserted. From the corner of the bay window she could see the sea-front. It looked as if spectators were gathering by the railings hoping to see another battle. But, in the other direction, not a creature in sight. And, by craning her neck, she could just see the awning outside the Little Shop. She'd be able to watch Marianne all the way.

"Take Sophie with you," she said. "I'll give you a list and ten shillings."

Marianne was too delighted even to complain about Sophie's presence. She put on her cardigan and took the list and the note.

"Come straight back," said Emma. "I'll be watching."

"I will," said Marianne.

Emma watched them walking up the road, hand in hand, like an advertisement for Start-Rite shoes.

From his balcony at the Grand, Max could also see the crowds converging on the seafront. The gangs of youths, some sharp-suited, some in studded leather, reminded him of the Montagues and the Capulets at the start of *Romeo and Juliet*. He'd played Mercutio at school, the best part because you got to fence — something he'd been rather good at — and have a

276

showy death scene before all the love stuff really started. As Max watched, four police horses passed by, their muscular rumps gleaming. Their hooves sounded a self-important tattoo on the tarmac, both stirring and rather sombre. The Four Horsemen of the Apocalypse. Max reached for his hat. Staying in his room wasn't going to make Ruby appear again. He might as well see what all the fuss was about.

"Going out, Mr Mephisto?" said the doorman. "Be careful. There are some ruffians out there today."

"I'll be sure to steer clear of them," said Max.

"They should never have stopped National Service," said the doorman. "That's my opinion."

It was a viewpoint that Max had heard rather often in the past few days. These young people had too much time on their hands, they needed some hard physical work to keep them occupied, some discipline, etc., etc.. For himself, he was glad National Service was over. He'd hated any kind of enforced discipline, at school and in the army, and was glad that, if the family returned to England, Rocco wouldn't have to serve. Would they ever come back to the country that Max couldn't quite think of as home? He'd thought so once, walking through the shrouded rooms at Massingham Hall. Now he wasn't so sure.

Max strolled along the promenade. The action was clearly taking place around the Palace Pier again. He could see the crowds and hear the whistles and shouts of the police. There were spectators too, hanging over the railings above and shouting encouragement as if they were at the races. He wondered what Edgar was doing. Presumably this whole operation came under his jurisdiction. If Max knew his friend, he'd be at the centre of it all, organising and worrying.

It was another beautiful day. A shame that all his favourite restaurants would be shut. But then, he didn't really feel like eating with Ruby still missing. Where was she, his beautiful, errant daughter? He remembered walking on the pier with Ruby before he knew their true relationship, thinking how young she was, how vulnerable to life's vicissitudes. Well, she was older now with a carapace of sophistication but he still felt that she could easily be hurt. And he, Max, would kill anyone who did so.

As he got nearer to the Palace Pier Max could see the gangs dividing; the mods in their parkas, some looking rather young and unsuited to such serious business, the rockers, older and more heavily built, some carrying bike chains. The police were trying to keep the two sides apart, he could see the white helmets on the beach, but the youths were running under the pier, throwing stones and shouting insults. The police line was wavering in places. On the promenade above, the horses were feigning charges at the rival groups, curvetting and snorting, unsettled by the noise.

Max reached a vantage point, a stone jetty that projected into the sea. The whistles were sounding again and the youths were responding with shouts and catcalls. Holidaymakers, curious or foolish enough to risk the beach, were running for the steps. Amongst the rush, Max spotted a blond head, a plaid jacket, American-style jeans. What on earth was Bobby

Hambro, Hollywood star, doing caught up in this imbroglio? Bobby seemed to be with someone, a slim man dressed in a mod suit with a pork-pie hat. Or were they just thrown together by the crowd? As Max watched, the two of them wove their way through the crowded promenade, heading for the arches. On impulse, Max started to follow but, at that moment, the mods and the rockers charged and the air was full of stones and missiles. Max stepped back onto the pavement. He didn't want to get concussed by a flying pebble. Think how ridiculous it would look in the next morning's papers.

"This is fun, isn't it?" said a voice behind him.

He turned. A woman was smiling at him; slim, short-haired, wearing trousers and what looked like a man's cricket jumper. She wasn't his usual type but there was something attractive about her, a directness of gaze, a certain humour in her expression. She also looked vaguely familiar.

"Sam Collins. Reporter. We met years ago when I was working on the Lansdowne Road case."

"I remember." He did. The snow-covered pier, a cup of black coffee in the café, a respite in the midst of hell.

"You're reporting from the front line," he said.

"They're just children playing games," said Sam. "This isn't real crime."

"It would feel pretty real if you were hit with one of those rocks." As if to prove Max's point, two mods walked past, holding handkerchiefs to bleeding heads. In the distance sirens sounded.

"I'm more interested in who abducted your daughter," said Sam.

Max stared at her, not knowing whether to be annoyed or not.

"We don't know for certain that she has been abducted," he said.

"I'm sure she has," said Sam. "Emma and I have a theory. He's kidnapping women with different hair colour. Rhonda's a redhead, Louise has black hair, Ruby's a brunette. Emma thinks that he reads about them in the papers and becomes obsessed."

It didn't surprise Max that Emma was more involved in the case that she admitted in her husband's presence. It struck him that, together, Sam and Emma made a formidable duo.

"How do we catch him?" he asked, really wanting to know what her answer would be.

"We have to wait," said Sam. "I'm almost certain that he'll make a move today. Look at all this." She gestured at the seafront. Someone had set off a smoke bomb and the air was full of vapour, like dry ice before an illusion, through which vague shapes appeared and discordant cries could be heard.

"It's the perfect camouflage," said Sam.

"Smoke and mirrors," said Max. He looked at Sam with new respect.

Meg was finding the front line rather less exciting than she had imagined. After she had spoken to the super, DI Willis had given in and dispatched her to the seafront. "You can be on hand to help anyone who gets hurt. Some of the girls might get overwhelmed and need a shoulder to cry on."

So her role was to be a nurse/confidante, not a policewoman. Well, it could be worse. Meg positioned herself on Marine Parade, where she could look down on the promenade. The mods were approaching from the Aquarium end, the rockers, appropriately enough, from Black Rock. The police horses were in the middle. Meg had longed to have riding lessons as a child. What would it be like to be on top of one of those restless, glorious creatures? Pretty terrifying, she imagined. As she watched, a dapple-grey half-reared as a mod threw a bottle at it. Bastard. She hoped he got trampled under its hooves.

She knew that her brothers Declan and Patrick were there in the crowd somewhere. She hoped they were safe. Declan had the sort of reckless high spirits that often led him into trouble. Patrick was quieter but still likely to be led astray by his older brother. She'd told them to be careful, that morning over breakfast, but neither of them had taken any notice. If they saw her there in her uniform, a head taller than anyone else in the crowd, they would be more likely to kill themselves laughing than be injured by a flying deckchair leg.

"Excuse me, miss?" It was someone asking the way to the railway station. They'd had enough of Brighton and who could blame them? People always asked the police for directions. Or the time. How did the old music hall song go? Her dad sang it sometimes, when he'd had a few drinks in the pub. *If you want to know the time, ask a policeman.* Time you got a watch, Meg wanted to say, but she couldn't, of course. The first rule of policing. Be civil to the public.

The public weren't being very civil today though. On the promenade below, the rival gangs clashed together with shouts and a hail of missiles. Then, a few minutes later, a smoke bomb went off and spectators staggered back from the railings, gasping and choking. Meg stayed put, wiping her eyes. And, as the smoke cleared, she saw a figure walking towards her, like something from a mirage. It was as if all the Bobby Soxers' dreams had come true.

She was looking at Bobby Hambro himself.

Emma watched until the girls reached the top of the street and went into the shop. It should only take them a few minutes. Mrs Minton was unlikely to be busy today. She looked at her watch. Ten forty-six.

Jonathan laughed suddenly. Emma turned round and saw that he'd somehow reached onto the table, got hold of the flour and emptied it over his head. He grinned at her, like some awful white-face clown act, blue eyes very bright amidst the powder.

"You horrible child! What have you done?"

She fetched a cloth and, when she next looked at her watch, it was ten fifty-five. The girls should be home by now. She was on her way to the door when she heard running footsteps. Thank goodness. Though it was silly of her to be worried. It was broad daylight and they'd only been to the end of the road. She opened the door with a welcoming smile, ready to relate Johnno's latest awfulness.

282

"Mummy!" It was Sophie, crying so hard that, at first, Emma couldn't make out her words. "Mummy! Marianne got in a car with a man. She's gone."

CHAPTER
TWENTY-EIGHT

"What do you mean, 'she's gone'?" said Emma, but her heart had turned to ice.

"She's gone," wailed Sophie. "She was cross with me because I wanted sweets. She left the shop first and I saw her getting into the car. Then it drove away."

"Sophie." Emma grabbed her daughter's arms. "Can you remember what the car was like? What colour was it? Was it like Dad's? Bigger? Smaller?"

"It had a flag on," said Sophie. "Like the Queen has."

Emma thought of a Rolls Royce with a flag on the bonnet. Her dad had once owned a Rolls. Who else in Brighton drove a car like that?

"You said there was a man in the car. What was he like?"

"I don't know." Sophie started crying again. "He was just a man."

"Stay here," said Emma. She ran up the road to Mavis's house and knocked on the door of the basement flat. Thank goodness, Mavis came to the door at once. She had her slippers on and was holding her knitting.

"Mavis. Marianne's gone missing. Can you sit with Sophie and Jonathan while I get Edgar?"

Mavis must have seen the panic in Emma's face because, for once in her life, she didn't ask any questions or start an anecdote. She simply followed Emma back to the house, still wearing her slippers.

Emma ran upstairs to the phone. She asked for Superintendent Stephens and, sure enough, soon Rita's supercilious voice was on the line.

"The superintendent is out. Who shall I say is calling?"

"It's his wife. It's urgent. Has he got his radio with him?"

"I couldn't say."

"Well, when he rings in tell him to telephone Emma immediately. Is DI Willis in?"

But Bob was out too. They must all be on the seafront trying to prevent the mods and rockers killing each other. But Bob did apparently have a radio set with him. "Tell him to go to Emma Stephens' house immediately. It's urgent. There's a child missing."

"Will do," said Rita. But Emma had no confidence in her.

Emma put the phone down. In the chaos of the seafront Bob might not even be able to hear his radio. Officers were meant to check at a police box every hour but that was impossible when you were being pelted by pebbles and deckchair legs. Emma couldn't just sit there waiting for the phone to ring. She had to try to find Edgar. She was sure that she'd be able to spot him in the crowd.

She turned to Mavis who was sitting on the sofa with Sophie on her lap. Jonathan had fallen asleep in his high chair, still covered in flour. "I'm going out," she said. "I won't be long. If the police come, tell them what happened." She squatted down to Sophie, who was still hiccoughing quietly. "Sophie, tell them about the man in the car. You're not in trouble. You're a very good girl. We've just got to find Marianne and you can help them. Understand?"

Sophie nodded.

"I'm going to find Dad," said Emma.

"Bobby?" said Meg before she could stop herself.

The man looked at her. Close up he was unmistakable, the clean-cut boyish face that she'd seen beaming down from the walls of Rhonda's bedroom. The man who was the intended bridegroom of hundreds of teenage girls.

"I'm sorry." The American accent was unmistakable. "You must be thinking of someone else. Excuse me, ma'am." He pushed past her and continued along the pavement, head down.

"You're Bobby Hambro," said Meg but she was speaking to empty space. There was a man with Bobby, a mod wearing a pork-pie hat, and he looked back at Meg. He was very young and she thought he looked scared.

The smoke bomb had frightened some of the crowds away. Down below, there seemed to be a temporary ceasefire. Meg watched as some PCs — she thought she saw Danny Black amongst them — bundled a few of the ring-leaders into the back of a police van. Four police horses cantered slowly along the promenade. There were shouts and catcalls from the remaining spectators by the railings. The mods and rockers were in small groups, nursing injuries or planning their next attack. Meg saw a girl, blood streaming from a cut on her forehead, sitting on the side of the road. Maybe she should go down and help. That's what she was there for, after all. She looked for the nearest steps.

"Stop!" A woman was running towards her. A blonde woman in a tweed skirt. There was something in her face, a kind of frozen terror, that made Meg move towards her.

"What is it?"

"Are you Meg Connolly?"

"Yes."

"You've got to help me. My daughter's been abducted. And I can't find my husband."

"Your husband?"

"Superintendent Stephens."

So this was the famous Emma Stephens, née Holmes.

Meg Connolly. The famous WPC Connolly. Emma had spotted her immediately. She really was incredibly tall, a head higher than anyone else in the crowd. She would know where Edgar was, and Bob too.

Meg led her to a bus shelter where Emma grasped her arm and poured out her story. Tramps sometimes slept in the shelter but now it was empty apart from an old blanket on one of the seats.

"Can you get hold of Edgar? Superintendent Stephens? Have you got a radio?"

"No. WPCs don't have radios."

"Well, can you find him? He must be down there somewhere?"

"He was by the pier earlier." Edgar had said that Meg was so bright but now she seemed maddeningly slow. She just stared at Emma as if she couldn't understand what was happening.

"My daughter's been taken!" Emma shouted. "Find Edgar. Hurry!"

"Emma? What's going on?"

She swung round to see, of all people, Max, elegant as ever in a pale grey suit and trilby hat. And, beside him — this was starting to feel like a dream — Sam.

"Marianne's been taken," said Emma. "I let her go to the shops on her own and a man took her away in his car."

"Did you get a description of the man?" said Meg, sounding like a detective for the first time.

"No. My youngest daughter, Sophie, was there but she just said he looked like a man. She said that the car had a flag on it, like the Queen's."

"Like the Queen's car? A Rolls Royce?"

"I don't know. I didn't question her very closely. I rang the station but Edgar and Bob are both out. So I came to find them."

"We'll find them," said Max. He sounded so confident and capable that Emma turned to him with gratitude. He put his arm round her. "I'll find Edgar. I'm good at finding people."

288

"A flag," said Sam. "Like the Union Jack?"

"What?" Emma was momentarily confused.

"The car. You said it had a flag on it. Like the Union Jack."

And Emma remembered. The drive along the seafront with Jonathan on her lap. His delight in the ramshackle car with the Union Jack painted on the bonnet.

"Harry," she said. "The photographer."

"Harry! He took photographs of you and Marianne," said Sam. "He must have taken the other pictures too. The ones of Louise and Sara. I bet he photographed Ruby loads of times."

"Where does he live?" Emma had left Max's side and was staring intently at Sam. Meg and Max were looking between the two of them as if they were watching a tennis match.

"Rottingdean," said Sam. "But I think he was in London yesterday."

"Where in Rottingdean?" said Emma, grasping Sam's arm.

"Above a shop."

"The Smugglers' Cave?"

"That's the one."

Harry had known about the smugglers' tunnels. Emma remembered him mentioning them that day. Was that where he had taken Marianne?

"We have to go there," she said. "Now. Has anyone got a car?"

Meg seemed to come to life. She stepped into the road, raised her fingers to her lips and emitted the loudest, most ear-piercing whistle that Emma had ever heard. Seconds later two Lambrettas were pulling up beside them.

"My brothers," explained Meg. "Emma, you get up behind Declan. I'll go with Patrick."

In a daze, Emma climbed onto the bike behind a brown-haired boy in a mod suit.

"Take us to Rottingdean," said Meg.

"You'd better hold on," said the boy to Emma. She put her arms around his waist as the moped moved forwards.

CHAPTER
TWENTY-NINE

Max looked at Sam.

"Who's Harry?" he said.

"Harry Payne. He's the press photographer," said Sam. "I can't quite believe it though. He seemed such a quiet bloke. Inoffensive."

"They're always the ones," said Max. "To commit a crime you need to be able to fade into the background."

"We need to find Superintendent Stephens," said Sam. "Tell him what's going on. He'll have to send some men after Emma and Meg. They could be in danger."

For all Max's words to Emma, it was harder to find Edgar than to make a woman disappear. The promenade seemed to be full of policemen in white helmets but Edgar, who would be in plain clothes, was nowhere to be seen. Sam recognised a few people and they all claimed to have seen Superintendent Stephens "just a few minutes ago". Eventually they found him, speaking to a group of officers by the entrance to the Palace Pier. Max could see the gypsy caravan in the background. Madame Astarte Zabini. Horoscopes. Tarot Readings. Genuine Romany Second Sight.

"Max!" said Edgar, looking up. "What are you doing here? Don't you know that this is a war zone?" He seemed tired but rather exhilarated, hatless, in shirtsleeves, a streak of dirt on his forehead. Max's heart was wrung for him.

"Ed," he said. "Something's happened. It's Marianne."

"What?" Edgar was at his side immediately.

"She's been abducted by a man in a car. Emma's on the trail of the man she thinks took her. They've gone to Rottingdean."

"Rottingdean? What the hell are you talking about?"

"It's Harry Payne, the photographer," said Sam. "We think he's the one who's been kidnapping the girls."

"What are you doing here?" said Edgar, sounding angrier than Max had ever heard him. "Looking for a scoop? Bloody hell, you people are like vultures."

"Ed," said Max. "The important thing is to go after Emma. Can you get hold of a car?"

"They're all full of casualties." Edgar looked round. "O'Neill," he shouted. "Get me a panda car now." A thickset man detached himself from the group and set off towards Madeira Terrace. "Where's DI Willis?" said Edgar to another man. "Find him for me."

"I'm here, sir." Bob arrived, out of breath and as anxious-looking as ever. Well now, reflected Max, he had something to be anxious about. "I've had a message to ring Emma," said Bob.

"Marianne's been abducted," said Edgar. "I'm going to Rottingdean after Emma. You go to the house and wait for me there. O'Neill, you come with me."

A panda car had drawn up. Edgar and the thickset man got in, leaving Max, Sam and Bob looking at each other while, behind them, a voice exhorted them to try the coconut shy on the pier.

It was the first time that Emma had been on the back of a moped and, at any other time, she might have enjoyed it. The wind flew through her hair as they passed Black Rock and Roedean, her old school high on the cliffs, as forbidding and impassive as ever. Emma now felt oddly numb. It was as if her brain had closed down, allowing her only room to breathe and to have one thought in her head. Find Marianne. Find Marianne. She thought of her daughter, the inquisitive tilt of her head, the way her nose wrinkled when she was thinking, the glorious softness of her cheek when Emma laid her face against hers. Marianne was Emma and Edgar's first child and for two years, until Sophie was born, she had been the absolute centre of their world. They used to sit in the evenings and just stare at her, marvelling at the back of her neck as she bent over her toys. She would go to sleep in Edgar's arms because neither of them could bear to put her in her cot. How different it was with Jonathan — sometimes Emma felt she only came alive in the rare moments during the day when he was asleep. Marianne claimed to remember those early years very well and said that she had never been that happy again. Certainly she had resented Sophie when she was born (such a funny, dark-haired little scrap, with none of Marianne's cherubic beauty). Should they have made more of Marianne, told her more often that she was their adored eldest daughter, the light of their lives? If they found Marianne, *when* they found her, Emma would tell her this every day.

Emma thought of Marianne going round the field on Toby. *Look at me, Mummy!* She thought of Marianne prancing around the room on the day that Harry took the pictures, desperate to be noticed, of Marianne with her tutu over her pyjamas, the evening that Edgar and Emma had gone to the Grand for dinner with Max. And she remembered Mavis's words, as she smiled indulgently over her knitting. "You look the spit of your mum." Emma had thought that she could lure the killer into action but she was too old, too faded, too much of a mother. But she had practically offered him her daughter on a silver tray.

They screeched around the St Dunstan's roundabout, Emma now hanging on for dear life. She could see Meg in front, leaning in unison with Patrick, seeming completely at ease. But presumably riding on motorbikes was nothing new for the intrepid WPC Connolly.

Rottingdean High Street was deserted. It was midday on a Bank Holiday Monday, everyone was probably indoors eating lunch. The little village was only four miles from Brighton but it could be on a different planet. All the shops were shut and the shutters were down outside The Smugglers' Cave. On the doorbell though was a piece of paper saying, simply, "Payne". Emma pressed so hard that her finger went white. Meg stepped back to see if she could see in the upstairs window.

"I don't think he's in," she said.

"Harry!" shouted Emma. "Harry Payne! It's the police."

A first-floor window opened and a head appeared. It wasn't Harry though, someone older and more authoritative.

"What's all this noise about?" Then the man seemed to notice Meg. "Oh, it's you. What do you want?"

"Tony," said Meg. "We need to speak to Harry Payne urgently. Do you know where he is?"

"He lives in the flat upstairs but I think he's out."

"Have you got a key?"

The head withdrew and, a few seconds later, a tall man appeared at the door with a key fob in his hand. "I don't suppose you've got a warrant," he said mildly.

"It's life or death," said Meg. She grabbed the key and ran up the stairs, two at a time, Emma on her heels.

The flat was small and smelt of vinegar and not-very-clean clothes. It seemed to consist just of a bed-sitting room with a sink and gas stove. Emma looked around wildly: the bed was unmade, there were fish and chip wrappers on the floor and about a month's worth of the *Argus* on a small coffee table. Nowhere for anyone to hide.

"Is this all there is?" said Emma.

"There must be a bathroom," said Meg, "or at least a toilet."

She went out onto the landing and Emma heard doors opening and shutting.

"Emma!" Meg called. She was standing at the doorway of a dark little space which housed a dirty-looking toilet, a sink and a rudimentary shower. The room smelled strongly of chemicals. Then Meg turned on her torch and thousands of eyes stared back at them.

"This must be his darkroom," said Meg.

The pictures were all of women. Hair, eyes, a hundred different smiles and poses. Black-and-white photos, with the occasional foray into colour, all stuck to the walls, overlapping and peeling at the edges. But Emma's eyes were drawn to a picture pinned over the sink. It showed her with the children, Marianne smiling like an angel. Someone had drawn a circle round her daughter's head.

"Louise is here. And Sara," said Meg. "And there are lots of Ruby. All circled."

"Oh my God. It was him. How did he do it? How did he lure the girls away?"

"I think he told them that they should be models. I think he got them to write notes and arrange to meet him, then he locked them up somewhere. The girls outside the Ritz, the Bobby Hambro fans, they said that a man had approached Rhonda. Trouble was, I couldn't get much of a description. "Tallish, oldish," that's the best they could do. I think he's been stalking one of the other girls too."

"Sophie said 'he was just a man'. But Harry is rather insignificant-looking, sort of colourless. I've met him a few times but I don't know if I could describe him."

"The girls said that the man had an American accent. Is Harry American?"

"No," said Emma. "But I think he could do the voice." She heard Sam's amused tones. *You should see him letting his hair down in the pub, singing Frank Sinatra songs and chatting up the girls*. Harry had been able to impersonate Sinatra, the American singer beloved of teenage girls, and he obviously liked to approach women. It probably helped too if they were young and naive. But Marianne was only eight. Her hands clenched into fists.

"Where are they?" she said. "Where is he hiding them?"

"Come on," said Meg. "There's somewhere else we need to look."

Outside, Declan and Patrick were still sitting on their scooters, awaiting further instructions. But Tony had gone into the shop and was standing by a cabinet full of glass animals. He didn't seem surprised when Meg said, "We need to look in the tunnels."

"Be careful," he said, getting another set of keys out of a drawer. He turned to a door behind the till but, before he could open it, a new voice said, "Police."

"Edgar!"

Emma threw herself on her husband. "Marianne's gone," she said, "There are pictures of her upstairs. It's all my fault, Ed."

Edgar's arms tightened around her. "We'll find her, Em. I promise." He addressed Meg over Emma's head. "What's going on, WPC Connolly?"

Meg told him and O'Neill, who had arrived with the super, about Harry Payne, his car and the photographs.

297

She was succinct and businesslike and Emma could feel Edgar relaxing slightly.

"There are tunnels under this shop," said Meg. "It's where we found the shoes. I was just about to search them."

"O'Neill, come with me," said Edgar. "Connolly, you wait here with Emma."

"But, sir," Meg began. "I know where the tunnels go —"

"Let me go with you," said Emma.

"Stay here," said Edgar. And he disappeared through the door, the burly man, who was presumably O'Neill, following him.

Meg and Emma looked at each other, then they pushed past the shopkeeper and through the door.

Edgar must have heard their footsteps behind him but he didn't look round. They were in a narrow, dark passage-way. The ceiling was low but Emma, unlike Meg, could walk without ducking her head. The walls were brick and the floor seemed to be concrete. It felt like a place that was in regular use. After a few minutes, Edgar stopped and Meg shouted, "Turn left." He did so and, following, Emma found herself in a different space altogether, a tunnel that seemed to have been burrowed out of the cliffs, the chalk walls uneven and clammy, narrowing so much in places that they had to walk sideways. The claustrophobia that had been looming ever since Sophie had spoken those fateful words now threatened to overwhelm Emma. She could hear her breathing becoming hoarse and shallow.

"Are you OK?" said Meg, looking round.

"Yes." Emma tried to take slower breaths. They were going downwards now and it was very cold. Eventually they stopped and Emma felt as if the walls were receding. She could stretch out her arms now. She did so and caught Meg's hand. Meg squeezed her fingers briefly and then let go. It was oddly comforting. By the light of the police torches, Emma could see a wooden door and an alcove cut into the chalk. Edgar was squatting to pick something up. Wordlessly, he held it out.

"It's a Roedean prefect's badge," said Emma.

CHAPTER
THIRTY

Bob turned and headed back towards Kemp Town.

"Come on, Barker," he said to the hovering policeman. "We're going to the super's house."

Uninvited, Max and Sam followed.

"If nothing else we can help with the children," said Sam. "Poor little Sophie must be terrified."

"Do you know the family well, then?" asked Max. They crossed the coast road, now fairly quiet, and walked up past the Regency terraces. Max remembered the other time he had searched for Ruby behind those smooth, respectable walls. He hadn't even known that she was his daughter then but she had been in danger and she had needed him. What if she needed him now? He hoped to God that finding this Harry Payne would mean that they found Ruby.

"Yes," said Sam. "Emma and I are good friends. We've got a lot in common. We're both as bored as hell and we both love crime."

She grinned at Max and he couldn't help smiling back.

They turned to walk inland. Above the rooftops Max could see the hospital and, behind it, one of the new blocks that seemed to be shooting up like weeds all over Brighton.

"Those new buildings are so ugly," he said. "I'd hate to live there."

Sam stopped in the middle of the road.

"What did you say?"

"I was just saying how horrible the new apartments — flats — were. Especially when you compare them with the old houses. You wonder if an architect was even involved."

Sam caught his arm. Max was surprised to feel a slight, but definite, electric shock.

"I went to those flats with Harry. Half of them are empty."

Max looked down at her. "You don't think . . ."

"They're like cages, that's what I said to Harry. Astarte said that he was keeping them in a cage."

"Not another one quoting that bloody mystic," said Max but his heart had started to beat faster. He looked up at the flats, towering over the Royal Sussex. And, from one of the highest windows, he saw a flash of light. On, off, on, off.

"Did you see that?" he said.

"No," said Sam. "Yes. In one of the windows. Something flashing on and off. Is it just a reflection of the sun?"

"It seems too regular," said Max. "Almost like a signal."

"Like Morse code," said Sam. "Let's go and look."

"Do you really think that's where he's keeping them?"

"I don't know but it's worth a try."

"Shall we tell Bob?" The two policemen were now a long way ahead, almost at the Stephenses' front door.

"No," said Sam. "He might try to stop us."

"We won't give him a chance. Hey, Bob!" He used his stage voice, well able to project over a few hundred yards. Bob turned and looked round.

"We're going up to the flats," shouted Max. "Tell Ed to meet us there."

And, taking Sam's hand, he started to run.

Sir Crispian Miles always had a proper lunch if he was at home. If he was in town he ate at the House of Commons or at his club. There was nothing so uncivilised as missing lunch or having something insubstantial like a sandwich. Today he was eating gammon, new potatoes and peas. He sat at the dining room table and read Saturday's *Times*, which he rested against the pickle jar. Valerie never ate much at midday and the nurse took her meals in her room.

The world was going to the dogs. That was the message that he got from the papers. Hippies in America protesting against the Vietnam War. Thousands of young hoodlums descending on Brighton and making trouble. The police should be concentrating on finding Rhonda — and the other girls too, of course — not stopping gangs of lay-abouts from killing each other. They should all be in the army anyway. He had his doubts about the Brighton police. The superintendent, Stephens, was a nice enough fellow but too mild for Crispian's taste. It wouldn't surprise him if he'd been a conchie in the war. Another thing that shouldn't be allowed.

He paused in his chewing and reading. The world might be going to the dogs but an actual dog was barking. It must be the Labrador three houses along. But Monty never barked unless he had a reason. He had barked last night too. Crispian went to the window and pulled aside the net curtain. The dining room looked out over the garden and through the small panes of glass he could see only the well-tended lawn and neat flower beds. Next door's cat, an idle ginger creature, was sunning itself on the roof of the greenhouse.

Crispian left his food and went to the front door. Sunlight was flooding in through the stained glass, making pools on the parquet, red, gold and green. Then, with terrifying suddenness, a shape appeared, blotting out the light. Seizing an umbrella from the stand in the hall, Crispian flung open the door.

A man stood facing him. It was a couple of seconds before Crispian realised that the man was holding a sack. And that the sack was moving.

"They're not here," said Emma. Her voice echoed in the cave-like space.

"But they have been here," said Edgar. "Or else it's a place where Payne keeps his trophies. This is where you found the shoes, isn't it, WPC Connolly?"

"Yes," said Meg. "The school badge wasn't here before, though. I'm sure of it. Payne must have found a way in from the undercliff walk. On the other side of that door is where we found Sara's body."

Emma wished Meg hadn't mentioned Sara. For the last few hours all that had kept her going was the thought that Marianne was still alive. But Sara had been alive and Payne had killed her, strangled her, Edgar had said. She found that she was sobbing. Meg put her arm round her but Edgar hardly seemed to notice. He pushed open the door and a shaft of light bisected the darkness. Outside, they could hear shouts of children playing on the beach. It truly seemed like another world.

"I'll take you back home, Emma," said Edgar. "I've told Bob to meet us there. We'll find this Payne. There are only a few places he can be. O'Neill, you wait here in case he comes back."

"Yes, sir."

"What about me?" said Meg.

"I thought I told you to stay in the shop with Emma," said Edgar.

"Sorry," said Meg, not sounding it.

"You'd better come back with us," said Edgar. "I'll need you to stay with my wife and children."

"Meg's been wonderful," said Emma. "We wouldn't have found the photos without her."

But Edgar seemed not to hear.

CHAPTER
THIRTY-ONE

Max was out of breath by the time that they reached the tower block. Sam was sprinting ahead like a gazelle. But then she must be at least fifteen years younger than him.

When he reached the entrance, Sam already had the door open. "It's got one of those entry phones," she said, "but I don't think it's working."

"They never seem to work," said Max, thinking of Ruby's London flat. He was trying not to pant. "Is anyone living here at all?"

"I think a few of the lower-floor flats are occupied."

"Where was the signal coming from?"

"It must have been at least the tenth floor, don't you think so?"

Max looked around. They were in a lobby, grey and featureless, with a staircase on one side and a lift in front of them.

"I wonder if the elevator is working?" he said.

"I wouldn't trust it," said Sam. "See you at the top." And she started for the stairs.

Max pressed the button but there was no helpful green light pointing upwards. With a sigh, he too began to climb.

It took longer than he could possibly have imagined. So many identical grey doors, the stairs, still smelling of paint and new plastic, snaking ever upwards. There was no noise at all apart from Sam's feet above him and, eventually, that sound too stopped. Max paused to catch his breath. He remembered getting breathless when he'd followed Ruby's mother Emerald up the stairs of her house in Hove. When he got back to America he would start exercising properly, maybe even go to the gym with Lydia. Obviously those lengths in the pool were having no effect at all.

"Max." Sam's voice echoed down the stairwell. "Hurry up!"

Sam wasn't exactly making a silent entrance, thought Max, as he forced himself to take the last flight two at a time. He sensed that she wasn't the sort of woman to do anything quietly.

Sam was standing by one of the grey doors. They were actually on the thirteenth floor and, from the window, Max could see all of Brighton spread out below him, the piers reaching out into the sea.

"I can hear voices inside," said Sam.

Max hammered on the door. "Ruby! Are you there?"

And a voice answered. "Dad? Is that you?"

Emma and Meg travelled back in the panda car, Declan and Patrick following like a guard of honour. Edgar sat next to the driver and didn't speak except to try to reach Bob on the radio. He seemed to be unsuccessful, eventually throwing the device down with an uncharacteristic curse, but by then they were at the house.

The sitting room was full of people. Jonathan, still floury, in his playpen, Sophie still on Mavis's lap, Bob standing by the window and another policeman sitting awkwardly on the sofa.

"I've sent two men to the *Argus* offices," said Bob, speaking to Edgar and ignoring everyone else. "And there was a message from Sir Crispian Miles, something about a break-in."

"The Surrey police will have to deal with that," said Edgar. "Our priority has to be finding Payne. I've left O'Neill at his flat in case he goes back there."

"Oh, and Max Mephisto has gone up to the new flats," said Bob. "He asked if you could meet him there. He had that reporter with him, the one who's always hanging round the station asking questions. Sam Collins."

"Why on earth have they gone there?" said Edgar.

Emma spoke from the floor where she was crouching next to Sophie. "Harry had been to the flats. That day he gave us a lift to the hospital, he said that they were half empty."

"Let's go," said Edgar to Bob.

"I'm coming with you," said Emma. "Mavis will stay with the children, won't you, Mavis?"

"Of course," said Mavis comfortably.

"I'm coming too," said Meg.

Emma thought that Edgar was going to tell her to stay behind, as he'd done in the tunnel but he said, "Very well, WPC Connolly. You may be able to help." Then he turned to Emma. She couldn't read his expression, it seemed remote and closed-off, as if he was concentrating hard on being a policeman and not a father.

"Emma, you must do what I say. Payne might well be dangerous. He may even be armed."

"All right," said Emma, but she clenched her fists in her pockets. Just let him try, she thought.

They crammed into the panda car, Emma sharing the front passenger seat with Edgar, Meg, Bob and the other policeman, whose name was Barker, in the back. It felt odd to be so close to Edgar and yet so far away from him. She clasped her hands together and thought of Marianne. Please let her be there. Please let us be in time.

Barker made some comment about Meg being too tall but Bob told him to be quiet. It felt strange, too, to hear Bob being authoritative.

"We should go in quietly," said Bob. "If Payne has . . . well, if Payne has Marianne with him, we don't want him to be panicked."

"We'll see his car outside the buildings," said Edgar. "What does he drive?"

"A Mini with a Union Jack on it," said Emma. She could feel Edgar's heart beating. "It's very distinctive."

"If it's there, you must wait in the car," Edgar said to Emma. "Promise."

Emma said nothing. She was not promising anything.

"We'll get you out of there," shouted Max. "Who's with you?"

308

"Rhonda and Louise." Thank God. But where was Marianne?

Max stood back, intending to run at the door but Sam caught his arm. "You'll never do it on your own."

"We'll see about that," said Max. He'd show Sam that what he lacked in sprinting ability he made up in brute strength.

"We have to wait," said Sam. "Harry will probably be arriving any minute. He'll want to keep Marianne with the others. He'll unlock the door and then we'll have him."

"Edgar will be here soon," said Max. "If Harry sees the police hanging around the building, he'll take Marianne somewhere else."

As Max spoke he heard footsteps, two sets of footsteps, ascending the stairs. They didn't sound like the heavy feet of the law. They were also moving surprisingly fast.

"Quick!" said Sam. She opened a door at random and pushed Max inside.

It was a tiny space, an electrical cupboard, probably. Max could feel levers sticking into his back. In the course of his career, he'd often had to fold himself into small spaces. He was no contortionist, like Sofija, the Bulgarian girl who had performed the Magic Box trick with him at the Empire Shepherd's Bush, but he was able to make his six-foot-three frame remarkably compact. Sam was another matter. She was a small, slight woman but she seemed to be everywhere, her hair tickling his nose, her elbow in his ribs, her foot treading on one of his. He could smell her shampoo, something clean and fresh, and hear her breathing; he even thought that he could feel her chest expanding.

The footsteps stopped and Max could hear another person breathing, breathless sobs that could only come from a child. "Quiet," said a man's voice. "Or I'll give you something to cry about." Max felt himself tensing and Sam grasped his wrist in warning. They heard a key going into a lock and then a door opening.

"Now!" They burst out of the cupboard and Max saw, as if on a magic lantern, a series of quick freeze-frame photographs. Ruby's white face by the open door. Marianne sobbing in Sam's arms. Another girl saying in a trembling voice, "What's going on?" Then Max was in the room with his arms round Ruby, dimly aware of two other human shapes in the background. Then he turned and found himself looking down the barrel of a gun.

"Get away from her," said the man, presumably Harry Payne, a thin, bloodless individual whose eyes looked almost red in the fluorescent light of the hallway.

Max raised his arms and the man backed out onto the landing, gesturing with the gun for Max to follow. Sam and Marianne were crouching on the top step, Sam protecting the girl with her body.

The man turned his gun on Ruby, still standing in the doorway.

"Did you let him in? You've been more trouble than the rest of them put together."

"Drop the gun!" shouted Max. "I'm armed." He drew something from his inside pocket and pointed it

310

at the man. Payne swung round and, before he could see what was in Max's hand, Sam had jumped up and pushed him down the stairs.

"Get the gun," said Max. It was lying on the third step. Sam picked it up and handed it to Max. He descended the stairs. Payne was lying on the twelfth floor landing, winded, his leg twisted under him. Max pointed the gun at him. "Stay where you are."

"You wouldn't dare shoot," said Payne.

"Try me." Max fixed him with the stare that had made thousands of women believe that their lace handkerchiefs had transformed into doves. Above him he could hear Sam talking to the girls. Thank heaven they all seemed to be unhurt. Where the hell was Edgar? He steadied the gun, still staring at the man on the floor. Then — thank God — there were shouts, heavy footsteps on the stairs, Edgar's voice yelling, "Police!"

Then Emma, like a whirlwind, racing past him. "Marianne!" "Mummy!" Then the tall policewoman loping past. "Is everyone all right up here?" Ruby saying something unintelligible. Other voices. Bob and another man putting handcuffs on Payne.

"I'll have the gun," said Edgar. Max handed it over.

"What did you point at Payne earlier?" asked Sam, who was now standing beside him.

Max reached into his pocket and drew out a piece of wood, hinged in the middle. "I think it's part of a deck-chair," he said. "I found it on the promenade."

"I really believed it was a gun for a minute."

"First rule of magic. If you tell someone that you're holding a gun, they see a gun."

"Fascinating. You must tell me the other rules some time."

They turned and walked back up the stairs. Emma was cuddling her daughter on the top step. She looked up as he passed. "Thank you, Max."

"It was nothing," he said. "Sam did all the brain work."

"That's true." Sam put her hand on Marianne's head. "All right, Mari?"

"He said that he'd give me a lift home," said Marianne. "I wanted to ride in his car. It had a flag painted on it. He said we'd just go round the block, so that I could see the mods and rockers."

"What did I tell you about getting into cars with strangers?" said Emma.

"He wasn't a stranger," said Marianne. "He was in our house, taking pictures of you."

Max left them to it and went into the flat. There, sitting on a stained mattress, were a red-headed girl and a black girl in a nurse's uniform. The policewoman was kneeling in front of them, talking gently. Ruby was standing by the wall. She came over to Max and he put his arms round her.

"It's all right," he said, speaking into her hair.

Ruby pulled away, smiling at him. "You saved me," she said.

"You saved yourself. I saw your signals."

"Did you?" Ruby looked pleased. Despite being in captivity for a week, her pink suit creased and dirty, her hair in tangles, she still had plenty of her old dash and energy. "That was me with the mirror on my compact. I hoped that someone would see it. We could see the seafront and there seemed to be loads of people around. What's going on?"

"The mods and rockers trying to kill each other."

"Was that what it was? Shame I missed it. I love a good fight."

"Thank God you're safe," said Max. "I've been going mad with worry."

"Have you?" Ruby looked at him with her head on one side. "What's everyone been saying? Has it been in the papers? I was worried that everyone would just think that I'd gone off with a man."

"I knew something was wrong when you didn't turn up for work," said Max. "I knew you'd never miss a rehearsal. I even went to your flat to look for you."

"Did you? How's Cleopatra? I've been really worried about her."

"The warden's looking after her."

"Oh, did you meet Celia? I'm surprised you got away with your life."

He wanted to ask about the mysterious man with the music case but thought that it might not be the right time. Looking back at the landing, he could see Edgar and Emma both with their arms round Marianne. Sam had moved tactfully away and was looking out of the window. Bob now appeared at the top of the steps.

"We're taking Payne back to the station. How are the girls? I've radioed for an ambulance."

"They seem remarkably unscathed," said Max.

"Girls are tougher than you think," said Bob solemnly. "I've learnt that over the years."

Max looked back into the flat. The two young women were standing now, hand in hand. Ruby went over to them and she, too, linked arms. The policewoman said something and they all laughed. Rather shaky laughter but laughter all the same.

"I think you're right, Bob," said Max.

CHAPTER
THIRTY-TWO

"It was just me at first," said Louise. "Harry told me that I could make lots of money as a model. He seemed so kind and sympathetic. I didn't want to leave nursing but Matron was so horrible to me and I thought, I'll get a bit of cash, just enough to be comfortable, then I'll start training again somewhere else. Serves me right for being so greedy."

"No it doesn't," said Meg.

Edgar and Meg were interviewing Louise in the hospital. All three girls had been treated for mild malnutrition and exhaustion but, in general, the doctors agreed with Max: they were in remarkably good shape. Edgar had telephoned Sir Crispian and decided that he wouldn't interview Rhonda until her father arrived. He felt sorry for Louise, she had no close family and no one to ring, but, halfway through the interview, Pete Chambers arrived and sat holding her hand in a very territorial way.

Louise told them that Harry Payne had taken her to his flat in Rottingdean and had made her a cup of tea. "It must have had something in it because I fell asleep and, when I woke up, I was in a tunnel underground. It was awful, freezing and dark. I thought I was going to die. I could only keep track of time by marking the days on the wall with a piece of chalk. Then, after a week or so, he brought Sara in. He'd told her the same thing, about being a model, and she believed him. It was lovely having someone to talk to. Sara was really young and she'd been through a lot but she was so brave, much braver than me. When Rhonda arrived, Harry told us he was moving us, one by one, to a different location. The tunnel was too small for the three of us and he said that he was going to 'add to his collection'. He said that he was moving Sara first — because she was the smallest — and so she worked out a plan. She put on Rhonda's school cloak and she was going to stab him with the pin and then escape. She said that the cloak would prove that we were all together. She said that people would care more about Rhonda because she was rich and her father was an MP."

Louise said this without rancour but Pete shot the police officers a reproachful look and Edgar didn't blame him.

"Then Harry came back. He brought Sara's shoes — he was funny about shoes, kept them all together in a separate place — and he said that she was dead. He'd killed her for trying to escape. Rhonda and I were terrified. Harry was more careful when he moved us, he made us drink some of the drugged tea first. I don't remember it at all, just being in his car, lights flashing and strange noises everywhere, and then walking up loads of stairs. It was better in the flat because at least it was light and we had mattresses and a proper toilet. Then Ruby came and somehow we had hope. She's famous, we knew people would be looking for her. But it was more than that. Ruby was so alive, she had energy, she had ideas. I think that, after Sara died, Rhonda and I had simply given up. Ruby said we had to fight back, she was full of plans for overpowering Harry. She answered him back. That's when he started carrying a gun."

And the gun had been loaded. It looked to Edgar like a relic of the Second World War. Could Payne have served? He looked too young but, then again, he had the kind of face that could be any age. "Oldish" as the Bobby Soxer, Isabel, had put it.

"Ruby had the idea of signalling with her compact. SOS. Save our souls. And then it seemed like the next minute Max Mephisto and the girl reporter were banging on the door. It was like a miracle."

Trust Max to make an entrance, thought Edgar. But he didn't begrudge his old friend the limelight. If he hadn't timed his trick to perfection, Payne might well have taken Marianne elsewhere, he might even have harmed her. He couldn't think of it without going hot and cold.

"I'm going to talk to Rhonda in a minute," he said. "But did Payne tell her the same thing, about making her a model?"

"Yes, Rhonda met him outside the Ritz. She used to go there in the holidays to wait for Bobby Hambro, the actor. Harry told her that she could be a model, he said that the magazines liked redheads. He said that, if she was a model, she'd move in fashionable circles and she'd meet Bobby. She loved Bobby."

Edgar thought of Meg saying: *They'd go off with the devil himself if he said he'd introduce them to Bobby Hambro.* Once again WPC Connolly had been right. Meg glanced at him as if thinking the same thing and then turned back to Louise. "I know," she said, "I spent some time with those girls and they're all obsessed with Bobby."

Louise smiled. "Rhonda did talk about him rather a lot. I feel like I could go on *Top of the Form* with Bobby as my specialist subject. I didn't mind though. It helped pass the time. Harry persuaded Rhonda to escape from school. That's how he put it. Escape. I think she loved the adventure of it. She got the keys to a tunnel from the caretaker and got out that way. Harry knew all about tunnels. Rhonda left her hat there to confuse the police."

"It did confuse us," said Meg.

"We were both so stupid to believe him," said Louise.

"It wasn't your fault." Pete put an arm round her. "Payne was a madman." He turned to Edgar. "Haven't you asked enough questions?"

Louise did look very tired, her eyes huge, her hands shaking slightly.

"We'll leave it there," said Edgar. "You've been very helpful, Miss Dawkins. If you could just read the statement that WPC Connolly's been writing out, and then sign it, we'll let you get some rest."

As Louise was reading through the pages, a tremendous commotion was heard in the corridor outside.

"What's that?" asked Louise in a rather tremulous voice.

"I think Sir Crispian has arrived," said Edgar.

Ruby refused to go to the hospital. "I've only been in the flat for a week," she said, "and I wasn't in the tunnels at all. I'm all right. Really I am. I just want to go home and wash my hair." Max could see Edgar wanting to argue but eventually giving in.

"I'll need to take a statement tomorrow," he said. Emma had already gone home with Marianne in the panda car. Louise and Rhonda were in the ambulance with WPC Connolly in attendance.

"I'll drive Ruby home tonight," said Max, "and bring her back in the morning."

"Oh, Max, would you?" said Ruby. "I really want to sleep in my own bed."

Max understood that and was glad that he could offer this comfort to Ruby. Even so, his back gave an anticipatory twinge at the thought of a night on the sofa and he felt slightly sad to hear the "Max". When Ruby had called out to him from behind the locked door she had spontaneously called him "Dad".

Edgar summoned another police car to take them to the Grand. Before she got in Ruby went over to Edgar and whispered something in his ear. Max would have given a lot to know what it was.

Max thought it might take a while to hire a car, especially on a bank holiday, but he explained some of the story to the hotel manager and the man immediately offered him "something from our fleet". The car was a

Rover, very smooth and luxurious. It reminded Max of his beloved Bentley, the car that had been his pride and joy in the 1930s and had survived the war on a girlfriend's farm. Selling the Bentley had been one of the hardest things about emigrating to America. He had a Cadillac over there but it wasn't the same.

"This is so nice," said Ruby, leaning back in her seat. "It's hard to believe that any of it happened."

They were on the A23, purring through the Brighton gates, occasionally passing little clusters of scooters as the mods made their way back to London. Otherwise the roads were empty, the Rover eating up the miles.

"How did it happen?" said Max. "I mean I understand how Payne lured the other girls away. Bob said that he had promised to make them famous models. But you're famous already. You're one of the most famous people in the country." He knew she'd like this.

"He told me that he knew where the girls were," said Ruby. "I recognised him. He's taken my picture hundreds of times. I trusted him. And, I know this sounds silly, but I wanted to solve the case."

"Why? You're not a detective."

"No. But I want to be one."

"What?" Max turned to look at Ruby, the car swerving slightly.

"Oh, not a real one," she said. "That would be too dull. But a TV detective. I've got this idea for a series about a woman private investigator. That's what I wanted to see Emma about. I thought she might be able to help with the research. I'm fed up with being Ruby Magic. I want to get into crime."

Why was everyone so interested in crime? thought Max. He could never see the appeal himself. He remembered Sam saying, "We're both as bored as hell and we both love crime." She had smiled when she said it too. He smiled now, remembering.

"Why are you smiling?" said Ruby. "Why is it funny for a woman to be a detective? Emma was a detective and a good one. I want her to be an advisor on the show."

Max was suddenly full of admiration for his daughter. She had had some setbacks in her life but she was always looking forward to the next thing, reinventing herself to keep pace with the rapidly changing world.

"I'm very proud of you," he told her now.

"Are you?" said Ruby. "That's nice. I can't wait to see Cleopatra."

Sir Crispian Miles was red in the face, eyes protruding. Behind him stood two nurses and the PC Edgar had left to guard the ward doors.

"What's going on, Stephens?" bellowed the MP. "Where's my daughter?"

Silently, Edgar opened a door and Rhonda sat up in bed. "Daddy!" It was enough to bring a tear to anyone's eye, even if you weren't already perilously close to breaking down. Edgar turned away as Sir Crispian put his arms round his daughter. "Sweetheart! Daddy's little girl. You're safe."

Meg wiped her eyes. "Isn't it sweet?" she said, beaming.

"Very sweet," croaked Edgar.

Crispian turned round. "You've got some explaining to do," he said to Edgar. "At lunchtime today a madman, an escaped criminal, burst into my house and threw a sack at me. A sack with a dog in it."

"A dog?" said Rhonda.

"Some mangy mutt," said Sir Crispian, warming to his theme, though he still kept his arm round Rhonda. "It was that nutcase who kidnapped Rhonda before. Ernest Coggins. He had escaped from prison, if you please. I ask you, why do I pay my taxes?"

"Coggins brought you a dog?" said Edgar.

"He'd heard about Rhonda going missing and he had some crazy idea that she'd run away and would only come back if I got her a dog. So the lunatic broke out of prison, went to a pet shop and bought a puppy. Man's a complete liability. A danger to society. Of course I telephoned the police immediately. You were unavailable, as usual," he said to Edgar.

"I was rescuing your daughter," said Edgar, though that wasn't strictly true. There had been nothing on his mind except his own daughter.

"Well, the local rozzers came eventually and they took Coggins into custody. He didn't even try to escape. Had the cheek to wish me well before they carted him away."

"And the dog?" said Rhonda, bouncing on the bed. "What about the dog?"

"It's a mutt," said Sir Crispian, "no breeding at all. A scruffy little black and white thing."

"Can we keep it?" said Rhonda. "Please, Daddy."

Sir Crispian looked away. "Well, your mother does seem to like the creature."

322

Rhonda flung her arms round her father's neck. "I'm going to call him Fluffball."

"No you're not," said Sir Crispian. "I've already named him Caesar."

By the time that Edgar and Meg returned to the station, Harry Payne had already confessed to the abduction of two women and three children and the murder of Sara Henratty.

"Did he say why?" said Edgar, looking through the transcript on Bob's desk.

"Just that he was a collector," said Bob. "He wanted a complete set, he said: a blonde, a redhead, a black-haired girl and a brunette. He's a complete nutter, if you want my opinion. I'm worried that he'll plead insanity and get sent to a mental asylum."

"Well, as long as he's not free to abduct and murder more women," said Edgar.

"He should be hanged," said Bob.

Edgar was opposed to the death penalty. He remembered Timothy Evans, wrongly executed for crimes committed by his landlord, John Christie. Edgar had caught murderers who had been sent to the gallows and, although he was sure that they were guilty, on the day of their execution he had felt like a killer himself. On the other hand, if Payne had harmed Marianne, he would willingly have torn him apart with his bare hands.

"Sir Crispian Miles was at the hospital," he said. "It seems that Ernest Coggins turned up on his doorstep with a dog in a bag."

"What?"

323

"He thought that Rhonda had run away because she wanted a dog so he broke out of prison and bought her one."

"Another nutcase," said Bob.

"Quite a well-meaning one though. Sir Crispian called the police and Coggins is back in custody. The funny thing is that Sir Crispian seems quite besotted by the dog. He calls it Caesar."

"Dog are good company," said Bob, who owned a border terrier called Scruffy. "Did Coggins say how he escaped from prison? It seems that Davies has an alibi."

"The Surrey police think that Coggins had some help from a group called Action for Animals. They're passionate about animal rights."

"Animal rights? What does that mean?"

"I was reading about it recently. There are groups who believe that we shouldn't eat animals or wear fur or test medicines on animals. They make good points although a few of them are a bit extreme."

"If these people helped Coggins escape from prison then they're more than a bit extreme."

"Yes," said Edgar. "We'll have some interviewing to do tomorrow."

As he said this, Edgar felt a great weariness sweep over him. It seemed impossible to think that, in a few hours, he'd be back at work again, chasing up suspects, tying up loose ends. He rubbed his eyes.

"You should go home, sir," said Bob. "See Emma. Mrs Stephens. She must be very shaken up."

Bob had been fond of Emma when they worked together, Edgar remembered.

"I've got some paperwork to do first."

"Go home, sir," said Bob. His voice was gentle but unusually firm.

Meg was touched to see Patrick waiting for her outside the station.

"Mum thought you might like a lift home," he said. The Lambretta was leaning against one of the monstrous columns that supported the town hall portico.

"She was right," said Meg. "I'm exhausted."

"Did you find him?" asked Patrick, wheeling the scooter over. "The man you were looking for?" Meg had parted company with Declan and Patrick at the Stephenses' house after the super had told the boys, politely but firmly, to go home.

"Yes," said Meg. "We found him and all the girls he'd kidnapped." She climbed on the back of the bike, pulling her skirt down over her knees. It seemed like years ago that she had ridden into Rottingdean. She hadn't worried about her knees then, it had been pure adrenalin, terrifying but also — she had to admit — very exciting. The moment when she had seen the darkroom, the women's faces looking out at her, eyes, hair, mouths, crazily over-lapping, had been one of the most frightening experiences of her life but also, in a strange way, one of the best. It had been the moment when she knew they were right, that they were chasing the guilty suspect. And she had shared that realisation with the super's wife, the famous detective Emma Holmes.

"That must have been very satisfying," said Patrick, kicking the bike into life.

That was one word for it, thought Meg. She held on to Patrick's parka, her face against the fox fur of his hood, and let the evening fly past her: the lights on the pier, the sound of the hurdy-gurdy, the cars and buses going past, their colours blurring like a dream kaleidoscope.

Edgar wasn't sure why he was reluctant to go home. He wanted to see Marianne for himself, to check that she really was unhurt, he wanted to watch his daughters sleeping, side by side in their beds, and rejoice that, for the time being at least, he could keep them safely under one roof. He wanted to cuddle his baby boy, the son he had secretly longed for, and thank his lucky stars for his home and family. But why did he not, at this moment, feel lucky?

He walked back along the seafront. It was eight o'clock but still not dark. On the promenade council workers were still clearing up the mess left by the mods and rockers. Beer cans, stones and rubbish littered the road along with other, odder, pieces of detritus like a single high-heeled shoe and an abandoned crutch. What was the story there? The shoe reminded him of Sara Henratty, the girl who had tried to outwit the kidnapper and had paid with her life. Who would be mourning Sara tonight? Rhonda had gone home with her father, desperate to meet the small, fluffy dog called Caesar. Louise had Pete Chambers, who had stayed at her bedside throughout. But who was thinking of Sara tonight? Edgar would remember her, as he remembered all victims of crime. He would remember Sara long after Rita had written "Case Closed" on her file. He made a mental note to send the photograph of Sara, the one she'd been so proud of, to Malcolm Henratty. He was her father, after all, and it was better than filing it away with all the case notes. Suddenly the weight of all those crimes, all those stories, felt like an unbearable burden, one that caused him almost to stagger as he walked. He felt so tired that he wanted to lie down on the stony beach and sleep for a year.

On the beach Edgar could see the remains of deck-chairs, like birds of prey, hunched frames with wings flapping. Max had managed to convince Payne that a piece of deckchair was a gun. It didn't surprise Edgar in the least. He thought of Max and Ruby driving back to London, Ruby going back to her glitzy celebrity life. Was Ruby happy? He thought that she probably was. "Cheer up, Ed," she'd said to him outside the flats. "You solved it. You won." But was it ever as simple as that?

Marianne and Sophie were in bed when he got home. "They were both exhausted," said Emma. She was holding Jonathan who looked like he planned to be awake all night. Edgar went upstairs to check on his daughters. They lay in their twin beds, facing each other, Marianne's fair hair fanned out on the pillow, Sophie sucking her thumb. He kissed them both, whispered a prayer to the God he only vaguely believed in, and went back downstairs.

Emma was waiting for him with a whisky and soda. Jonathan was sitting, wakefully, in his playpen. "Are you hungry?" she said. "Shall I make you something to eat?"

"Have you been reading the *Argus* again?" said Edgar. He had meant it as a joke, something to lighten the atmosphere that still seemed to hover in the air, but Emma crumbled. She literally fell to the floor and knelt there, sobbing.

"What is it?" Edgar pulled her upright. "It's all OK. Marianne is fine. I've just checked on her and she's sleeping peacefully."

"Oh, Ed." Emma pulled away from him. "It was all my fault. I planned that article to tempt him. Astarte said that the kidnapper wanted a blonde so I thought I'd make myself into bait. I thought that he might try and abduct me. But Harry saw Marianne. He saw her that day when he came to the house to take my photo. She had her hair loose and she looked so lovely, like an angel. Harry Payne abducted her and she trusted him because she'd seen him here, in her home. So it really was all my fault."

Edgar put his arms round her. "It wasn't your fault. Harry Payne was a madman. He told Bob that he was a collector, he wanted a set of girls, all with different hair colour. You can't predict what a person like that will do."

"Astarte was right," said Emma, brushing tears from her eyes. She used her sleeve like a child would. Edgar felt his heart bursting with love and pity. "She said 'he hasn't got a blonde'. That's what gave me the idea."

Thanks very much, Edgar told the medium silently. Not content with encouraging my daughter to predict my death, you encourage my wife to take on a murderer single-handedly. Aloud he said, "You helped solve the case. You thought of Harry Payne. You went to his house."

"That was Sam," said Emma. But she brightened slightly. "Meg too. She was brilliant. Will you promote her?"

"I might make her a DC," said Edgar. "She's only young though. She's got a lot to learn."

"Not a DS?" said Emma. She was smiling now.

"A woman detective sergeant?" said Edgar. "Who's heard of such a thing?"

"You told me that I wasn't a detective any more," said Emma.

"You'll always be a detective," said Edgar. He was rewarded by the warmth in Emma's eyes but he wondered why the words gave him a distinct twinge of unease.

CHAPTER
THIRTY-THREE

Once again, Max was meeting Ruby for a meal. But this time they were eating at the Grand so at least the food would be good. It was Saturday, almost a week after Harry Payne, "The Brighton Kidnapper" as the papers called him, had been caught. Ruby had shared in most of the headlines. In fact, a lot of the press seemed to think she had apprehended the killer single-handedly. "Ruby's Magic Escape" screamed the *Argus* in massive letters. The article had been written by Sam Collins, the woman who had actually solved the mystery and thrown Harry Payne downstairs to boot.

"How can you write this stuff?" said Max, when they met for a quick coffee on the pier. It was three days after the rescue at the flats but Sam still seemed to be on a high from all of it. She was glowing with energy and vitality. Max remembered the electric shock he had experienced when they had touched.

"'Reporter Solves Crime' is on page three," said Sam. "'Beautiful TV Star Solves Crime' is front-page stuff."

"And will the reporter get the credit she deserves?"

"Probably not," said Sam, blowing the froth from something purporting to be a cappuccino — the coffee

330

craze had really hit Brighton with a vengeance. "But it doesn't matter. I've got other plans."

"Have you?" said Max. "What are they?"

"I can't tell you now," said Sam. "But I will one day. When we meet again."

But when would that be? Max was due to start filming next week. Lydia and the children would be joining him and then they would be spending the rest of the summer at Massingham Hall. He doubted that he would come back to Brighton. And, even if he did, he could hardly see Sam with Lydia in tow. He didn't want to think of the reasons why this seemed impossible.

Ruby was due at twelve but he knew she'd be late. Max was quite happy sitting in the bar with a whisky, watching Brighton go by. The town was no longer a battleground, although you occasionally saw a flock of mods or a pack of rockers slouching past. Today it was full of families enjoying the sun: fathers in panama hats, mothers holding the hands of fractious toddlers, teenagers — that newly discovered breed — torn between the excitement of the seaside and the mortification of being seen in public with their parents. Max missed Rocco and Elena, who were still young enough to find him fun and entertaining. He wanted to hug them and do tricks for them (what did fathers do who couldn't produce an egg from their daughter's ear?). He was looking forward to showing them England, where everyone "talked funny" like he did. He was even looking forward to taking them to Massingham Hall. Going back the other day had softened his feelings towards the house somehow. It was a place where you could have fun as a child; there were woods and streams and endless rooms where you could play hide-and-seek. It was just that Max had had no one to play with and, at the age of six, his world had been plunged into darkness with the death of his mother. Maybe Rocco and Elena would let the light back in. He touched the blue cat that he now always kept in his pocket. Perhaps everything would be all right with Lydia too.

"Max?"

He was so far away, lost in the grounds of his ancestral home, that he actually jumped. He looked up and saw a blond man dressed in jeans and a check shirt.

"Bobby! What are you doing here?"

"Looking for you. Is there somewhere we could talk?"

Max looked around the bar. It wasn't full but a few people were looking in their direction. Whether it was because they recognised Bobby, or because they disapproved of his clothes, he wasn't sure.

Max looked at his watch. A quarter to. Ruby would be at least another half an hour, by his guess.

"We could go for a quick walk. I'm meeting someone at twelve." He didn't want to tell Bobby that he was seeing Ruby. It wasn't that he thought the pair had been deeply in love, more that Bobby wouldn't want to be reminded of the one woman who had finished things with him.

"Nah." Bobby glanced out of the window. "Too many people about. I'd get hassled." He was wearing dark glasses but Max thought that he was right. Bobby was famous; people would think that it was acceptable to approach him and ask him for autographs or to pose for photographs. Max had experienced some of this himself in the course of his career but he was hardly in Bobby's league. Girls were unlikely to start screaming if they caught a glimpse of him crossing the street, for example.

"We could go up to my room," he said.

"That would be great."

They went up in the lift. It felt odd to be taking another man to his room though Max had made this journey with many women in his time. The thought made him feel old and rather sleazy. Bobby didn't speak until they were in Max's suite. Then he sat on one of the many sofas, took a deep breath, and said, "I know you saw me that day. The day when all the hoodlums were fighting."

Max had almost forgotten his glimpse of Bobby on the beach. It had been entirely eclipsed by the events that had followed: running into Sam and Emma, the dash up to the flats, the discovery of the girls, the show-down with Payne.

"I was meeting a friend," said Bobby.

"Really," said Max. "It's none of my business."

"I figured that it might become your business if we're going to work together," said Bobby. "The thing is, Max, I'm gay. I'm a faggot, a pansy, a fairy. Call it anything you want."

"I certainly wouldn't call it any of those things," said Max. "And, as I say, it's entirely your business."

"It's why I like Brighton," said Bobby. "People are more relaxed about that sort of thing here. I can meet a guy in Kemp Town or by Duke's Mound and we'll both know the score. I usually go out at night but I thought there were so many people out and about that day that I could get away with it. But I know that you saw me and I wanted to be sure you'd keep the secret."

"Of course I will," said Max.

"If anyone knew," said Bobby, "it would be the end of my career. The end of everything."

Max was about to protest; homosexuality was illegal in Britain but people did seem more accepting these days; he'd heard comedians on the wireless who would have been considered shocking in America. But then he thought about Bobby Hambro; he was a heart-throb, his whole appeal rested on the fact that girls wanted to marry him. That's why screaming fans waited outside his hotel, it was all part of some hormonal crucible. Bobby was the perfect man, the perfect boyfriend, the perfect husband. If this illusion was shattered, what would be left? Had Ruby known? he wondered. Thinking of her letter (*I think you'd be happier with someone else too*) he thought that she had probably guessed.

"Of course I won't say anything to anyone," he said. "I'm honoured that you told me."

"Thanks, Max. You're a gent. Wilbur knows, and my American agent, but no one else."

Bobby looked so relieved that Max felt a surge of pity for him. It suddenly felt unbearably sad that Bobby would not be able to find love with the person of his choosing. Bobby might be fairly free now but he was (officially) only eighteen. Max guessed that, before long, he would be forced into marriage with some starlet and made to pose for articles entitled "Hollywood Star's Domestic Bliss".

"I'm sorry that you have to live like this," he said. "I hope it won't be for ever."

Ruby was late but not impossibly so. They drank martinis in the bar and then moved through to the restaurant. Heads swivelled towards her as they had with Bobby but this time the reaction seemed universally favourable. Ruby was looking really lovely in a yellow minidress and, since the kidnapping case, she had acquired an almost goddess-like status in the eyes of the British public. "Well done, Ruby," said someone as they passed. "God bless you," said another.

"You are now officially the nation's sweetheart," said Max when they sat down.

"I know," said Ruby. "Isn't it lovely?"

"I don't know," said Max, thinking of Bobby. "Fame can be a straitjacket sometimes."

"Are you in one of your gloomy moods?" asked Ruby, smiling at the waiter as he proffered a basket full of rolls. He blinked, dazzled.

"Of course not," said Max. To prove it he ordered champagne. The maître d'hôtel appeared, to tell them that the bottle was on the house "to celebrate the lady's safe return". Ruby twinkled and thanked him. Ruby was the queen of entrances and exits, thought Max. They had once performed an act together called the

Vanishing Box but Ruby didn't need a magic cabinet in order to disappear and reappear. She and the other girls had recently performed their own vanishing trick. Now you see them, now you don't.

"What are you going to do now?" asked Max.

"I'm back in the studio on Monday," said Ruby. "If it's the last series of *Ruby Magic*, I want it to be a good one."

"Are you really going to leave?" said Max.

"Yes," said Ruby. "The show's been good to me but I think it's run its course. And I want to call the shots. I'm sick of smiling sweetly and saying stupid lines. I've got a fantastic new writer lined up for the detective show. I'm going to direct it as well as star in it. It's going to be great."

Max looked at his daughter with admiration. There were no TV shows directed by women but he had no doubt that Ruby could be the first. And, of course, it was the perfect moment to launch a detective series, when everyone was still obsessed by the kidnapping case.

"And I've met a new man too," said Ruby, spreading butter on a roll. "He's a jazz musician, black as the ace of spades. You'll like him."

That explained the music case, thought Max. It also explained why Ruby had told Joe that people would be shocked at her choice of boyfriend. The ace of spades, just as the ace of hearts was the blood card. Max wasn't shocked but he did hope that the jazz musician would be good to Ruby. And that he wouldn't have to listen to too much of his music.

The waiter poured the champagne with a flourish. Max raised his glass to Ruby. "Your future is bright," he said.

"I think it is," said Ruby.

Emma and Edgar were also having lunch, although the setting was slightly less glamorous. Sam had offered to babysit while they "talked things over" but Emma couldn't face a restaurant with people whispering, "That's the police superintendent and his wife, their daughter got kidnapped, you know." It was another lovely day so they took a picnic to Cuckmere Haven, a beauty spot near Eastbourne, where the river meandered lazily to the sea. They parked by a convenient pub and then walked along the shingle path. The land was marshy and flat with secret pools fringed by reeds. The sky was a bright, clear blue reflected in the still waters of the estuary. Birds flew overhead, dark against the sun. Were they coming home for summer? Emma wasn't sure although she remembered being taken to this very spot for a biology field trip when she was at Roedean. There were no school parties today, only a few other couples walking in companionable silence. You couldn't see the sea until you reached the dunes but you could hear it, hissing against the stones.

"The girls would love it here," said Emma.

"Johnno too. Although he'd be sure to fall in the water."

"He does have an uncanny ability to get wet."

They sat on the grass by the sand dunes and ate their sandwiches. The tide was coming in, racing to join the river mouth, creating runnels and rivulets through the pebbles. The Seven Sisters were on their left, whiter by far than the cliffs of Dover. *There'll be bluebirds over the white cliffs of Dover.* But bluebirds, Emma had read somewhere, were native only to America. Typical wartime propaganda.

"Ed," she said. "I want to talk."

"Yes?" He turned to her but she thought that he sounded wary.

"I love being your wife," said Emma, "and I love being a mother. I love the kids. And you."

"I sound like a bit of an afterthought there."

"You're not," said Emma. "I've loved you since I first saw you. But it's not enough. My life isn't enough. I can't bear *just* being your wife and the children's mother. I want to do something else."

"Like what?"

"I want to go into business with Sam and become a private detective."

"What?" Edgar raised his hand to shield his eyes from the sun but it felt as if he was warding her off somehow.

"We've thought it all through. I know how to investigate a case and Sam knows how to get information. Sam's fed up with the paper. They never give her any good stories and they keep asking her to make the tea. Harry Payne was the final straw. She'd liked him, trusted him. She wants a change and so do I. We're going to set up a company. Holmes and Collins. Sam's even offered to change her name to Watson."

"Holmes and Collins," said Edgar.

338

"Well, I couldn't use your name, could I?"

"No, I suppose not. It'll look odd, though, a superintendent's wife becoming a private investigator."

"Well, I don't mind if you don't."

"I don't mind," said Edgar. "But I haven't got much choice, have I?"

"No," agreed Emma. They sat in silence for a moment watching the sea advancing, turning the beach into a bay.

"Just be careful," said Edgar at last. "It's a dangerous world out there."

But it didn't seem dangerous today, it seemed golden and full of possibilities. Emma laughed and leant against her husband. He kissed her while the seabirds called wildly from the waves.

Acknowledgements

This book describes some real events, including the battle between the mods and rockers in Brighton on 17th and 18th May 1964, but I have changed some details and invented others in order to fit the plot. I'm very grateful to Peter Conroy for sharing his experiences of being a teenage mod. I hope that I have done Peter and his Lambretta justice. Thanks to Graham Bartlett, ex-chief superintendent of Brighton Police, for showing me round the old police cells where you can still see graffiti from the mods and rockers. Thanks also to Marjorie Scott-Robinson, my aunt in Seaford, for her memories of being a student in 1960s Brighton and frequenting the town's coffee shops and cider bars.

I pass Roedean School almost every day but had never been inside. I approached Grace Cather, the Alumnae Relations Manager, to ask if I could visit and was amazed at her generosity and helpfulness. Thanks to Grace for showing me round Roedean and to Jackie Sullivan for taking the time to show me the school's archives. Jackie also lent me a wonderful book entitled *Memories of Roedean: the first 100 years* compiled by Judy Moore. Many of Emma's memories come from this book and I'm most grateful to the Roedean staff for being so generous with their time and resources. I need hardly say that all the events in this book are fictional and that I have invented a whole new school personnel. The tunnel is real though. Many thanks to Ivy Robin for the initial contact.

Rottingdean was once famous both for smuggling and for being the home of Rudyard Kipling. There are meant to be many tunnels under the village but The Smugglers' Cave and its secrets are purely imaginary.

Thanks as ever to my wonderful editor, Jane Wood, and to all at Quercus, especially Therese Keating, Hannah Robinson, Bethan Ferguson, Laura McKerrell, Katie Sadler, Ella Patel and David Murphy. Thanks also to Chris Shamwana from Ghost Design for a really beautiful cover. Thanks to my fantastic agent, Rebecca Carter, and all at Janklow and Nesbit UK. Thanks to Kirby Kim at Janklow in the US and to my American publisher, Naomi Gibbs, and all at HMH.

Love and thanks always to my husband Andrew and to our children, Alex and Juliet.

This book is for Lesley Thomson, my dear friend and sister in crime.

Elly Griffiths
2019